W9-ATZ-246

BREATHING

WATER

BREATHING
WATER

T. GREENWOOD

ST. MARTIN'S PRESS ☙ NEW YORK

BREATHING WATER. Copyright © 1999 by T. Greenwood. All rights reserved. Printed in the United States of America. No part of this book may be used or reproduced in any manner whatsoever without written permission except in the case of brief quotations embodied in critical articles or reviews. For information, address St. Martin's Press, 175 Fifth Avenue, New York, N.Y. 10010.

Design by Maureen Troy

Library of Congress Cataloging-in-Publication Data

Greenwood, T.   (Tammy)
    Breathing water / by T. Greenwood.—1st U.S. ed.
        p.   cm.
    ISBN 0-312-20283-0
    I. Title.
    PS3557.R396B74   1999
    813'.54—dc21   99-17450
                                                                   CIP

First Edition: May 1999

10 9 8 7 6 5 4 3 2 1

With love and gratitude to my grandfathers,
one for poetry and the other for music.

ACKNOWLEDGMENTS

I would first like to thank my agent, Christy Fletcher, and my editor, Joe Veltre, for their enthusiasm about this novel and for their thoughtful insights and suggestions during the revision process. I would also like to thank Erika Fad for her patience and helpfulness.

I am deeply indebted to the following people for their ceaseless encouragement and incredible faith. Without them, this book would neither exist nor matter: Lon deMatties, Warren Doody, Janet Dunphy-Brown, Ann-Britt Malden, Howard Mosher, Nicole Norum, Ron Ross, Samantha Ruckman, Esther Stewart, Beya Stewart, and my many wonderful teachers.

I offer thanks to my grandparents—Don Craig, Eunice Craig, and Clifford Greenwood—for their love and support. To my sister, Ceilidh Greenwood, for her generosity and humor.

To my parents, Paul and Cyndy, for believing.

And to Patrick, for listening.

PROLOGUE

～ ～ ～ Do not ask me for haunted. Do not ever ask me for haunted, because I will give you haunted and you will never be the same. I will turn a nursery rhyme room into a prison of rhythmic sighs. Of mice screaming and clocks that will not stop their tick-tock, tick-tock. The closed eyes of dolls and animals will not open here, not even if you try to pry them awake with gentle, pleading fingers. I will make the record skip; the arm won't lift from the only song that has ever made you sad.

I will tear each blade of grass from the green velvet of your memory, leaving only the empty stems of dandelions gone to seed. I will burn the wooden castles of your remembrance, set the forest where all of your remaining dreams reside on fire. The branches you swung from will be nothing more than steaming bones in the cold morning air.

I will hold the baby bird that you brought back to life with an eye dropper of your breath. I will be careful with its wings, of its softly beating chest. I will hold it in the palm of my hand, close my fingers gently around its wings. I will close my fingers so gently you will think that you are safe. But then, quite suddenly, I will squeeze my fist tightly around its quickening heart. Squeeze until beak crumbles, until bones crack. And this will be the one thing that you can't forgive.

I know now what you will and will not tolerate. I know from watching you, from inflicting pain, that you are capable of great forgiveness. You forgive without waiting for apologies. You forgive tremendous cruelty, each cruelty, until this one. I am certain of this. I will make you trust, and then I will crush the bones of your credulity.

Do not ask me for haunted, do not ever ask me for haunted. Because I will give you haunted and you will never be the same. You may think that exorcism is as easy as words, but it's far more complicated than that, much more dangerous and ultimately unkind. Do not ask me for haunted, don't ever ask me to recollect, because the collected remains I will give you will be more real to you than I am.

Lake Gormlaith, Vermont
August 1991

ॐ ॐ ॐ Blue night. I am standing at the edge of the lake, shivering in my summer dress when they pull her body out of the water. I am shivering and tearing at my cuticles when they lay her on the moon-drenched, indigo grass. At the edge of the lake, I tremble with cold as I watch Max's shadow pulling the boat out of the water and hear the scream of the wooden bottom scraping against the rocks.

A woman who lives in the small cabin nearest to the landing covers the girl's small dark body with a blanket the color of morning sky. There are about five of us standing close to her now, closer to her than most of us have dared to go before. But now we circle her with our own bodies, as if to shield her from harm.

Mrs. Forester, her caretaker for the summer, is still standing waist-deep in the water, holding the hem of her white cotton nightgown. I can hear a low moan coming from somewhere deep inside of her. The sound of an animal. The sound of loss and pleading. The moon makes her almost transparent as she stares toward the center of the calm lake. She too is shivering in the cold, her body shaking. She wraps her arms around herself and continues to moan. Mr. Forester ignores this and kneels down next to the dead girl.

As Max ties the boat to a rotten tree stump at the shore, I stare at the strange pink of the girl's upturned palms. She could be asking for something with this gesture. Answers, perhaps. To be left alone now. I look at the girl's small face, still full of color, and envy this. I envy the way she seems to sleep, warm and quiet beneath the blanket of light. I envy her, because I am colder than the water, colder than the air. I am colder than the dead girl whose mother thought she was sending her somewhere safe.

No one speaks as Mr. Forester covers her face with the blanket. And when her small face, her strange dark face is covered, I am tempted to pull the blanket back. I am tempted to pull the blanket from her and carry her away from this place. To take her somewhere she belongs. But there is no such place. Not here. And so instead, I find my fingers pulling the satin edge of the blanket further so that her hair, beaded with glistening drops of water, is covered too.

Mr. Forester stands up slowly, his knees creaking. When he sees his wife still standing in the lake, he walks toward her, wading into the lily-laced water. When he reaches her, she seems not to notice that he is there. She is rocking and moaning in her transparent nightgown. He puts his arm across her shoulders and waits patiently until she collapses in his hands.

After the dust from the cars and ambulances has settled, I find Max's old leather suitcase in the musty closet in the loft. After someone has called her mother in New York, I fold his shirts, gather his shoes. After he has calmly lied to the police who wanted to know where he found her and why he was in the middle of the lake in the middle of the night, I decide.

I come down the precarious stairs from the loft into the dark living room. I walk through the darkness and into the kitchen where I set the suitcase by the back door. When I return to the living room, I see him sitting in the corner on the dusty wooden floor. The air still smells of basil and garlic from dinner.

"Go," I say. It is all I can manage.

He doesn't look at me and he doesn't speak. Slowly, he begins to bang his head against the wall, each strike leaving the wet imprint of his hair. I look away from him to the window. The moon is full and bright, reflecting and trembling on the dark surface of the lake. All of the voices from this night have faded; even the crickets, usually restless, are quiet. The only sound is the water lapping the rocks at the edge of the lake and the rhythmic banging of bone on wood.

"Please." I plead.

He stands up slowly, still stumbling and stinking of too much drink. His jeans are damp, his bare feet caked with mud from the lake. He reaches toward me.

I walk to the kitchen and push the screen door open, my arm shaking.

"No more," I say.

He comes closer then, and my shoulders shrink in remembrance of all the other times. My spine recollects and recoils.

"If you touch me, I'll kill you," I say. "I swear to God I will."

He pulls me toward him. I can feel him both asking and demanding that my body give in to him. When my shoulders remain stiff, when I fail to yield, he shoves me away. I stumble with the force of his push and the screen door slams shut. I put my hands on my hips to steady myself, and I feel quite suddenly like a stubborn child. He veers past me toward the door. He pushes it open and lets it slam behind him. He grabs awkwardly at the suitcase, knocking it over, and then kicks it clumsily into the driveway.

"Stop," I say, and my eyes feel wide and strange.

He turns toward me and then comes close enough to the door that separates us for me to smell the stink of drink on his breath.

"You know it's not all my fault," he says, pointing his thick finger close to my chest. "Weren't the Foresters supposed to be watching her?"

I feel the fire, warming me, filling me with remarkable heat.

"How was I supposed to know she'd be out there?" he asks, his voice softening in the still night. His chin is quivering. He opens the door.

My heart thuds softly, and I start to feel sick. He seems vulnerable now, incapable of causing harm. His eyes plead and promise. I imagine him pleading with his mother to *Stop, stop*. I imagine the cigarette burns in the palms of his hands, the stigmata of his mother's cruelty. And I reach out to touch him; I watch my hand in disbelief. His shoulder trembles under my touch.

"And where the hell were you?" he asks, his voice growing louder and louder. "If you hadn't decided to run off to your grandmother, *Oh save me, Gussy, from my horrible life*, then maybe I wouldn't have been out there in the first place." The softness of his face and his voice is gone now, and my hand returns to my side. Now I can only think of myself pleading with him to *Stop, stop*.

"I hate you," I whisper. "I hate you, hate you."

"You can't pretend that I'm the only one at fault. You think that if you send me away that I'll be gone. You think you can put this, this night, away into a pretty little box, shove it under your bed, and forget what's inside. But you're wrong. Because you were there with me, Effie. You were inside my head when I went out there. You were there too. And you won't get away with this." He cups my chin in his palm and looks at me with disgust. "You won't get away."

He slams the screen door again and walks to the car. When I hear the engine start, roaring with his anger and impatience, I shut the storm door and hook the ridiculous latch. He has already broken it once this summer. I lean all of my weight against the door and listen for the sound of the tires crushing gravel and grass. The radio pierces the quiet night. The motor hums, and I wait.

But suddenly the car door slams again. I hear his heavy footsteps coming back. Closer and closer. I hear him breathing on the other side of the door. I will the lock to hold. I close my eyes.

"I love you, Effie. I'm sorry. It was an accident. You know that."

I put my hands over my ears, listening to the blood thudding dully at my temples and in my chest. I wait for him to push. I listen and wait. Any moment now, I know he will push and send me flying backward into the sharp corner of the stove or the cupboard. I wait for glass to break, for something, anything, to shatter.

It could be hours that I lean against the door, listening to my heart and his breath through the wood. It could be minutes. But then, suddenly the engine roars again and the headlights sweep through the windows. The yellow beams touch the bookcase, the worn fabric of the love seat, and my clenched hands. And then the light is gone.

I move away from the door; my shoulders are cramped. I walk slowly through the dark kitchen and living room, quietly up the stairs to the loft. I almost slip as I reach the landing, feeling in the darkness for the mattress. I sit down on the edge of the bed and stare out the window at the road that has taken him away, at the road that could bring him back. The sheets still smell of his sweat. I stand up then and tear the pillowcases off the pillows and the sheets off the bed. The hems are strewn with Gussy's embroidered sunflowers. My chest aches as I stuff them in the cedar chest, and I can't stop shivering as I lie down on the bare mattress.

I try to rest, to slow the fluttering of my heart. I try to imagine something else: that I am not here. Not now. But every time I close my eyes I see her limp body, her limp dress on the grass. On the back of my eyelids, I see all of the faces white with moon, staring at the girl like a discarded toy underneath the late summer sky. And I see Max walking calmly back to the camp with the policeman, his hands gesturing toward the place in the lake. His false heroism as transparent to me as water, but an answer the police find easier than the truth. I watch them scribble his words onto their pads, ink turning his explanation into indelible history. He has always had the ability to make people believe. No questions. I see his hands steadily pouring coffee. I see hands reaching for me, promising tenderness, and then fingers threatening to tighten and not let go.

And so I keep my eyes open and stare out the window at the lake until the sky fills with light, and I listen for the sounds of his return.

PART
ONE

Seattle 1994

໑ ໑ ໑ I fled. When the sun came up the morning after Max left, I was perched at the edge of the bare mattress. And in the half-light of early morning, I took flight. I ran as far away from the familiar as I could. I brought only the bare essentials and told only a few people where I intended to go. To Gussy, I muttered *Arizona, California*. To my mother, I said *Just away*, and *I'll write*.

I didn't know where I was going. I only knew it had to be far from this place. I took trains and buses so that I could be certain I had left that world behind me. Through windows, I watched Vermont disappear in the distance. I didn't sleep, because I was afraid that while my eyes were closed we might change directions and I would wind up back where I had started. Every night, while the other passengers slept or read under the soft lights above their seats, I looked out the windows to make sure I was still headed *away*.

I didn't stop traveling until the sky no longer resembled the one over Gormlaith that night. Only then did I stop moving, did I trust that I had gone far enough. In the mountains of northern Arizona, I was grateful for the closeness of stars. For the brand new shade of night. I stayed there for a month, thought about looking for an apartment, a job. But the sound of the train passing by the hostel where I stayed lured me back. I wasn't ready to stop.

I arrived in Seattle two months after I left Vermont, drawn by the stories of dew-drenched grass and gray skies. I got off the bus downtown and walked through the throngs of tourists at the Pike Place Market, across Alaskan Way, and out onto one of the long wooden piers. Standing at the edge of the water, it could have been the edge of the world, and I knew I was finally far enough from home. Max thought I was in New York in graduate school as I had planned; he didn't even know that I had fled.

Even after I had settled in Seattle, I couldn't stop moving. It had become a habit, I suppose, this fugitive life. Living alone in this city of rain, I feigned anonymity. I came and went from my apartment when I knew that no one in the dusty building would see me. In every new apartment, I became what I hoped was just a curiosity: a newspaper disappearing each morning, the smell of coffee escaping through the cracks in the woodwork, someone softly snoring. As soon as people began to recognize me, I found myself searching the newspapers for a new place to live.

Soon, I imagined, I would disappear altogether. That eventually no one would be able to see me at all. When I first fled, I was careless. I was accustomed to people speaking to me, noticing me, touching me. I talked to the other travelers on the trains. I made up stories about where I was headed and why. But after I stopped moving, I had to learn how to fade. I was becoming more ethereal as each day went by. Diaphanous. I was losing my dimensions. I was becoming small.

It's easier to live like a fugitive than someone with nothing to fear. Boxes get moved from place to place. After three years, I didn't even bother unpacking anymore. I dragged the boxes with me to each new apartment without even bothering to undo the packing tape. There could have been books or dime-store dishes, clothes or fragile sentimentals inside. It didn't matter anymore; I could have been carrying around cobwebs or air for all I knew.

I was living in my third apartment in Seattle when I found out about Max. I had just moved in. At first I thought this might be a place I could stay for a while. It had a deep clawfoot tub and a view of Elliott Bay. A bed pulled out of the wall, and the ceilings were twice my height. I liked the way it smelled. I liked how quiet it was. But when you are a fugitive, you never sign leases. That way there's nothing to break. I knew moving again would be easy.

It was May, and my mother's voice at the other end of the line sounded like snow melting. At home, in Vermont, spring was late. I listened to my own voice, raining on her from three thousand miles away.

"I'm coming home," I said.

"Are you okay?" she asked.

"I want to live at the lake again. I can help Gussy."

"You're coming home?" my mother asked softly, hopefully. "Gussy will be so happy. It's been so long—"

"Max is dead, Mom. I just found out."

Her sigh: ashamed relief, the same relief. I have always shared my mother's breath and shame.

I found out that Max was dead when the university's alumni newsletter arrived. It was stuck in the narrow metal mailbox like any other flyer for groceries or tune-ups, sweepstakes promises or postcards with blue photos of lost children. It had traveled all over the country to find me: the layers of yellow forwarding address stickers a testament to my flight.

Inside my new apartment, I curled up on the couch and stared at the glossy cover. Shiny blond coeds dissected by cartoon lacrosse sticks, hallowed halls, and impossible trees. It was something that should not have found me at all. In the three years since I'd run away, I'd been able to avoid most reminders like these. Fugitives rarely get mail.

Near the end of the booklet, I found my own name, highlighted as *MIA*. There were ten of us who couldn't be found. There were nine others who, for whatever reason, had also disappeared. And between us and the stories of our more successful classmates were the newly dead, alphabetized like books in the musty library where I *used* to hide. Bingham, Cane, Doyle, Findlay, and then him.

It wasn't until later that day that I learned the details of his death. Of the needle that was found still stuck into the lean crook of his arm. Of the vomit that stained his chest and linoleum. Of the cats that had multiplied and then starved to death in his studio apartment above the bar where he worked and ate and drank himself to sleep.

It was raining. While the voice of my only old friend, Tess, described with almost morbid glee the supposed color of his skin and stench of his carpet, the decay of his small life, it rained. Incessantly, gently, and I didn't cry. Instead, I hung up the phone and felt my chest heave and then fall with a vague sense of freedom. The way a child feels when the puppy who messes on the floor more than he bargained for is suddenly struck by a car. Or the way a man feels when his own father who rarely remembers his name stops breathing. Terrible freedom. Freedom tainted by guilt.

I curled my knees to my chest, pressed my face to the watery pane of the window and concentrated on my breath. Below, on the slick dark street a bus stopped for no one and then lurched forward, exhaust rising in a cloud behind it. A girl without an umbrella appeared then, running and just a moment too late, and the driver didn't see her or didn't care and left her behind. She slumped down on the bench, and threw her fist at the sky. A ridiculous gesture. Futile and small.

I hadn't even lived in this apartment for a full week yet. I was still having a hard time remembering which faucet in the kitchen meant hot instead of cold. Sometimes they were backwards; you never knew in the older buildings. And maybe because everything was so new, the newness of his death didn't create panic or pain. It wasn't any different than the smell of newly painted cupboards or the new view from the kitchen window.

After I put the newsletter down, I went to the kitchen and washed my hands. I let the water run over my skin until my palms flushed red with the heat. It was almost dusk; the streetlamps had just turned on outside, casting strange shadows on the street below as the backs of my hands burned. I held my hands under the water until tears welled up in my eyes. Wrong tears, but tears no less. It was raining that day.

When he was still alive but no longer in my life, I dreamed that he was making bread in my kitchen. Over and over, in each new apartment, I'd fall asleep to different sounds and smells and have the same dream. I'd open the door and he would be standing there busily making bread, flour on his hands and face. He always found me in my dreams and made himself at home. But that night, as I listened to the rain tremble against the window, I dreamed that I was in the elevator of this new building. I was ascending and then heard the loud snap of the cable above my head. And I was suddenly, sharply, plummeting. It wasn't as simple as begging him to stop spilling flour on the floor, as taking the hot loaves and throwing them away. In this dream, there was nothing I could do except tear at the walls as I fell.

"Gussy is talking about selling the camp," my mother said.

"What?" I asked, my throat constricting.

"Since Daddy died, she doesn't have the energy to keep it

17

up. It's a lot of work, Effie," she said. "It's too much."

"I'll help her," I said, my words struggling past the new growth in my throat. *To watch the loons, to tame the dandelions, to keep the break-in kids from staining the floors with strawberry wine.*

"It's just talk, Effie. Maybe she'll change her mind."

"Tell her I'm coming. I'll be there by Monday."

When you live like a fugitive, you don't make friends. There's never the danger of becoming too familiar or attached. Of course, I knew faces. I recognized plenty of faces, but they didn't recognize mine. It made me pleased, and it made me sad. I had become every face, or no face at all.

Working at a library lends itself to anonymity, especially when you're not in Circulation. The Circulation girls all wear lipstick and stand in huddled circles outside smoking cigarettes on their breaks. I worked at the oceanography library at the university for an entire year before one of them noticed me. And even then, after the quick hello, there was a moment of uncertainty. There was the flash of fear in the girl's face that she had mistaken me for someone else.

It was the smallest library on campus, in the basement of an old building. The small windows in the archives where I worked were level with Portage Bay. When it rained, all you could see was water through the glass. I had become attached to this place despite myself. I emptied the drawers of my desk: paper clips, gummy erasers, aspirin.

Estelle said, "Have a safe trip home, Effie."

"I will." I smiled.

"It'll be nice to get out of the rain I suppose," she said. Her teeth were small, her eyes shifty.

"Um-hum." I nodded.

I had thought about taking a bus the whole way back to Vermont. But this time, I was going home. I was returning instead of running away. There was no need to watch through windows to make sure I was headed in the right direction. And so I packed my few boxes, mailed them to Gussy, and bought a one-way plane ticket home.

As I waited for the bus to take me to the airport, I grew dizzy with the heady scent of freshly cut flowers in the market, each bundle competing with the next in the endless parade of impossible colors to ward off the gray. It was 10:00 A.M., but it looked like twilight. Cars shined their lights, and the streetlamps glowed eerily in the darkness.

I've heard that this rain is enough to drive some people to madness, to their medicine cabinets, or to the tops of the tallest buildings and bridges. That these are the martyrs, the sacrificial lambs, who die so that others may be reminded of the slender distance between *pain* and *rain*.

Lake Gormlaith, Vermont
Late May 1994

෨ ෨ ෨ The bus from the airport dropped me off in Quimby. The bus doesn't go as far as the lake, so I waited in front of the drugstore for an hour for a taxi to take me the rest of the way. Gussy offered to pick me up, but I wanted to get settled in at the camp first. I wanted a little while to be alone before I saw my family.

As we drove away from town, the road turned from pavement

to dirt. The foliage became thicker and thicker, but finally through the trees I could see the blue of the lake. And then there was the camp. The paint was peeling, and the grass was overgrown. It looked abandoned.

Gussy has always kept the key to the padlock underneath a large gray rock by the back door. It's a good hiding place, because moss crawls across the smooth surface of the stone, making it look as though it has never been moved. I found the key, and my fingers remembered the simple trick of a tug and twist before the lock relented. Then, there was the familiar sound of lazy hinges waking. The scent of the camp when you first open the door to May air is thicker than cigar smoke, sweeter and mustier than the thrill of a bonfire.

I was dizzy with the scent of Grampa's old books and homemade candles and moth-eaten sweaters stuffed into drawers for colder evenings. I breathed the smell of the kitchen, stopping to open the cupboard doors, opening empty tins and running my fingers over the rows of spices, salt, and pepper. Dusty brown bottles of vanilla and molasses. The refrigerator was empty except for a fresh, unopened orange box of baking powder. I found Gussy's wooden rolling pin and rolled it between both hands. I remembered clothes powdered in flour and sugary wild blueberry pies. I lingered in the kitchen, rifling through drawers, so that I could hold on to the sweet anticipation of the rest of the cabin for a bit longer.

The living room was dark; the wooden shutters were closed. I walked slowly across the floor, careful not to trip over any forgotten piece of furniture. The threshold to the glassed-in porch came more quickly than I expected, and it startled me. This was my favorite room in the camp. I would spend the entire summer here if I could, watching the lake, reading myself to sleep each night.

The wooden floors, faded the rust color of autumn, were worn smooth with time. The metal-framed daybed was up against one wall, the sheets tucked tight. The heavy feather pillows were covered in blue and white ticking and propped up expectantly. The wicker chair, the small table for Chinese checkers or chess, and Grampa's desk were all there, as if unmoved in so many years. The door from the porch to the front yard was sealed shut; I don't remember ever using it to come and go from the cabin. It would have disturbed my grandfather as he worked at his desk if I'd been able to run in and out through the front with my muddy feet and constant chattering. By going through the back door, Gussy was always able to keep me in the kitchen long enough to dry off and calm down before I greeted Grampa.

The air in here was warm, the sunlight pressing persistently against the closed blinds. But there was something pacifying about the stagnant air, as if all past summers had been captured there. I felt like a strange puppeteer as I pulled the strings that controlled the sunlight. Dust rose and fell gently. Dead insects lay in piles as if slumbering after an orgy of wings and stingers. I brushed them into my cupped palm and opened the neglected door to the front yard. I walked all the way to the shed and tossed their dead bodies into the bushes.

I didn't remember the camp looking so run-down, and it was hard to imagine that the paint could have weathered so much in only three years. The grass tickled my shins. I wondered if Gussy had succumbed to a power mower yet. Grampa had always used the old hand mower that looked to me like an iron-toothed monster.

They call summer homes *camps* here. I suppose it's because the houses used to be so rustic: no electricity, no running water, each with a wooden outhouse instead of indoor plumbing. Of course, over the years they've become less primitive. Even Gussy and Grampa gave in and put a toilet and shower in, had the camp wired and plumbed. I could only vaguely remember the outhouse with the crescent moon carved out of the door, the earthy smell of excrement, and my fear of what might reach up and grab my naked bottom in the middle of the night. Now Gussy's compost heap stands where the outhouse used to, chicken wire and last summer's grass clippings and garden skeletons.

I walked across the dirt road to the bank where Gussy kept her wooden boat. The oar locks were rusty; the oars were probably inside the shed. Gormlaith was still today. The blinds in the windows of the other camps around the lake were still drawn. It was too early for there to be children and noisy motorboats; May was too cold, and the black flies of June kept most summer people away until July. I picked a dandelion from the shore and plucked the bright yellow head off. It landed in the water.

I heard a car coming up the winding road that circled the lake and saw Gussy in her old Cadillac. I walked back toward the camp as she drove past me, waving and grinning. She pulled into the driveway, stopping just short of the shed door.

"Effie," she said. "When did you get here? Are you hungry? Look at how small you are."

"I've always been small, Gussy. Since I was little." I laughed as she opened up the trunk and struggled with a grocery bag brimming with green leaves.

"I stopped by Hudson's, because I didn't know if you had planned supper yet. You haven't planned supper yet, have you? I figured you would want to get settled before you went shopping," she said, and I opened the back door for her.

"Well, let me look at you," she said. "You're starting to look like your mother, you know."

I hadn't seen my mother in three years. Three years can change a person. It had changed Gussy. Her silvery braided bun was finer, her body thinner.

I smiled and kissed her quickly on the cheek. She tasted like baby powder.

"I thought we could make a salad and cook up some of the fish your grandfather caught about a million years ago. It's just been sitting in the freezer, and I didn't know what to do with it, so I brought it along. I imagine it's still good. No freezer burn or anything."

It had been a year since my grandfather died. Gussy called me in Seattle to tell me. She said that he went fishing in the morning, came back to the camp for his usual lunch, a liverwurst sandwich and a glass of bourbon, and then laid down for his daily nap. She said she went on with her afternoon: working in the garden, putting a jar of raspberry tea outside on a wooden saw-horse to brew in the sun. But when she went to wake him for dinner, he had already gone. She said she ate dinner by herself and then called a neighbor to take care of the rest. While I shook and sobbed on the other end of the line, she said that the tea was sweet; that it had been a sunny day. I didn't go home for the funeral. I didn't want to confuse my grief with all the other emotions that were certain to accompany my return. I also had the irrational fear that Max would be waiting for me at the airport. That he'd be standing there with a bouquet of black-eyed Susans. That he'd find me if I came home.

As Gussy sliced the bright lemons into quarters, flicking the slippery seeds into the compost bucket with a knife, I washed the lettuce.

"Thank you, Gussy," I said.

"It's just fish. Your grandfather would have had a fit if we left it in the freezer forever."

"Not the fish," I said and patted the wet leaves with a dish towel. "I mean, letting me stay here. Letting me come back again."

"You don't need to thank me for that," she said and stopped unloading the groceries. "That's what this place is for, you know."

"I can do some work on it this summer. Painting and stuff," I said.

"That would be nice, honey." She smiled. "I can always hire someone to get the place in shape, though."

"Mom says you're talking about putting it up for sale," I said and the thickness returned to my throat.

"Oh, I don't know. It's just that now that Grampa's gone, I don't know how to take care of all the things that need attention. The roof, the plumbing, all that stuff. And since the ski resort opened property taxes have shot through the ceiling."

"I can help," I said again. "Really."

"Well nobody's going to buy it in the condition it's in right now. It needs some paint, the weeds have practically taken over the front yard. The tree house is falling down."

"I'll help, Gussy. It will give me something to do," I said. I couldn't believe that I was offering to help make the camp attractive to a prospective buyer. What I really wanted was for her to say, It will always be here. You can always come home.

"You need to keep busy," she said suddenly and started washing the tomatoes under cool water in the deep porcelain sink. "Last year when your grampa died, I had blisters on my fingers from all the work. I knit sweaters, I tore up linoleum, I polished brass and silver. Even the doorknobs."

I imagined my grandmother, alone for the first time in fifty-one years, polishing doorknobs and tearing up the old yellow linoleum in their kitchen. I didn't know how to tell her that it wasn't the same. Because this was not grief; this was something different.

I cut into a shiny green pepper, the seeds spilling onto the cutting board. The smell of the tomato was pungent and sweet. Quietly, we prepared a salad too big for the two of us.

"I forgot vinegar," she said suddenly, her face dropping. "I can't make dressing without red wine vinegar."

"I'll go get some," I said, relieved almost to be able to be alone for a minute. "While I'm at the store, the fish can defrost."

The closest store was Hudson's, six miles from the lake. I took my old Volkswagen Bug out of the garage where it had been sitting since I left Vermont. I was embarrassed now by the bumper stickers advertising who I once thought I wanted to be.

The sky was bright; the sun shone through the dusty windshield. Max hated this car. He said it made him feel claustrophobic, that it was made for midgets. It was perfect for me, though. I even had plenty of room to stretch my legs out. Max ended up buying a car that summer so he wouldn't feel so cramped. But when we moved to the camp we drove the Bug, with all of our things in a U-Haul trailer we pulled behind us. He complained the entire way, making me stop in Montpelier, St. Johnsbury, and West Burke so he could stretch his legs.

At the far end of the lake, I drove past my favorite camp. I didn't know who lived there, but I had always loved it. It looked like a fairy-tale cottage. And it, like the Bug, seemed to be made for little people. The yard was filled with rose bushes that would bloom in surprising colors in early summer. Peach, yellow, silver, and red. There was a separate building off to the side that had round windows, like portholes looking out at the lake. Stained glass, in colors too vivid to describe with crayon box–color words. Near the treeline was a swing set made from old barn boards, the red paint now chipped and peeling like Gussy's camp.

The sky and water were achingly blue. Perhaps that is why the red swing was so startling. There was never a child living at this house. I was certain of this. I longed for a child my age to live there when I was young. I imagined that if a little girl lived there then I wouldn't be stuck tagging along behind my older sister, Colette. But it had always been a still, empty swing. Now, as I drove slowly, almost stopping, it seemed to stand as a testament to a child grown quite suddenly too old.

It was the first thing I showed Max as we drove toward Gussy's that day. Even before the lake, I wanted him to see this nursery-rhyme cottage and the red swing. As we drove toward the cabin, I pointed toward the swing. But as I motioned to it, suspended by a thick rope from its wooden frame, there were no words to accompany my gesture. There was no way to articulate the red empty familiarity of the swing's stillness. Instead, I recollected something about someone who might have lived there a long time ago. I think now that I must have lied.

I played with her. We caught crayfish with hot dogs on the end of a stick. She had a locket with a picture of her dead mother inside. She stopped coming to the lake the summer I turned nine. Felicity. A girl without a mother named after happiness. Later that summer when I began to feel his hatred like heat, the swing became the same color as the geraniums I tried to coax from the reluctant soil. And I noticed then that there wasn't nearly as much blue as I had thought. The sky was white with humidity, the lake gray.

I drove past the cottage and onto the main road into town. When I was little, the Hudsons actually owned the store. They were an elderly couple, both covered with so many enormous liver spots I once told my mother I thought that they were really Frog and Toad from my favorite books at the time. But both of them must have either died or hopped away when I was in high school, because the Moffetts had owned it since.

I used to kiss Billy Moffett for hours and hours in the woods between Hudson's and the camp when I was sixteen. We snuck away to the same spot for an entire summer. I would wait for him to get out of work, and then we would ride our bikes through the woods to the junkyard. It wasn't really a junkyard, but for some reason deep in the woods there was a mountain of old stoves and refrigerators, washing machines and dryers. After we lay our bikes down on the ground, carefully avoiding the sparkling mountains of broken glass, we would spend hours tearing the appliances apart, smashing the glass oven doors, ripping knobs off the washing machines. And then we would collapse, exhausted from our destruction, and make out. We would kiss and kiss until our lips were chapped and our clothes dirty from rolling around. We pretended that we were lovers instead of kids and that the junkyard was a lovers' hideaway instead of our playground. And then he accidentally broke my nose when he was swinging a metal pole at a Freon tube. My father called his father and made him apologize to me in front of my mother, Gussy, and Grampa after I told him that Billy had done it on purpose. How else was I supposed to explain a bloodied and misplaced nose? They would never have understood our bizarre mating ritual of wreaking havoc on a bunch of broken-down appliances.

The store used to be a one-room schoolhouse. My mother went there when she was in the third grade, before they built the K-8 in Quimby. There was still a bell on the roof, and inside there was a desk near the freezers that they couldn't get unbolted from the floor. As I walked through the familiar yellow door, I noticed a big green Megabucks machine near the counter. An ATM machine and a self-serve espresso machine. But the postcards in the stand by the door were the same. They had probably been there since the fifties; not many tourists come this far into the woods.

The girl behind the counter was terribly pretty, probably no more than fourteen. She was watching a soap opera on the TV mounted on the wall by the window. She was sitting on a stool absently swinging her legs, speckled with scabby bug bites. The color of her skin was like the color of early summer itself. Sunshine and hope.

I grabbed a red plastic basket and picked up a few things that I knew I would need later. An economy-size can of Off, chocolate kisses, half and half. I found the vinegar next to the diapers and motor oil. The price tag said $3. I counted the crumpled bills in my pocket and put the can of Off back on the shelf. Things at Hudson's have always cost more than in town. The Hudsons started a tradition of jacking up prices back in the seventies when the first tourists discovered Gormlaith. They were used to city prices, willing to pay $4.50 for a gallon of milk. The old school-house store was *quaint,* and the tourists (the Hudsons quickly discovered) were frivolous.

A man came into the store as I was trying to get the girl's attention. The sleigh bells hanging on the door jingled. He had to lower his head to avoid bumping it on the doorway. He looked like Sidney Poitier, only much taller, and I forgot for a moment where I was. In Seattle, there were so many different kinds and colors of people. Japanese ladies in the U-District, black children playing in the streets, Muslims and Hindus. Clothes like costumes. Faces like dreams. But here, in the northeast corner of Vermont, his dark skin made him look transported from a foreign land. Even his clothes and posture looked like a magazine cutout. Definitely a tourist. He grabbed a newspaper from the stack by the counter.

"Excuse me," I said to the pretty girl whose mouth had fallen open as she stared at the screen. She absently scratched a bug bite on her shin without looking away from the TV.

"Melissa." He reprimanded her. His voice was thick and deep, like gravel and molasses.

She looked away from the screen and scurried off the stool to the counter.

"Sorry, Mr. Jackson," she whined and blushed. "But it's my *soaps.*"

He grinned at me.

"Thank you." I smiled.

He tipped his baseball hat and disappeared behind the giant display of charcoal and lighter fluid.

"Twelve ninety-five," she said and turned to look again at the TV.

I handed her the bills and she reluctantly made change.

"I don't need a bag." I smiled and grabbed the awkward items to avoid annoying her further.

On the way back to the camp I thought about how I used to wait for Billy to get done with work that summer. He would watch basketball while I pretended to be shopping for Gussy. I read all of the magazines that summer. Even *Good Housekeeping* and *Sports Illustrated*. I felt sorry for what I did to Billy.

After dinner, Gussy started to clear the dishes.

"Stop," I said and pulled at the sleeve of her cardigan. "I'll get them later. Sit with me."

"Just let me get them in the sink," she said and pulled away, balancing the salad bowl and the plates laced with transparent fish bones.

I went to the porch and turned on the small lamp by the daybed. It wasn't dark outside yet, but the sun was starting to fall slowly into the water. I took off my sandals and laid down on the bed. It was as soft and lumpy as I remembered. The blanket was pilly; I tore absently at them as I waited for Gussy. I could hear her running water, washing dishes. She has never been able to leave a mess. She can't rest until everything is clean and tidy.

From the porch you can see the ragged shore of the island. As the sky grew dark, the edges blurred, and it looked like an inlet rather than a separate place. While Gussy wiped down the counters and dried the dishes, I began to plan a trip to the island to see if my tree was still there.

"Would you like some tea?" Gussy's voice swam to me from the kitchen.

"No thanks," I said, and then realized it might settle my stomach. "I mean, yes. Please."

I put my face into the blackberry steam, and smelled other evenings. I supposed this tea bag came from the same tin I had sent Grampa two Christmases ago when he was alive.

"It's quiet tonight. The summer people haven't come yet," Gussy said and raised the teacup to her lips. Her hands were remarkably steady. Grampa's hands hadn't been steady for several years before he died. His fingers trembled with even the smallest gesture: holding a nail steady, grasping the slender handle of a teacup.

"Do you miss him, Gussy?"

She set her cup down on his desk and leaned back in the wicker chair. She pulled her cardigan around her and held her breath. When she breathed again, her chest fell gently. "Did I tell you how I met your grandfather?"

"I think so, but tell me again," I said and looked away from her to the sun that had slipped away without my noticing.

"I was sixteen then. A girl." She smiled. "Not much younger than you."

I didn't interrupt. I was far enough from sixteen now to be sentimental.

"He had a brand-new car. A Dodge he bought from his uncle's shop. It was beautiful."

"What color?"

"Black," she said. "Dark as night and shiny."

"What happened?" I realized I hadn't heard this story. I didn't remember there being a car.

"I was walking to school with my girlfriend, Jessie. It was springtime. I think we were thinking about skipping school and coming up here to go swimming."

"Did he give you a ride?" I asked.

"Oh lord, no." She laughed. "I stepped off the curb to cross the street, you know where the pet shop used to be?"

I nodded.

"Well, before they put in the stoplight there weren't even any signs or anything. People were just slower then, more careful. But your grandfather, in his brand new Dodge, comes down the road and doesn't stop. Just as I'm stepping off the curb he hits me, knocks me to the ground." She pulled her sweater tightly around her and picked up her tea again.

"He hit you with his car?"

"Uh-huh." She nodded. "And he drove me all the way to the hospital in that car too. I was out of school for six weeks. He came to see me every afternoon, parking that monster in front of my house so everybody knew he was there. A year later we were married."

"Jeez," I said.

I looked at her for some sort of nostalgia or melancholia, but she was concentrating on a run in her stocking.

"The fish was good, wasn't it?" she said after a while, tracing a thick blue vein underneath the sheer hose.

"It was good, Gussy."

After Gussy left, I took my suitcase upstairs to the loft. The sheets were pulled back, waiting for me it seemed. I opened the curtains and let the moon fill the room. The ceiling was slanted, and I bumped my head as I leaned over to pick up a crumpled piece of paper from the floor. It looked as though it had been through the wash, and crumbled as I unfolded it, disintegrating before I could read the blurred ink. I laid down in the bed and wondered if it was a grocery list or a note. I wondered if it belonged to Max. If it had somehow avoided years of Gussy's meticulousness only to arrive and crumble in my hands.

October 3, 1987

❧ ❧ ❧ I find Max when I am only looking for a quiet place to read.

I lock the door to my dorm room and wander down the concrete corridor to the stairwell. It is Sunday morning, and the air is still thick with the smell of cigarette smoke, spilled beer, and the fading perfume scent of hopeful girls. Last night I listened to them dancing and flirting. For hours, I eavesdropped until the sound of their laughter inevitably turned to the violence of vomiting and toilets flushing. One girl was crying and, on the other side of my wall, were the faint squeaky rhythms of making love. I hate this place. I hate this limbo between adolescence and whatever is supposed to be on the other side.

My backpack is heavy, the hard spine of *The Riverside Shakespeare* digging into my tailbone as I make my way down the stairs, holding my breath against the stench. When I open the door, the autumn air is clean and brisk. The sunny sky through my sliver of a window was deceiving; it isn't summer anymore. But the sharp wind and the cloudless sky make everything beautiful today.

The trees on the quad of my building look like they are on fire. I can hardly see the pavement walkway for all of the colors littering the ground. I would study under one of these trees, but the same voices from last night will burst through open windows soon enough. Frisbees and Hacky Sacks will make it impossible to concentrate. There will be too many distractions here for Shakespeare.

I walk through the park, my feet crushing the brittle leaves, leaving a trail of fiery dust in my wake. The library isn't open yet, so I walk down Main Street, down the steep hill from the campus to the lake. I walk past Victorian houses whose widows' walks are strewn with beer bottles and boxer shorts. Whose gingerbread trim has been replaced by painted Greek letters.

The bakery next to the movie theater is open, and inside the scones are still hot from the oven. The girl behind the counter smothers mine with raspberry jam. Outside, the brown paper bag is warm in my hands. The sun follows me out of the bakery, past the shops and restaurants to the park at the edge of the lake.

I have found the only truly quiet place in this town. The only noise here is the shrill arrival and departure of the ducks. It may very well be the only spot that remains unmolested by students. Undiscovered, except by an occasional child who has wandered from his mother. You have to be small to find this place. You have to think like a child to get here.

Behind an old brick wall strangled with ivy is a tunnel of leaves. The foliage is thick, camouflaging the entrance. You might not know that you could crawl into its green darkness unless you were looking for a place to hide. The cave of ivy and shrubbery must be six feet deep. I crawl on my hands and knees through the leaves. The smell is deep and green. Branches tickle and scratch my arms and face. This is the only way to get to this particular inlet of the lake. The only entrance and exit. When I emerge on the other side, I am startled to see someone standing at the edge of the water.

I don't know what to do. I am frozen at the opening of the tunnel. Part of me thinks I should go back, crawl backward through the dark cavern to the park, try to find a quiet bench, forget about solitude today. Part of me is curious. How did he get here? He could never have fit inside the secret entrance. And so, for several moments, I just watch.

He is turned toward the water; I can't see his face. He is tall and thin, his straight dark hair falling over the back of the collar of his faded denim shirt. His khaki pants are rolled up, his feet bare. He is holding a stack of papers; it's hard to see what they are. He kneels down, setting the papers next to him on the grassy shore, and begins to fold one of the pages. His hands are tan, his fingers long and thin. He is careful, methodical in this task. Soon, the page has become a boat, the paper boat a child makes. He sets it in the water, and a small current carries it away from the shore. He keeps folding the pages until there is an entire fleet of paper ships.

I watch until there are no pages left at all. I am quiet, and he is quiet, and the pages look like white leaves instead of paper as they drift away. I wait to see what he does, and I don't move from the mouth of the cave.

"I hear you," he says, standing again.

I think for a second that he is only talking to the water, certain that I am obscured by the leaves.

"I said, I hear you. You can come out now."

"Excuse me?" I say softly.

He turns around, and I fall forward onto my hands, the weight of Shakespeare on my back pushing me forward. I can feel the gravel and dirt making pinpricks in the palms of my hands. When I look up, he is reaching out to help me. I accept his hand, and he pulls me up. His eyes are wet, his eyelashes glistening as if drops of rain had fallen there. But his eyes are strangely dimensionless: flat, black circles without light.

"What are you doing?" I ask. It's easier to ask this stranger why he has launched those pages like small ships into the water than to ask about his tears.

"Do you have a mother?" he asks.

"What do you mean?" I ask. "Everyone has a mother."

"I mean, is she alive?"

"Oh. Yeah, of course. Why?"

"My mother is dead," he says. "Today."

"She died today?" I ask in horror.

"For me, she's dead. I *decided* today." His voice is soft.

I am quiet.

"Letters. From my psychotic mother," he says, gesturing toward the lake. "Every day since I left home, pleading with me to come back. All the guilt in the world is in those letters."

"I know what you mean." I smile. I think of the care packages my mother has been sending me. The boxes of my favorite cookies, the aspirin and coffee beans and Tang. About her silly reprimands to write more, call more. Collect, if I need to.

"You do, huh?" He laughs, shaking his head. His expression tells me there is more to this story. That I am a little foolish, maybe.

He sits down next to me at the water's edge. He smells clean, like wind and grass. I open up the bag from the bakery. I take the scone out and split it in half, handing half to him. Quietly we eat the sweet scone, watching the water carry his mother away.

The next day I arrive after my Shakespeare class, and he is already there folding more paper boats. This time I bring him blueberry muffins. Coffee. The day after that, I offer him a chocolate croissant and freshly squeezed orange juice in a plastic cup. Every day for six days, I meet him there after a stop at the bakery and watch him let go of another piece of his mother. But each day, I get a sense that it is not as simple as this. That setting sail to her letters is only a gesture. That she is still with us on the shore, between us as we share another breakfast. His flat dark eyes suggest that his sadness is heavier than Shakespeare on my back. Heavier than the dark clouds that move across the sky when I hold out an apricot danish and he refuses.

Instead, he sits next to me on the grass without saying a word. For a half an hour we sit like this. When he finally speaks, he tells me about what happened after his father left them.

"You have to understand a few things," he says.

I nod.

"This is who I am. That won't change."

He tells me about the boy who cowered inside the locked closet, when she put him there to teach him about darkness. About the way her dresses enclosed him and the heels of her shoes bruised his ribs. About the boy whose legs bled from the belt she swung to remind him that no one is immune to pain. Not even children. About the boy who stood at the edge of the road as his mother drove away to teach him a lesson about how it feels to be left behind. About the smell of gasoline and the way her hair looked as it blew out of the driver's side window.

When he rests his head in my lap, I stroke that little boy's hair. I touch the pulsing vein at that little boy's temple. Each touch, I think, might help to erase the scars. I run my finger along the thin line of his lips, across the ridge of his chipped tooth from the first fall.

The next day, he brings *me* a present. He hands me a pocket watch on a silver chain as delicate and fragile as a spider's web.

"For being patient." He smiles.

He puts the watch in the palm of my hand, closes my fingers around it. His hand is strong, larger than mine, pressing my fingers against the cold, smooth silver.

"Thank you," I say.

I don't know until later that it is broken. That the hands don't move. That time is frozen inside this gift from Max.

June 1994

∾ ∾ ∾ In the morning, I woke up before the sun. I had been dreaming the sound of Grampa's bagpipes. Every morning he would stand at the end of the dock in his pajamas, waking the world with his music. He was terrible, but persistent. His own grandfather had played, and he said he was just carrying on tradition. My childhood mornings are made of this sound: bagpipes, water, and Gussy in the kitchen.

I searched the shed for the oars and wished that I had shoes on. Rusty nails threatened tetanus with every step. Behind the plastic lawn chairs and the old mower were the oars as well as a stack of orange life jackets. I grabbed the oars and one of the smaller jackets and stepped tentatively back out onto the driveway. I knew I should eat breakfast, but I was eager to get out to the island to see if the tree was still there.

There were clouds covering most of the sky, but the weather forecast on the public radio station had predicted afternoon sunshine. I went back into the camp and grabbed a peach from the blue bowl on the counter. It was too early for peaches. It was hard, the skin taut, reluctant.

I rolled the cuffs on my jeans up and stepped into the water; there was the carcass of a crayfish in the sand. Tess and I would lure crayfish with bits of hot dog when we were little. Grampa would cook them up in one of Gussy's big silver pots. When they emerged from the pot, red and steaming, he would arrange them on one of Gussy's platters. *Delicacies*, he said. *The rare miniature lobsters of Gormlaith.* I couldn't eat them because I was allergic to shellfish.

When I untied the boat and set the oars inside, I realized that I had never been in a boat alone on Gormlaith. I felt the way I did the first time I went grocery shopping. The first time I wrote a check, drove a car.

I awkwardly put the oars into the oars locks and started to push myself away from the shore. The sun shone brightly on my arms and then disappeared behind the clouds. The island was less than a half mile away, and I was glad. I tried to remember the rhythm of this task, dipping the oars into the water and pulling them out at the right time. The boat turned left and then right. Slowly and steadily, I made my way to the island.

I was seven the first time I went to the island. It was my birthday, and Grampa told me that he would take me to his favorite place. We set out after my chosen breakfast of banana and chocolate chip pancakes, one Gussy must have made against her better judgment. I had a small allergy to bananas, and later we both knew my arms would be covered with blotchy hives. As we rowed out to the island, Grampa was quiet. I pointed and asked questions, and he quietly rowed. But when we got to the shore, his face lit up. He took me by the hand as we hiked through the woods to the other side. He named all the trees by genus and species, comparing the more mysterious ones to the pastel drawings in the dog-eared book he kept in his back pocket. He snapped the slender stalks of ferns and held the fresh dewy green to his nose. He left me picking wildflowers to bring back to Gussy, while he lit his pipe and disappeared behind a tree. He emerged wearing only his boxer shorts and undershirt. Then he stepped carefully across the rocky shore and waded into the water, still smoking his pipe. For almost an hour he floated on his back, smoking. The smoke curled up in perfect spirals of liquid fire.

My arms were tired, and I stopped rowing for a minute as I passed two loons dipping and flapping their wings against the glassy surface of the water. The bottom of the boat sunk and crushed the sandy bank at the shore of the island. I struggled to pull the boat up onto the grass so that it wouldn't float away and leave me stranded. I tethered it to a tree trunk to make sure it wouldn't disappear, and then began to make my way through the woods.

My heart raced as I walked through the trees, the burrs and branches scraping my bare ankles. No one lived here. It was too rocky to build a foundation, too small for a home. But it took me nearly ten minutes to find the place. As I wandered through the trees' gnarled branches and tangled leaves, I wondered if I had been mistaken. Some things still felt too much like dreams to be real. But this was vivid. I dreamed this tree, I dreamed that day over and over. And soon, I began to recognize the landscape. The archway of birches, architecture of white bones and transparent leaves. Just when I was ready to give up, I saw the willow.

When I was a child, the willow curved gently over the spring, making a perfect veil under which I could hide as Grampa and Gussy picnicked near the shore. I made its umbrella my cave of leaves. While Gussy pulled plates and utensils, wineglasses and a corkscrew from the picnic basket like Mary Poppins from her magic bag, I lay on the cool ground beneath the tree and pretended I was invisible. But now, the willow remained the way it had since that afternoon with Max.

The wood was blackened, split down the center. Leaves no longer grew from the willow's fingertips. Its charred limbs couldn't hide me anymore. Because that summer, kissed by a gentle summer storm, trusting the sky, lightning came as a surprise, and its graceful back was quickly broken by the light.

June 1991

ᖇ ᖇ ᖇ Blue morning. This is a perfect day, and I wake up feeling full. When Max sleeps I love him. He is like a child in slumber, vulnerable and kind. When we first shared a bed, I would stay awake all night sometimes watching him sleep. The window is open, and soft wind brushes my bare shoulders. I consider kissing him, but know this will reverse the magic. I have been disappointed before, and I am learning how to make the spells I cast in the middle of the night linger.

I walk quietly down the wooden stairs that spiral from the loft to the living room and am dizzy when I reach the floor. On the sunporch the shades are drawn, rolled all the way to the floor, enclosing us inside. I open them now, letting in the morning. It's only the night that he fears. The lake is rough, white caps like frothy milk render it a small sea.

I open the bread box and reach for the loaf of sourdough bread he made yesterday. I cut thick slices and cover them with brown honey mustard, smoked Gouda, avocado, and turkey. I scoop mounds of tomato, mozzarella, and red onion salad into a plastic container. I grab a bottle of white wine from the case he bought at the liquor store in town and search through the silverware drawer for a corkscrew.

"Morning," he says and pads into the kitchen. "Coffee?"

"I haven't made it yet." I smile. "I was making lunch. I thought we could row out to the island today."

"Um," he says and sits down in the breakfast nook.

"Kenya or Maxwell House?" I ask. I am accustomed to simple food, student food. But because Max cooks, I am learning to distinguish croissant from biscuit. Gouda from Velveeta.

The coffee fills the kitchen with smells of African coffee plantations, and Max tries to find music on the small radio Gussy keeps on the counter.

"What's on the island?" he asks and sips at the bitter coffee that is too strong for me.

"Not much. A spring, blueberry patches, trees."

"Hmm," he says.

Coming here was my idea. After we graduated I thought we could leave everything behind: the empty classrooms where we went to argue so that no one would hear; the dormitory where he stood and screamed into the night air that he would die unless I loved him back, almost falling down the treacherous fire escape as I stood below weeping in my pajamas. I thought as we drove away from the blossoming campus, the air redolent with lilacs and finality, that I could transform fear into love at the lake.

And, I suppose, it has worked. He sleeps more deeply here. The nights are quieter, and his chest rises and falls more slowly. The dreams of his mother come less frequently. His angry fists beat dough into compliance now, and vegetables offer their suppleness to his sharp knife.

He struggles with the oars, complaining that one is longer than the other, as we make our way slowly toward the island. The air is cooler out here on the water. I let my hand dip into the thick dark surface, watch it change shapes and colors. There are clouds overhead as I tilt my head back and peer at the sky.

"Shit," he says when I tip over the picnic basket while trying to crawl out of the boat onto the shore. The wine bottle breaks and the sharp smell permeates the air.

My chest tightens, and I reach over to pick up the pieces.

"I'll get them," he says, brushing my hand away.

I grab the basket and jump gingerly out of the boat. Max follows behind as I start to walk toward the other side of the island, where I know the willow will make a perfect picnic spot. I can hear him breathing heavily behind me, feel the soft earth yielding beneath our feet.

I spread out a sheet that I found in Gussy's closet and set the picnic basket down. Max sits down and looks into the basket. "Turkey?" he asks.

"Um-hum," I say. I know this is his favorite sandwich.

He peels back the bread and looks at the slices of turkey.

"You shouldn't get the packaged kind," he says. "The kind you get at the deli is better. Fresher."

"I'll do that next time," I say.

"It's full of preservatives. It's *pressed* meat. Not much better than bologna, really."

"Sorry," I say. "I'll get the deli kind when we go into town."

"Did you bring another bottle of wine?" he asks. He knows that I broke the only one.

"No," I say, lowering my head, staring at my hands.

Quietly, I eat my sandwich. He picks the meat out and lays it on a napkin.

"I can't eat this," he says. "It makes me sick."

"Max, I told you I would get the kind you like next time. Why do you do this?" I ask.

"I do this because if I don't tell you how to do things, you have a tendency to screw them up."

My heart thuds dully in my chest. The air feels thick, pregnant even. I can't finish my sandwich, and the mozzarella in the salad is warm. There are crumbs from the hard crust of the sourdough in my hair.

"It feels like a storm," I say.

"Maybe," he says. "We should get back anyway."

"Don't you want to go swimming or anything?"

"Not really."

"Well I do," I say. I pull my shirt over my head, trembling when the cool air touches my skin. I hope that I will be able to distract him with this.

"Jesus," he says.

"There's nobody here," I say and run toward the shore. I step across some slippery rocks until I am far enough out to dive.

"Effie, damn."

I look back at him sitting below the willow. The sky is growing dark. The breeze trembles across my shoulders.

"We'd better get back," he says, crooking his finger at me, luring me back like a child.

"Just a little swim," I holler. "Come in with me."

"I said we'd better get back. I just felt some rain," he says and stands up.

I move further out on the rocks. The air is cold on my bare chest; I shiver.

"Fine," he says and kicks the picnic basket. A bunch of red grapes spill out onto the clean white sheet. "I'll fucking leave you here."

I don't move. I try to imagine what it would feel like to jump into the lake, the first shock of cold and then the water slowly warming, encircling me. As he starts to walk away, the sky rumbles, threatens. I put my arms around myself and look at the black clouds swarming overhead. I can't see the red of his shirt anymore, and I begin to panic. I am suddenly running across the rocks, scraping my ankle when I slip near the shore. I struggle to put my shirt back on and I call after him. He doesn't answer.

I sit down under the willow and wait, stubbornly hoping that he will return. The rain begins to come down in hard sheets; my hair sticks to my face. The thunder explodes, and my heart races. He is not coming back. I start to fold the wet sheet, to put the dirty plates and containers back in the picnic basket. My hands are shaking. The rain blinds me, my eyes filling with tears and rain. I trip on a fallen tree branch and scrape my wrist. A thin trickle of blood stains my shirt as I hold the sting closely to me. I find him in the woods.

"Are you crazy?" he asks. "Come with me and get in the goddamn boat."

"Max, it'll be safer to wait out the storm here. If there's lightning we could get in a lot of trouble out there." I plead.

"Well, I'm going back," he says and starts to walk away again.

"Max, don't," I cry and drop the picnic basket. "We can wait under this tree," I say and motion to the willow.

"No," he yells into the rain.

I run after him, stubbing my toes and scraping my legs. At the landing, he steps into the boat and grabs the oars. "Are you coming?"

I stand still for a moment, as he sits down in the boat and begins to push away from shore.

"Fine," I say and reach out to the edge of the boat. When I step into the boat, it rocks with my weight, threatening to spill me.

"Sit down," he says.

He raises one of the oars and pushes us violently away from the safety of the island into the cold gray water. A flash of light and more rain. I sit as far away from him as I can and pray. I recite bedtime prayers each time the lightning strikes. I am shivering and the wind keeps blowing us farther and farther away.

"I'm scared," I say as thunder cracks like old bones. I know he won't hear.

We finally get turned around and Max rows frantically until I can see the red of the camp. I feel lightheaded, dizzy, and cold. My T-shirt is stuck to me, and my hair tastes like rain in the corner of my mouth. The sky is no longer blue, but almost black.

When the bright bolt of light strikes, the island is illuminated by the flash.

I lie down on the daybed in my wet clothes, staring at the lake, until Max climbs up the stairs to the loft. I wait until I hear the sounds of his sleep and then climb the stairs and curl myself around his familiar body.

Later that summer, when Max is in town grocery shopping, Gussy and I go to the island and I find the tree that the lightning kissed. I touch the cold black wood and start to cry. He made me believe that day that he knew where lightning would strike. And I realized that the places I thought were safe weren't safe at all.

June 1994

ᔕ ᔕ ᔕ I began painting early each morning and worked straight through until noon. Then I would swim to wash the salty sweat from my skin and begin again. The first week I could barely lift my arms in the morning, but now they weren't even sore anymore. I planned to finish the front of the camp by the Fourth of July. It was an arbitrary deadline, really. But I wanted the front of the house to look nice by the time the summer people started to arrive.

I was reluctant to get out of bed that day. I was working on the area near the loft window, and got a touch of vertigo every time I was up that high on the ladder. I swung my legs to the edge of the bed and stared at my pale skin; another hazard of painting is that the sun touches only the back of you. I looked like a half-roasted marshmallow: golden on one side and white on the other.

The phone rang. I scrambled down the stairs, almost tripping on my long nightie to get to the phone in time.

"Effie?"

"Hi, Mom."

"Want some company?" she asked.

"Sure," I said. "What time?"

"I thought I'd leave in a few minutes. We could have break-fast," she said.

"Okay, Mom."

I couldn't believe how long my parents had waited to see me. My mother had called once right after I arrived. She said my father was busy finishing up his semester. They would see me soon. What she meant was that it had been three years, that I shouldn't expect them to just drop everything to see me when I had hardly written or called. That Colette would never have done this sort of thing.

I got the bucket of paint from the shed and found my brushes, clean and dry, on a piece of newspaper on the picnic table out-side. I brought everything to the front of the camp. The ladder was still leaning against the wall. There were curled pieces of paint littering the green grass like crayon shavings. I needed to move the ladder over to the left-hand side of the camp. I almost tripped on the wooden steps that led up to the unused front door. I started to cuss, and then something caught my eye.

I knelt down and saw a robin's nest with a tiny blue egg inside. I picked up the broken shell, in two perfect pieces, and looked over my shoulder for a clue as to how it had arrived on my step. Nothing. I would have noticed if a robin had made the steps its nesting place. It must be a gift from Magoo, I thought. He used to do things like this for Gussy and Grampa all the time: a story found in the newspaper, a feather, jars of marmalade. But it was still too early for Magoo to be up. He didn't start splitting wood until after he had his morning pipe and a full breakfast. He probably left it for me the night before, after I had gone to sleep. I turned back to the nest and picked it up gently in my hands.

It was the size of a saucer, the egg even smaller inside.

I forgot about painting and carried the nest inside. I set it on the windowsill above the sink next to three green tomatoes. I went back outside and walked down the road a ways, looking for something to give Magoo in return for this odd gift. But as I walked away from the camp, all I could find were pebbles and ferns tickling the edge of the road.

When I got to Magoo's house, I could see that his curtains were drawn. Rather than wake him up, I decided to go to the tree house. Maybe I would find a gift along the way. The path was overgrown. I wrestled through the waist-high foliage until I could see the rope ladder. As I climbed, I remembered the feeling of rope in my hands. The urgency of climbing quickly to get away from Colette and her friends below. When I reached the small wooden landing, I stepped off the ladder and opened the door. It was warm and stuffy inside. This will be my next project, I thought. Fresh paint, maybe new hinges on the door. No one but me fit inside here anymore. When I was a child, Tess and I made all of our plans here, made pacts and fabricated dreams. There weren't any children anymore, though, and everyone else would bump their heads on the low ceiling. Max and I tried to spend the night here once, but his legs were too long for the bunks. We walked back to the camp in the middle of the night so he would be able to sleep.

The bookcases built into the wall were empty and dusty, the books probably in storage in the shed. The bunk mattresses were also gone; only the bare rusty frames remained. No curtains, and I recognized the blackened wood where a careless candle from my adolescence left its scar on the windowsill. Through the window I could see Magoo's house. He opened the door and waddled slowly toward his mountain of wood. He sat down on a tree stump and began to load his pipe. Then as he puffed, he took off his thick glasses and rubbed them with the soft corner of his flannel shirt. When Grampa was alive they would sit together for hours by the woodpile, smoking quietly, occasionally gesturing toward a new cabin going up across the lake or to a family of loons. Earwigs on a plant, skid marks from a teenager's car.

I closed the door of the tree house and crawled back down the ladder. It seemed so much higher up when I was small. I started walking toward Magoo's house, waving and smiling.

"Good morning, Heidi," he said, waving and squinting at me.

"It's Effie, Mr. Tucker," I said.

He put his glasses back on and smiled. The air smelled sweet around him.

"Effie Greer. You've brought sunshine with you today."

"For you," I said, motioning to the sky.

I thought of thanking him for the robin's egg, but I was a bit afraid that it would ruin the magic. I decided, instead, to bring him something later.

I could hear my mother's car coming up the road. I went into the camp to make lemonade. I needed something to keep my hands busy.

"Hi, honey," she said. She was holding a big cardboard box.

"Hi, Mom," I said and stirred the powdered lemonade with a wooden spoon.

She set the box on the table in the breakfast nook and stood awkwardly in front of me. I stopped stirring and let her hug me. Her back was stiff, her skin cold. When we parted, I smiled nervously.

"It's sticky today," she said, tugging at the long sleeve blouse she was wearing.

"You want some lemonade?" I asked.

"Sure."

I opened the freezer to look for ice. I filled two plastic tumblers with ice and lemonade.

"The camp looks great," she said. "How long has it taken you?"

"A couple of weeks," I said, handing her the glass. "I'm pretty slow."

"Well, it looks good. And there isn't any hurry. I think Gussy is just grateful that you are helping out."

"How's Daddy?"

"Good. He's teaching two classes this summer. A light load." She sipped the lemonade and though her lips puckered, she nodded. "This is good."

"What's he doing today?"

"Grading papers. He said to give you a hug though. He's planning to come visit you soon."

I drank my lemonade quickly and stood up from the table to get more.

"He was asking if you've thought about what you'd like to do this fall yet."

"No, Mom. I haven't. I just got here."

"I'm sure Daddy could pull some strings at the college. Maybe you could start the graduate program. Part-time even."

"That's not why I came back here." My heart was racing, and her face was getting red.

"I know, it's just that we're so worried about you. What happened to all of your plans?"

"I left my boyfriend. Three years later he dies of a heroin overdose, Mom. I guess maybe some of my plans don't seem too goddamned relevant right now." My hands were shaking. I dropped an ice cube on the floor. I could feel the cold against my bare feet.

My mother was staring at her hands. "It's not your fault,

honey," she said looking up, her eyes pleading with me. What she wanted was for me to stop. If she could, she would have put her hands over her ears.

"I know it's not my fault. That's not exactly the point," I said softly.

She held the empty glass to her lips; I could hear the ice cubes hit her teeth.

"It's more complicated, Mom. You need to let me . . ." and then I let my words fall away from me. I could almost see them fade into the air in front of my face.

Her eyebrows settled into soft arches again. Her fear of hearing what I had to say was gone. She was safe again. She could pretend again that I had not made so many terrible mistakes.

"Colette is coming in a couple of weeks," she said softly.

"Why?" I asked, suddenly furious again. The last thing I needed right now was to see Colette.

"To visit. She's stopping by on her way to visit Justin in Saratoga."

"Great."

"Effie," she said, scowling, and went to the sink with her empty glass. Then the nest distracted her. "This is beautiful," she said, forgetting to finish her reprimand. She picked up the robin's egg and cradled it in her palm. "Where did you find this?"

"By the tree house." I lied. "I found it when I was sweeping out the dead flies. On one of the branches. I wouldn't have taken it unless the egg was hatched."

"You should keep an eye out for the baby." She smiled. "Maybe put a feeder up or something."

"I will," I said.

"Well, I just wanted to check in with you. I brought some of your books from Gussy's." She motioned to the box.

"You're leaving already? I thought we were going to eat breakfast."

"I need to get back pretty soon. Your father wants to go to the farmer's market when he's done grading papers. Tomatoes." She nodded. "We need tomatoes."

"You've only been here a half an hour," I said, but she was already moving toward the door.

"We'll come see you next weekend. How about that? Maybe we can have a Fourth of July picnic with Gussy. Did you find the grill in the shed? Gussy said it should still work just fine. Maybe we can pick up some watermelon at the market."

"Okay," I said. "Next weekend."

As I painted the trim near the bedroom window, I caught a glimpse of my reflection in the glass, recollecting the glance I gave a photographer one childhood afternoon. Elbow deep in prickly white fabric freckled with silver to look like snow, I wore a dress the color of rust. He kept counting to three before he flashed the bright lights. He had a sock puppet and dandruff on his glasses. The lights were almost blinding, and the paper forest backdrop kept curling down behind me from the heat of the lamps.

When the photos arrived three weeks later, I knew something was wrong as soon as I looked through the plastic window of the envelope. My mother sat cutting apart a hundred likenesses of me; the room smelling of her patience. She pretended that nothing was wrong with the pictures, that they were perfect little Kodachrome portraits. But in each and every picture, duplicated in three or four different sizes, the flat winter forest behind me was falling down. Behind every glossy evergreen backdrop was autumn. Where the edges of the evergreen forest fell was the wrong forest where the leaves were dying. And in the picture, you couldn't tell the difference between my hair and my dress and the shiny dead leaves. I was six years old and caught between seasons, falling quietly into fall.

At the kitchen table, she cut away the wrong backdrop, the wrong season (these photos were to be Christmas gifts for everyone we knew). She cut and cut until she had not only cut away the careless photographer's trees, but my hair, my shoulders, and my rust-colored dress. All that was left was my somber face.

It is this glance, this expression that I saw reflected in the bedroom window, the lake shimmering behind me. And it was the same expression I gave him each time he banged his fist into the wall over my head, no matter how much plaster fell like snow into my hair. I was still caught between the seasons of his fury, but in the glance you couldn't see his winter, you would only see me falling into fall. Fading into the wrong backdrop.

August 1991

∾ ∾ ∾ I ride my bicycle slowly back from the blueberry patch, careful not to spill the basket brimming with blueberries. My fingers are stained, my lips (I am certain) are blue. The road twists and turns, and I stop to gather wildflowers for the table and stones to use as paperweights. I stop several times just to prolong this tender feeling I am having about my life today. It is late afternoon by the time I get home.

I see Max's car in the driveway, the car he bought to spare his long legs from my Bug. He must have gotten back from the grocery store while I was huddled in the blueberry patch gorging myself on the plump, sweet berries. My chest aches as I get off the bike and open the screen door.

"Here are the blueberries," I say and set the basket down away from where he is working.

"Can you put them in the fridge?" he asks.

"Uh-huh." I smile and pour them into a colander. Each berry tumbling down, each wearing its own small crown. That was how you could tell that they were blueberries instead of the other, poisonous, ones. My grandfather had shown me this, shown me the regal blueberry and the evil blue imposter side by side.

"What are you making?" I ask and peek into the pot he is stirring.

"Ciappino."

"What's that?"

"Italian seafood stew. With whole crab legs, mussels, salmon, scallops."

"Decadent," I say. I don't remind him that I am allergic to shellfish.

"I suppose." He smiles.

I am tired from hiking through the blueberry patch, from riding my bicycle up hills. I hug him softly from behind so as not to disturb the rhythm of his stirring. Then I go to the front porch to lie down. The sheets on the daybed are embroidered with orange sunflowers. I imagine Gussy sitting alone on the porch, patiently threading her needle. As I run my fingers over the raised petals and leaves, I imagine that when Grampa went for his nightly swim, Gussy lit a thick green candle and watched her fingers rise and fall. These sheets had been here since my mother was a child. Gussy was my age when she patiently coaxed sunflowers from clean, white cloth. I used to rub the floss and cotton between my fingers to fall asleep.

I lie down and listen to Max's kitchen sounds. The scratchy radio, the ciappino bubbling, the hiss of a beer opening. I feel almost happy. The lake is choppy; the rhythm of the small waves tapping the shore lulls me to sleep.

Soon I awaken to darkness. I am lying on top of the blankets, cold and disoriented. I reach over to the nightstand and turn on the lamp. Its orange glow casts strange shadows across my thighs. My heart races at the silence in the kitchen. There is an odd scent in the air.

I go to the kitchen and see pots and pans strewn all over the stovetop and counters. Red sauce splattered on pale Formica. The sink is full of shells, gray and pink carcasses. There are seven empty beer bottles lined up on the table in the breakfast nook. My heart pounds thickly in my chest. I knock on the closed bathroom door and push it open gently. Empty. I go back to the living room and up the stairs to the loft. I expect to see him, hope to find him asleep in the soft bed. But the bed is empty, the mountain of quilts and blankets deceiving.

I return to the kitchen and gently push the door open.

He is sitting in an Adirondack chair facing the lake. He has dragged the heavy wooden chair from the shed to the front yard without me noticing. His arm rises and falls. I think about how to approach him. I practice my words. *Pick a door, pick a door.* If I'm lucky, I will say the words that will make him cradle his head in my arms. Or, better still, the chosen words might make him laugh. But more likely there is only one door and behind that, opened by any words I might choose, is the tiger.

He doesn't hear me approaching. I watch his arm rise and fall. There is a rhythm to everything he does, it seems. Breathing, stirring, drinking.

"Max?"

He is quiet.

"I'm sorry I fell asleep," I say.

I sit down on the ground next to him and when he doesn't speak, I lean my head against his soft arm.

"Have you thought about this fall?" he says, not looking at me but straight ahead.

"What do you mean?"

"I mean, what do you think will happen to us this fall?"

"I don't know," I say. My heart is skipping beats. He is asking me a question I don't want to answer.

He frowns.

"Don't worry," I say.

"You're going to leave," he says.

"Why would you say something like that?" I ask, lifting my head.

"Because it's true, Effie. You'll go off to New York this fall, meet some cocky bastard who sweeps you off your goddamn feet with a glance, and then I'll get the phone call. He'll probably be lying right next to you, sticking his tongue in your goddamned ear, while you make up some excuse. You'll cover the receiver, but I'll still be able to hear you giggling, telling him to stop. And then you'll lie." He is not looking at me. He is staring at the lake.

"Of course, you'll tell me what you think I want to hear. Tell me what you think will keep me from tearing the phone out of the wall and throwing it across the room. And all the while he'll be sitting there."

"Max, why are you doing this?" I ask. I am shivering.

"But I *will* hurl the phone across the room. I'll rip the phone out of the fucking wall so you won't have to hear me. And because all you'll get is a dial tone, you'll always wonder. You will always wonder what happened after the jack came out of the wall," he says.

"Why are you doing this to me?" I ask, allowing tears that I hope will evoke some sort of tenderness from him.

"I'm telling the truth. Isn't that what you want, Effie? You're not pissed off because I'm accusing you of something but because there's *truth* to everything I'm saying. You're looking for a way out. I can see it in everything you do. From the very beginning you've been trying to figure out how to get out of this."

"I am not," I say. But I realize I am lying. I dream the man he fears. "Where did this come from? I'm here aren't I? Why can't you let yourself be happy?" I stare into his eyes, which frighten me with their vacancy.

"Why don't you let yourself be happy!" he cries suddenly. His voice is shrill. He raises his arm to drink, suckling the bottle with his pale lips. "It must be great, to be so simple and small. You have an easy life, Effie Greer. All you need to do is wave your magic Tinker Bell wand and make everyone happy. You spread your fairy dust, and everything is A-OK."

"I don't have to listen to you," I say and start to get up.

"Of course you don't have to." He smiles. "But you will."

"What happened to the ciappino?" I challenge him.

"Fuck you."

"Did you burn it? Did you forget a pot while you were busy opening another bottle? Did you leave the burner on while you were fabricating ways for me to leave you?" I am growing. In the darkness, I feel my bones expanding to accommodate me.

He stands up and knocks the chair onto its side.

I start backing toward the house, slowly. I am trying to make the tiger angry. I want him to attack.

"Did you singe the sauce while you were imagining me with someone else?"

I am certain that he will strike this time. That these bruises will be real. As he puts his hands on my tightened shoulders I will him to hit where it will show. I want his careful kicks, his soft fists to leave marks this time. This will be the proof I need. The violet blossom of broken blood vessels, the blue berry, the evil imposter, will be my proof. But instead he strikes with his words, pushes me softly into the camp, and, later, into the bed, covering my mouth to keep me from telling anyone that there is only one door and it opens to this again and again.

June 29, 1994

౿ ౿ ౿ The clock said three-thirty when I heard someone walking on the front lawn below my window. The sound was heavy, watery, and thick. I was too afraid to sit up. The curtains were open to let in the breeze, and he might have been able to see me. I squeezed my eyes shut and concentrated on the sound of his feet. But behind my eyelids, I saw Max's face. I saw Max watching me as I plucked the oyster shells from the sink, as I dumped soggy cigarette butts from the empty beer bottles. On the back of my eyes, I saw Max walking slowly toward the camp to find me, to make me go back with him again. I forced my eyes open, forced Max away. He was dead. He couldn't come here anymore. Suddenly, I realized that it might be the break-in kids: high schoolers who broke into empty cabins to drink and smoke pot. But it was too late for that; it was that strange spot of time between deep night and dawn. The sky was black, but the air smelled of morning. I pulled the blanket away from my ears so I could listen for voices.

I heard the steps again, the swish of pant legs and dew-drenched grass. My heart was pounding so loudly, I swear I could see my chest rising and falling. I inched my way slowly to the edge of the bed and crawled carefully onto the floor. The wood was hard on my knees as I made my way to the window. There was silence.

I peered out the corner of the glass, trying to see the yard below. It was too dark. There were no streetlamps here. I heard the sound again, and shrank back down to the floor. I looked through the window and it was like peering into nothing. I sat on the floor until I was certain that whatever was making the noise was either gone or just part of a dream I was having, and then I crawled back into the bed. I drifted in and out of sleep until Magoo's rooster started his cockadoodle-dooing at five-thirty and the sun was warm on my bare shoulders.

As I carried my coffee with me outside, I decided that I must have imagined the invasion. It's something I have done since I was little, talking myself into a fearful frenzy. I walked to the edge of the water and felt calm. Silly. I put my feet in the water and drank the hot coffee. It was a strange sensation, terribly hot and terribly cold at the same time. I enjoyed this odd equilibrium of hot and cold, frightened and calm until Magoo started up his chain saw.

I walked back to the camp, whistling loudly over the chain saw's roar. And then I saw a glass jar on the steps to the unused front door. I walked slowly across the yard, thinking that maybe it was just the jar I kept the paintbrush in, stinking of turpentine and speckled with red paint. But there was something odd about its shape. Something unfamiliar.

I bent down and picked it up. It was a jelly jar, the kind with beveled edges. For marmalade or raspberry preserves. But there was no lid, and it was filled with murky water. The shape of the glass made kaleidoscopes of whatever was inside. I peered down through the top and realized that the water was teeming with polliwogs. I ran into the kitchen and set the jar on the windowsill next to the nest. I would need to get an aquarium if I wanted them to grow up. I picked up the jar again and looked inside. There must have been twenty or thirty of them.

I should have told Magoo thanks, but his chain saw was too loud for him to have heard me hollering through the open window.

I forgot about painting and drove into town looking for yard sales. I figured I could probably find an aquarium if I looked hard enough. When I hit the pavement and the houses grew closer and closer together, I realized I hadn't been into town for almost three weeks. I never thought that my small hometown would feel like a metropolis, but today, with the main street closed off for the farmer's market and people milling about everywhere, Quimby could have been Seattle for all of the traffic and noise. I decided to pick up a paper and have breakfast at the Miss Quimby Diner before I set out on my search.

When I walked into the diner, I could feel eyes on me like black flies. Glances swarming. The difference, I supposed, between this place and the city is that there is no such thing as anonymity here. And it had been way too long for me to blend in anymore. Faces were familiar, most I knew from high school. Faces grown longer, more tired. Eyes widened by time. Lips drawn. I kept my head down, some sort of Hester Prynne I imagined.

"Hi, Effie." The waitress smiled. My eyes darted quickly to her name tag. *Maggie*.

"Hi, Maggie." I smiled. I recognized her.

"Coffee?" she asked, but she was already pouring the thick black diner coffee into the small white coffee mug.

"Thank you," I said and watched her hands. Her nails were painted carefully, that shade of red I've always associated with being grown up. And I wondered, was it possible that she was my age? This girl, Maggie, who used to sit next to me in biology in the ninth grade, drawing endless circles on the brown paper cover of her textbook. Softly snoring during the dreary films of spiders spinning their intricate webs.

"Did you and that guy, what was his name? Mac? Max?"

I nodded.

"Did you get married?" she asked and took her notepad and pen from her apron pocket.

I shook my head.

"Oh, I'm sorry." She blushed. "It's just you too looked so cute together when you used to come in here on Sundays. I was sure you'd be married by now."

"Nope," I said and sipped the hot coffee. It burned my tongue, but I wouldn't swallow it. If my tongue became ignited, I wouldn't have to speak.

"Probably better off without him anyways." She smiled. "Dog?"

"Huh?" I ask.

"Was he a dog? You know, good-for-nothing. Good for *one* thing maybe." She winked. "I'm just foolin' with you."

After she handed me the laminated menu, I watched her walk away. I tried to imagine how Max and I must have looked to her. It amazed me that she remembered us that way. I remembered Sundays as silent. The long drive into town, Max bleary-eyed and sober. The newspaper a wall between us. The bitter grapefruit and cold silver spoon. Max's plate spilling syrup and strawberries. Texas-style French toast, batter dipped and deep-fried. Ice cream. This sweet decadence of his nauseating me. How must this have looked to Maggie? I didn't seem to recollect her ever looking at us longingly, the way I used to catch myself peering at couples with interlaced arms and that gentle contentment of being together. I didn't remember ever feeling envied. I only remembered the white of vanilla ice cream on Max's stubbly chin and the sting of citrus in that place inside my mouth where I bit the skin away to remind myself that I wasn't dreaming. That all of this was real. That I was still alive.

I ordered eggs and toast, but couldn't bring myself to eat the shiny yellow yolks floating on the milky sea of eggs whites. And so I punctured each embryo, let the yellow run across my plate and ate the buttery toast while I read the paper. I circled the yard sales and left enough money for my bill and a tip for Maggie before she even came back to the table. On the way out I saw her at the cash register. I was afraid she would think that I was skipping out on the tab, so I stopped and said, "I left the bill on the table."

"That's fine. Are you livin' up to the lake again this summer?"

"Um-hum." I nodded.

"I live up there now too. I gotta work weekends, but maybe sometime we can get together. Play poker or somethin'. Have a few beers?" She shrugged.

"Sure," I said and waved as I headed toward the door.

The first yard sale was at a trailer park on the edge of town. I pulled in through the gates, past the rows of mailboxes, and parked in the dirt parking lot. I walked through the maze of trailers, waving happily to people sitting on their steps drinking coffee and hanging clothes on makeshift clotheslines. I used to love the idea of mobile homes. The notion of a home on wheels was like something out of my storybooks when I was little. But as I wandered looking for the sale, I noticed that most of these mobile homes had not moved. Most of them had rooms attached, windowless afterthoughts. Front porches made of concrete. Most of them didn't even have wheels anymore.

I found the sale at the end of one of the rows. There were about four people bent over mountains of clothes and card tables littered with knickknacks and trinkets. TV trays, milk crates, a bean-bag chair. And an aquarium. I could barely believe my luck. I looked around for the owner of the trailer, and checked the glass for cracks. It seemed perfectly intact.

"Tropical or saltwater?"

"Excuse me?" I said.

A man was hobbling down the steps of the trailer, holding a pair of roller skates in one hand and a cigar in the other. His face was tanned and wrinkled like a shrunken apple–head doll.

"Freshwater or saltwater? Whatcha want the tank for?" he

asked and started to cough. It sounded as if his lungs were turning themselves inside out.

I felt suddenly, terribly, sick. "Tadpoles."

"Whatcha want to keep tadpoles for?" He put his hand over his mouth and stifled another cough. "You must live up to the lake. Which camp you staying at?"

He had mistaken me for a summer person. "I'm Gussy McInnes's granddaughter," I said defiantly.

His face lit up. He set the roller skates down and offered me one shrunken hand.

"Well, you don't say. Gussy and I go way back. All the way to grade school. How is she? How about that old man of hers? Frank it is, isn't it? Quiet man."

My heart thudded in my throat. "He's fine." I didn't know why I was lying. Maybe it was too hard to say *passed away*. "He and I are repainting the camp this summer."

"Well, you give my love to Gussy. Tell her Kaz says hello," he was coughing again.

Breakfast turned in my stomach.

"How much for the tank?" I asked.

"For Gussy's girl?" His chest rumbled. "I'll tell you what. How about you go into town and get some tropical fish from the pet store? Bala sharks, neons. Some rocks. The filter's already in there. No polliwogs. Let them live in the lake. If you promise to let them go, you can have it."

"Free?" I asked.

"Sure thing."

"Thank you," I said. "Let me look around and see what else I might need."

"Sure thing," he said and lifted the aquarium up. "I'll set this aside for you, while you browse."

I found three cobalt jars, covered with dust. A daisy pin made of colored glass. A box of children's books for a dollar and a piece of antique lace big enough to cover the daybed. Gussy would love it.

Kaz put all of my treasures in a plastic grocery bag and stuffed them into the aquarium. "No frogs." He smiled and helped me put everything in the back of the Bug.

I felt guilty about the tank all the way home. But what was the difference between keeping fish and keeping tadpoles? They were more apt to die in the lake than they were in my care.

I took the long way home, around the lake past the cottage with the red swing. I drove slowly with the windows down so that I could inhale the smell of wildflowers. The tree next to the swing had spilled purple petals all over the lawn, making a violet carpet. The shades were drawn; whoever lived here had probably not arrived for the summer yet. Except the wooden flag on the mailbox was up. I stopped the car and looked at the house. There was no car in the driveway. The shades were drawn. What harm could it do? I wouldn't take anything. I just wanted to know who lived there. I got out of the car and closed the door quietly. I looked down the road to see if anyone was coming, but the coast was clear.

I ran quickly across the road and pretended to inspect some wildflowers. I picked a bunch of daisies and looked down the road again. I walked slowly to the mailbox, and my heart was pounding. I touched the metal latch, which was hot from the sun, and gently pulled the door open. It made a terrible sound of rusty hinges, and I jumped. My hands were shaking, but it was too late now, I reached in and pulled out a bundle of mail, mostly bills. There was also a large manilla envelope addressed to Columbia University Visual Arts Division. I struggled to read the return address, and then heard a car. I quickly shoved the envelopes back into the mailbox, crushing the corner of the manilla envelope in the process. I could feel sweat trickling down my sides. I pushed the door closed, stood the flag back up, and returned to the daisies. The car slowed as it approached me. My heart settled as I saw that it was only Magoo driving down the middle of the road in his big blue Fairlane. He rolled down his window.

"Nice day," he said.

"It's beautiful." I smiled nervously.

"I'm goin' into town for the night. Visiting my grandbabies," he said. "You keep an eye on my place?"

"Sure." I smiled. "How old are they now?"

"One's six. The baby just turned two."

"It sounds like Lucy's got a handful," I said.

"Sure does. That's why she needs me to visit every now and again," he said and started to roll up the window. "We'll see you tomorrow."

I waved as he drove away. I crossed the road and got into my car. I set the flowers on the passenger's seat and turned the key. Nothing. I pumped the gas pedal and tried again. "Shit," I muttered. Since the meter had broken, this was the third time I'd run out of gas. I slammed the door, opened up the trunk, and hauled out the aquarium. It was heavy, the box of books still inside. I could barely lift it, and I knew I wouldn't make it home. I unloaded the books back into the trunk and lifted the aquarium again. It was heavy but manageable. My arms were stronger since I had started painting the camp. I dumped the daisies in the aquarium and started to walk home.

By the time I got back to the camp my arms were numb and my hip sore from where the edge of the tank had been banging against my bone. Inside, I went straight to the jelly jar and looked to make sure the tadpoles were still alive. A couple of them had died, but most were still swimming around. I figured I'd deal with the car later. I needed to get the aquarium put together first.

When I finished setting up the aquarium and putting away my treasures, I was tired. My skin was prickly with the heat, and my scalp itched. My hair had grown long and heavy again. When

I pulled off my T-shirt to put on my bathing suit, I got tangled up in it. I figured a swim would help cool me off. I wrapped a towel around my waist, but as I was about to head out to the lake, the phone rang.

"I am so pissed at you."

Tess. Beautiful Tess. Like a pre-Raphaelite painting come to life, but with a tongue sharper than a bitter lover and less forgiving.

"Tess!" I said, unable to hide my excitement despite her condemnation. "I've been so busy, I haven't had a chance—"

"You've been back for a whole month and you haven't had a *chance* to call me?" she asked. "I called your new number in Seattle and it was disconnected. I called your mom and she said you were *here*. Damn, Effie."

"I'm sorry."

"Well, are you still going to be there in a couple of weeks?"

"Uh-huh," I said.

"I'll see you in two weeks. There's an eight o'clock bus every Friday from Boston. It gets into Quimby at midnight. I'll get a cab to Gormlaith."

"Midnight?"

"Hey Geezer. It's me, your best friend. And I haven't seen you for two years. Shut up and get ready for me." She hung up before I had a chance to protest.

Tess and I met in the sandbox at the state college day-care center while our fathers taught history and our mothers took macrame, pottery, and stained-glass classes. We suffered through the torture that was elementary school and high school, and escaped here, to the lake, every summer until we left the cozy nests of our parents' split-level homes. And then we couldn't bear to be apart. We roomed together our first year in college, took the same classes. Kissed the same boys. Until Max.

She was there before Max, and during Max. Like the faint

sound of a foghorn, a storm warning. A gentle voice of reason, a faint tap on the shoulder reminding me that something wasn't right anymore about my life. Sometimes the only thing that made sense in the mess of my life then was Tess. Even when I fled to Seattle, I still called Tess every other week and pretended I'd made a new and better life for myself in the rain. I couldn't remember life without her, but now I was nervous. I hadn't called her because facing Tess meant facing Max.

When we graduated, Tess moved to Boston to work at a publishing company. At first she had to edit cookbooks. She said that every day in the office felt like being in her mother's kitchen: Jell-O molds, casseroles, and things to do in a Crock-Pot. But that was only at the beginning. Now she was editing real books. She had her own office with a sliver view of the Charles River and a brass nameplate. She had an apartment in Cambridge with wood floors and a neighbor who was a masseuse. She was a grown-up.

And I had become a fugitive. She flew out to see me once in Seattle, but I had forgotten by then how to be around other people. We went out to a noisy club on Capitol Hill and ended up staring into our drinks for hours. When she left, I felt I had lost her for good. But it wasn't Tess that was lost; it was me.

I tried to imagine what she would look like. I imagined soft jade-colored suits and pale hose. Delicate heels and hair that belonged to someone on TV. It was funny, her face used to be as familiar as Colette's, as my own reflection, but now I couldn't conjure her face at all. When I closed my eyes I could only see braids traveling down her back and black eyelashes glistening with the tears of a tumble. The knobby knees and bloody bug bites of childhood.

I hung up the phone and went outside. I waded into the water, walking slowly until I couldn't touch the bottom anymore. I let my body relax, rolling over onto my back. I thought of my grandfather smoking his pipe, lying on his back on a bed of water.

I closed my eyes. I let my body move with the small waves, felt myself changing directions. I was becoming disoriented, but I refused to open my eyes. Small fish nibbled at my ankles, but I didn't flinch. I heard someone's lawnmower, Magoo's old cat, Matilda, crying for food or love. But I felt nothing except sun on my face and water, like a cradle, beneath me.

July 1991

∿ ∿ ∿ The first time I see her she is floating on her back in the dark blue water.

"She's a real little fish." Mrs. Forester smiles, crossing her arms and gesturing to the girl in the water. I see nothing but a bright pink bathing suit bobbing in the water by the sand dunes.

"Who is she?" I ask and help her spread the vinyl red and white checked tablecloth on the picnic table.

"Fresh Air kid. We try to take one in every summer." Mrs. Forester runs her hand across the tablecloth, smoothing out the wrinkles. "We had the same girl for a couple of summers in a row, but she's too old now."

"What's a Fresh Air kid?" I ask.

"That program for city kids? Inner-city kids. She's from Harlem. Or the Bronx. I can never remember. It's all city to me."

I help her carry the bowls of potato salad and macaroni salad and the plates with wet sweet slices of pink watermelon. Soon, Mr. Forester has lit the grill and people from the surrounding camps start arriving.

"Is your boyfriend coming?" she asks as she molds ground beef into perfect patties.

"No," I say. "He doesn't feel well. Flu."

"In the middle of the summer?" she asks.

"Um-hum."

At home Max is listening to a Red Sox game on Grampa's radio. It is ten-thirty in the morning and he is drinking Bloody Marys. He drove all the way to Hudson's for celery before I woke up. When I rolled out of bed the house smelled rotten. Pungent tomato juice, clams, pepper, and vodka. The glass sitting next to him is empty, the sides coated with thick splotchy red sauce.

When I left him he grabbed at my legs as I passed, carrying the bag full of corn on the cob. "Where are you going?"

"The barbecue starts at two," I said.

"I'll be there," he hissed. "With bells on."

I don't like to leave him in the house alone. I am afraid of the damage he might do. But today I have no choice. Gussy will be here. My mother and father will be here. They come to the Foresters' every Fourth of July.

I sit down at the picnic table and start to peel the husks off the corn. The silky strings tickle my bare legs. I watch the water where the girl is still lying motionless. The Foresters' real children are playing in the water, diving off the dock, splashing each other viciously.

"She's a real loner," Mrs. Forester says. "Not like Ariana. She was always making up games for our kids to play. Teaching them stuff. But this one hasn't said more than ten words since she got here last week. All she wants to do is float on her back. I think she's afraid of the boys. They can be a little rough. She's so little. She's eleven, but you'd never guess it by looking at her. I'd say seven, eight maybe."

"What's her name?"

"Keisha, Ky-esha? Damn, I can't pronounce it. We've just been calling her Fish ever since the first time she got in the water. Can you believe it? Her mother didn't even send a suit with her. I gave her one of Stephanie's old one pieces, but it hangs off her. I told her we'd take her to Rich's to get a new one next week."

I look toward the dock where one of the Forester boys has got Stephanie in a headlock. She is squirming, trying to get away. She is only ten, but she is pudgy and already has breasts larger than mine. There is something terribly pathetic about the Forester kids. They are loud and stupid. Cruel and fat. I feel guilty thinking this way about children, but I can't help myself.

When I have shorn two dozen ears of corn I tell Mrs. Forester that I need to go back to the camp for my bathing suit.

"Can you bring some of those little plastic things to hold the corn with if Gussy has some lying around?" she hollers after me.

"Okay," I say and trot back toward the camp.

I walk into the camp quietly and look for him. The empty can of juice and the half-empty bottle of vodka are on the kitchen table. A book lies open next to the sink. I start to put it back on the shelf (it is one of Grandpa's leather-bound editions of the Great Works), but carefully mark the page with a slip of paper in case Max truly intends to read it.

I find him passed out on the daybed, the radio still on, the distant sounds of a crowd, the voice of the announcer pacifying and deep. I slip his shoes off and cover him with a blanket. I look at his slightly opened mouth and fluttering eyelids. I go to the bathroom and find the thermometer in the cupboard, a bottle of aspirin, cough syrup. I arrange the medicine next to him on the nightstand. I watch my hand reach for his head, feel his cool skin against the inside of my wrist. *He has the flu.*

"He's got the flu," I tell my father when he asks where Max is later that afternoon. "When I left he was konked out on the porch wrapped up in a blanket. He's got a fever," I say, nodding.

"That's a shame," my mother says, stroking my hair with her fingers. "Maybe we can put a plate together for him and bring it to him later."

"I'll do that." I smile. "Hopefully he'll have his appetite back."

My parents leave before dark because my father has a faculty party to go to. "Take care of Max," my mother says. "Chicken soup. Lots of liquids."

Mrs. Forester has extra blankets for everyone who wants to stay for the fireworks. I walk to the water with a thick green blanket, and spread it out on the ground. It is chilly now. I am cold in my T-shirt and long skirt. A lot of people have returned to their camps. Gussy and Grampa are out in the boat to watch the fireworks. They asked me to come along, but I would rather be alone right now.

I lie on my back and stare up at the sky. I close my eyes and imagine that I am floating on the water. I lie still and quiet, barely letting a breath escape from my lips.

"You have pretty hair," a voice says, startling me.

I open my eyes and sit up quickly. The little girl is sitting next to me on the blanket, touching the tips of my hair.

"Thank you." I smile.

"My mama makes me cut my hair short cause it gets too nappy. Does your hair hurt when you comb it?"

"Sometimes," I say.

She keeps touching my hair, but she looks out at the water.

"Aren't you cold?" I ask.

"Nah," she says. She is still wearing Stephanie's pink bathing suit. It gapes open at the legs and chest. She is small inside the pink nylon.

"Are you sure you don't want a blanket or something?"

She shakes her head.

"Mrs. Forester says you're here for the summer," I say.

"Uh-huh." She nods.

"Do you like it so far?"

She shrugs her shoulders.

"It's hard to make friends here," I say, thinking of the miserable Forester children.

"Except the other Fresh Air kids. I see them at the park when we go into town," she says. "They're okay."

"Are there a lot of them?" I ask and then blush. "I mean, are there a lot of kids in the program?" I imagine a swarm of children, plucked from their world and plopped down in this strange world of cows and endless fields and white people.

"There's six or so. Mostly boys though."

"Maybe there will be some other kids at the lake this summer," I say.

She frowns. "I've seen you," she says, still playing with the curled ends of my hair.

"You have?" I ask.

"Uh-huh. With that guy," she says.

"Where?" I ask. My words feel thick in my throat.

"This is a pretty barrette," she says then, touching one of the barrettes that Gussy gave me for my birthday. It's a silver sliver of a moon.

"I have another one at home," I say. "Would you like to have this one?"

"Can I?" she asks, her eyes widening. The whites of her eyes are bright against her dark skin, against the dark night. If she were to close her eyes, she might disappear.

"Sure," I say and undo the barrette. "Come here and I'll put it in your hair."

She leans toward me and I touch her curly hair. It feels strange in my fingers, softer than I thought it would be. I clip the barrette to a curl. It looks pretty, a moon in her night sky of hair.

"Thank you." She smiles.

"You're welcome."

Fireworks explode overhead, splattering the sky with specks of pink and purple and yellow. *Oohs* and *ahhs* echo across the water. She looks at the sky expectantly. It must seem as if the neon of her world has followed her here. That the city lights of

71

her nights have broken through the uneventful skies of this strange world.

She sits with me until Mrs. Forester calls her in.

"Fish?" Her voice breaks the spell of colored lights. "Where is that girl? Fish!"

She finds us, and pulls Keisha up by her arm. "You scared me half to death."

Keisha looks over her shoulder at me as Mrs. Forester takes her hand and leads her back to their camp.

After the fireworks I linger by the water, not wanting to go home. But after everyone has left, the air is damp and I am chilly. I walk home, letting my hair fall around my shoulders, letting it cover me like a blanket, hoping that I can disappear this way. I think of her small fingers and wish I could become small again. That could become a sliver, something that slips through small places. Dark like her so that I could disappear into the night.

July 3, 1994

ᔕ ᔕ ᔕ I woke to the sounds of the summer people. The sun was hot on my legs. I had thrown off the covers and the fan at the foot of the bed spun hot air around and around the room. I heard cars and people, the roar of a motorboat and the squeals of children. I pulled on a T-shirt and cutoffs, lifted my hair off my neck, catching it with the other silver moon barrette.

It was too hot for coffee. I yawned and filled a glass with ice cubes, pouring hot coffee and milk into the glass, watching the sugar melt and crystallize on the ice. I remembered the Bug, still parked down the road in front of the Hansel and Gretel house, and looked at the big yellow clock to see if it was too early to call Gussy: eight-thirty. She would be taking her morning bath, lukewarm water and lavender soap. Afterwards she would eat a peach and a soft-boiled egg balanced in a flower-edged china egg cup. I would call her at nine-thirty when she had had time to solve the crossword puzzle and put sugar water in the humming-bird feeder outside her kitchen window.

The front of the camp was finished now. The summer people might comment on how nice the McInnes camp looked. It was now time to start the sides, to paint the places no one could see. I got my brushes from the sink and checked on the polliwogs. They were alive, swimming furiously in the murky water. I rubbed a fingerprint smudge from the glass and peered at the water. I felt something like anticipation, like hope. I was remembering kind-ness. The way Magoo would shield the wind from my grandfa-ther's match. His hand appearing to help Gussy out of the boat onto land. Magoo's gifts, these simple generous gestures filled me with a sense of expectation that I could only vaguely recollect. But beneath this, deeper than that night-before-Christmas sort of feeling was something sad. Anticipation of disappointment. Ma-goo was at his daughter's house, so there would be nothing on the step for me this morning. I opened the window and leaned out to look at the step anyway. No robin's egg. No tadpoles swim-ming in a jar. I leaned further, but all I saw were the curls of old paint and grass that needed to be cut.

I went back into the kitchen to gather my painting tools. I could probably get the shutters done before I called Gussy to help me go get gas. The ice in my coffee had melted, and the milky liquid was warm. I gathered paintbrushes and jars, slipped on my sneakers, and went outside into the humid morning.

There was an envelope tacked to the front door. I couldn't imagine who would be leaving me a note. I took it down and tore it open. Inside were my car keys, dangling from the tacky Space Needle key chain I had bought in Seattle. I went around the side of the camp and saw my Bug parked in the driveway. I ran to the car and opened the door. I looked for a clue, opening the glove box, the ashtray, looking in the very back where I usually kept a blanket, a flashlight, and a warm pair of socks. (I'd been stranded before, and had learned.) All three items were there. I sniffed for an unfamiliar scent, but it only smelled of the pine tree air freshener I had hung on the rearview mirror in June.

I closed the door and opened the trunk.

Inside was a small bookcase. And inside the bookcase were the children's books I had bought at the yard sale. I lifted it out of the trunk and set it on the grass. I sat down and looked at every side. The wood was painted pale violet, the shelves forest green. I turned it around and caught my breath again when I saw the pictures painted on the sides. Alice falling down the rabbit hole, Huck Finn on the raft with Jim, Frog and Toad planting seeds, and Willy Wonka holding Charlie's hand. My eyes started to swell. My throat was thick. I ran my fingers over the intricate pictures, the smooth violet wood, the crumbling spines of the old books. I wiped at my eyes quickly, and looked toward the lake afraid that someone might see that I was crying on the lawn. Crying because there was no explanation. The gifts were not from Magoo. Crying into my hands because I had forgotten how to understand kindness.

As I painted the shutters the shade of blue Gussy had chosen from the chips at the hardware store, I plotted how I might catch the gift giver. I could barely wait until the sun set so that I could begin with my plan. I felt like a child. Like a hunter, like a spy.

I painted until the air grew cooler, until my back ached from the day's work. Until the summer children were lighting sparklers, imitating fireflies in the night. I hadn't eaten anything and my stomach was begging me to feed it. It was the first time I had felt hunger in a very long time.

In the kitchen I cooked as if I were going to feed a family instead of just one very small person. I thumbed through Gussy's cookbook, held together with old flour, sugar, and rubber bands. I searched through the cupboards and refrigerator for the necessary things. Pasta, cream of mushroom soup, sour cream, mushrooms, thick red steak. I brushed the ice from the package of meat Gussy had brought over a month before to fatten me up.

In no time the sauce was bubbling in one pan, water in another. I had cooked enough for five people. I sat down and felt suddenly, sadly, alone. I thought about asking Magoo to come over, but it was well after ten o'clock, and his lights weren't on anymore. It was times like this that I thought about Tess, missed the familiarity of her. I even thought, in a panic, of calling Maggie from the diner. Inviting her entire family over for dinner. I wanted someone familiar here. Finally I spooned the stroganoff onto a big red plate and sat at the table trying to eat. After only a few minutes, my plate was still full and so was I. I scraped everything into a large Tupperware container and put it in the fridge. It took me two hours to make dinner and two minutes to eat it. I turned on the radio and checked on the tadpoles.

I turned off the light over the makeshift aquarium and started to gather the things I would need. In the closet I found an old army sleeping bag and an extra pillow. I took a book from Grampa's bookshelf, a bag of popcorn, a nightgown, and a sweatshirt. I found some candles in Gussy's junk drawer and got Grampa's binoculars from the loft. I turned out all of the lights in the camp and pulled the shades. After I got the flashlight from the car, I quietly walked through the wet grass to the tree house.

I closed the door after I had lit a candle and spread the sleeping bag out on the floor. There used to be mattresses on the bunks, but now there were only the metal springs. I didn't plan to sleep, though, until after I had figured out who was coming to my house in the middle of the night.

I tested the binoculars; I could see the front lawn perfectly. There was nothing left to do except to wait. The lake was calm; the summer people had all gone to bed.

I woke up when I heard a car coming up the road. A radio was blaring Led Zeppelin, and I struggled out of a dream. My back was throbbing. I must have fallen asleep on the floor. My pelvic bone was sore from the wood. My head, at least, was cushioned by the pillow. The candle had burned down, and the wax had created a solid yellow puddle on the floor. I searched in the dark for the binoculars and knelt by the window. The car was parked on Gussy's front lawn. The headlights reflected off the porch windows. The door opened, and the music became louder. I looked through the binoculars, but it was still too dark.

I was confused by the noise. There had been no noise before tonight. I hadn't even heard my own car pull into the driveway. I pressed the binoculars against the glass and saw four dark shapes get out of the car. They stumbled across the grass; I heard *shhh* and then giggles. It took me only a moment longer before I realized that they were teenagers.

They opened the porch window quickly. They had been here before. They disappeared into the house, and in only moments I saw lights go on and their shadows moved behind the shades. I stared in disbelief at their figures. I was paralyzed. I watched them from the tree house window until they were finished with my home. Until the girl was vomiting by the picnic table, and one of the boys was streaking down the road toward the lake. It felt like hours before they stopped setting off fireworks. Until they all piled back into the car and the song resumed as they drove away.

I felt sick as I walked back to the camp in the early morning light. I left the sleeping bag and flashlight in the tree house. My hunt had been interrupted by poachers. I was still wearing my nightgown and my sweatshirt. I didn't care what the summer people thought.

The kitchen smelled of cigarettes. The Tupperware container with the leftover stroganoff sat on the counter with three forks sticking out of the stiff noddles. The refrigerator door was open. The bathroom smelled of hair spray, and the toilet seat was left up. I picked up the empty beer cans, threw the rest of the stroganoff away, and poured bleach into the toilet.

I walked slowly to the porch, afraid of what they might have done to the polliwogs. But I found them safe inside their artificial world. I grabbed a garbage bag to go clean up the mess the girl made as well as the empty shells of the fireworks from the front yard.

Sitting on the steps were three terra-cotta planters. They were each filled with soil, but there were no plants in them. I picked each one up, inspecting it for something, some evidence of who had put it here. Could they have arrived before the break-in kids? I could only have been asleep for a little while. But surely they would have broken them when they crawled in through the window. I brought them inside one by one and set them next to the nest. I trusted that something was planted in each pot. I trusted that something would grow.

My family descended on me like a swarm of black flies at 10:00 A.M. I wanted nothing more than to go back to bed, to ignore the holiday and be left alone. The commotion of my family was too much for me today. But when my father's car pulled up, I found myself feeling excited to see him despite myself. It had been such a long time.

"Hi Effie," he said. He closed the car door and came to me.

"Hi," I said and hugged him. Unlike my mother, he held on to me.

"I missed you, Daddy," I whispered.

"Let's get the charcoal burning." He smiled and pulled away.

He opened up the trunk and started to unload everything.

The Foresters stopped throwing the Fourth of July picnic after the little girl drowned. They sold their camp and bought a condo in Tucson. Since then, Gussy and my parents have had to throw their own Independence Day celebration. I think it's ironic, really. My father, the history professor, the man who claims to know the truth about what really happened way back when. The man who equates the word *forefather* with *rapist*. With *pillager*. The first to criticize all American traditions, particularly Thanksgiving, the so-called Feast of the Uninvited. We ate chickens in protest each November when I was growing up. But he loves to barbeque. To marinate. To tend the fire, to coax the coals. It is primitive, this need to cook over an open flame. While my mother unwrapped the deli packages of potato salad and made careful platters of graham crackers, marshmallows, and Hershey bars for S'mores, my father donned the apron of his ancestors.

In the kitchen I helped him with the grocery bags.

"Honey, get me the Worcestershire sauce?" he said, grabbing bowls from the cupboards.

I got the brown bottle from the refrigerator and handed it to him.

"Thanks." He smiled.

My father looks like a comedian. He always looks as though he is about to present a punch line, eager and smiling. He is always smiling. It's hard to tell sometimes what he's thinking.

"How does it feel to be home?" he asked.

"It's good to be back here," I said, nodding.

"I talked to Roy Oliver the other day. He knows the chair of the English department," he started. "He helped Colette get into Bennington. He's very influential."

My heart dropped. Why couldn't they leave this alone?

"Are these fish?" My mother's voice floated from the other room.

I left my father peeling garlic cloves in the kitchen and went to the porch where Gussy and my mother were staring earnestly at my aquarium.

"Frogs," I said.

"Tadpoles?" Gussy asked, taking my hand. I could feel her veins, like thin ropes of blood under her skin.

"Um-hum."

"Do you remember the sea monkeys?" my mother asked.

"Colette killed them," I said and sat down in the wicker chair. The wicker was cool against my back.

"She didn't mean to," my mother said.

"She did *too* mean to. She poured Clorox into the fishbowl."

"That's not what she said. She said she was feeding them."

"Feeding them *bleach*," I said.

"The point I was trying to make," my mother said, "is that you were so cute with them. I bought them for you at the drugstore, and you treated them like they were pets. You even named them."

"Bow Top Green and Purple Monkey," I smiled.

"That's right." My mother nodded.

"How is Colette?" I asked, sitting down on the daybed. I hadn't talked to my sister since I arrived back in Vermont. She was living in New York with her ballet dancer boyfriend, Yari.

"Good," my mother said. "Yari just got promoted to principal."

"How's her asthma?" Gussy asked.

"Terrible. She's seen three doctors now, and there's nothing they can do for her. Weak lungs." She shrugged.

"She should come home where the air is clean," Gussy said, frowning.

"She should quit *smoking*," I said.

The last thing in the world I needed right now was my frail-breathed, protégé sister coming to visit. Colette is only two years

79

older than me, but she has always been old. Even when we were little, she was always giving advice, always condescending. The last time we spoke she told me that I should consider going into advertising. I wasn't dancing for the New York City Ballet. I wasn't writing books or painting canvases. I wasn't living my life like a movie. *You have such a way with words*, she said, breathing into her inhaler. *What else are you going to do with an English degree?*

"It'll be nice to see her," I said, though I knew that it wouldn't.

My father burned the steaks and undercooked the hamburger, but Gussy's deviled eggs, German potato salad, and baked beans melted like butter in my mouth. I pushed the charred T-bone around my plate. I was anxious to be alone again. I was tired from all the conversation. My father noticed that I wasn't eating my steak.

"So Effie, you don't eat anymore? Is that the new hip thing in Seattle?"

"I ate," I whined. Every time I am around my parents I find myself behaving like a child.

"You can't weigh more than a hundred pounds," he said.

I shrugged.

"She was always picky." My mother nodded. "That's all it is. Remember when she wouldn't eat strawberries or bananas?"

"I wasn't being picky. They gave me hives," I said. "God."

"What?" she asked, looking hurt.

"I'm not picky. I'm just not hungry," I said and grabbed my plate. I stood up, the greasy paper plate flimsy in my hand, and threw the plate into the trash barrel by the door.

"Effie," my father said, reprimanding me. He wasn't smiling anymore.

"I feel sick," I said.

Gussy stood up and put her hand on my shoulder. "It's okay, honey."

I felt like I was going to cry. I kept walking back toward the camp. I walked up the stairs to the loft, and I could hear Gussy talking softly to my mother. I pulled the covers over my head to block out the hushed whispers. The soft cotton of the quilt reminded me how tired I was. I couldn't have slept more than a couple of hours in the tree house. I feigned sleep when my mother came up the stairs to check on me.

"Effie?" I heard her whisper. "We're going home now. Call if you need anything. I hope you feel better."

When I heard the door close, and the sounds of their departure, I started to sob. I sobbed until my hair was wet around my face and the pillowcase was soggy. I pulled myself out of bed and walked down the stairs. The clock said 3:45, but it felt later. The kitchen didn't look as though anyone had been there. The coals on the grill had turned to dust. I felt suddenly, horribly, guilty. I thought about calling my mother, my father, Gussy, and apologizing.

Instead, I decided to drive to Hudson's and buy a six-pack of beer. I was overcome with a sense of purpose. I gathered change from the nightstand and pockets. I found my keys and slipped on my sandals. When I turned the ignition, the gauge didn't move, but there was gas. It was running. Whoever returned the car to me must have put in enough gas to drive it into town.

There were a lot of cars on the road. Kids with fishing poles, teenagers giggling and holding hands. I swerved to stay clear of a group of cyclists. There were no parking spaces at Hudson's.

I grabbed a six-pack, a bag of ice, a pack of cigarettes, and a box of sparklers. The man behind the counter was Billy Moffett's father. I looked at the stuff I was buying and hoped he didn't recognize me. Luckily, he was too busy to notice that I was not a summer person but rather the girl who accused his son of breaking her nose. He was operating two cash registers and the

MegaBucks machine for the line of people that curled all the way back to the freezers.

Back at the camp, I changed into my bathing suit. I filled a cooler with ice and beer and dragged and old lawn chair out to Gussy's dock. I opened a beer and watched a group of people at the Foresters' pile into a big motorboat and take off with a water skier in tow. I pulled off my T-shirt and ran my fingers over my ribs. My skin was so pale it was nearly blue. It was a strange contrast to the skin of my arms and legs, which was dark from days of painting. My bones were sharp, my stomach sunken. After a few minutes, I covered my body up again so I wouldn't have to look at it.

I went back inside and checked to see if anything had started to grow in the terra-cotta planters. Not yet. I checked on all of my gifts and then felt hungry. There was a platter of food in the refrigerator, intended for me, I supposed. I sat down in the breakfast nook and ate as if I hadn't eaten in days. Potato salad with thick red potato skins, sweet white corn cold and salty. Cold steak, sweet and red inside. When the food was gone I sat back, leaning against the cool hard wood of the bench seat and peered out the window at the cotton candy sky. There were still boats out on the water. Everyone was trying to squeeze another drop of sunlight from the day. I smelled barbecue, burning cedar and meat. I imagined my parents linked arm and arm at the faculty picnic. My mother's lips stained with faculty wine. My father's hands strongly shaking faculty hands. I imagined they'd carefully forgotten my small illness by now.

Warm and slightly dizzy with the beer and sun, I picked up the phone and dialed information.

"Hello?"

"Hi," I said. "Maggie?"

"Yeh?"

"This is Effie," I said.

I heard rustling and then the heavy clunk of plastic on linoleum. "Alice, leave the cat alone! Hello?"

"Maggie? It's Effie. Effie Greer."

"Effie! Are you up to your Gram's camp?"

"Uh-huh," I said. My palm was sweating on the phone.

"Well what're you doing for the Fourth?"

"Nothing much," I said. "I mean, my folks were here earlier, but they're not anymore."

"I'll be over in ten minutes. I've been dying to get out of this house. I'll drop Alice over to my mother's," she said.

My hands were still sweating; I could barely hold on to the phone. "Okay," I said.

"I'll bring some beer. I could use one. Sounds like you could too." She laughed.

She pulled into the driveway in her station wagon, snubbed out a cigarette, and turned off the ignition. "Hey there." Maggie's voice sounded like crackling fire. Everything about her suggested a certain smoldering. Her eyes were black but bright, like glowing embers. Even her hair, a mess of willful curls, looked like flames licking her face. She looked more like she had in high school without her waitress uniform on.

"Hi," I said. I was standing barefoot on the grass. It was already damp with dew, and my feet were cold.

"I never break a promise." She smiled, reaching into the back of the car and pulling out a brown paper bag. "Hudson's was sold out of the light stuff I usually drink. But you hardly need light beer, do you? And, hell, it's a holiday."

"Come on in," I said, motioning awkwardly to the camp door.

"Sure thing," she said. "This is nice," she said, peering into the living room.

I took the bag of beer and put it in the fridge. "It's bigger inside than it looks from the outside."

I tore open the box of beer and handed her one. The sharp cap stung my palm as I tried to twist it off. I covered my hand with my T-shirt and tried again.

"Aren't these a bitch?" she said, shaking her head. "Gimme, I've got calluses."

I handed her the beer and she easily pried the cap off. A thin cloud of white smoke rose from the bottle.

"I am so glad you called. I was about to tear my hair out with boredom. It's not like I mind sitting around on my ass any other night, but on a holiday? No way. You should be out doing something, dontcha think?"

"Definitely." I nodded, swallowing a mouthful of bitter beer.

"I mean it's *Independence Day*." She grinned. "I love the whole idea, you know? Our forefathers breaking out of England. Sure, they were convicts and lunatics, but they were *escaped* convicts and lunatics." She sat down in the breakfast nook and leafed through a newspaper. She shrugged. "I don't know. I don't mean to get all philosophical or nothin'."

"I hadn't thought about it too much," I said. "But you've got a point."

"So whatcha want to do tonight?" she asked and stood up.

"I don't know," I said. "Don't they still do fireworks?"

"Yeh, but they suck," she looked at the ceiling, contemplating the pattern of knots. "Let's go for a hike."

"A hike?"

"Yeh. We can climb up to the lean-to on Franklin. Start a fire, roast some marshmallows. Tell ghost stories. Shit, I don't know. Get drunk and fall asleep outside?"

"It's already dark," I said.

"So? You got a flashlight?"

"I can't stay the night," I said, vaguely remembering my plan to catch the night person. "Last night some kids broke in."

"Fine then. Let's go up and watch the lame fireworks and then come home," she was tugging on my arm like a child. "Please?"

If you have ever hiked in the woods at night, you know the strangeness of familiar places in the dark. As we climbed through the cold forest, I held on to the back of Maggie's flannel shirt with one hand and a small disposable flashlight I found in Gussy's closet with the other. Maggie was carrying the good flashlight, casting a narrow yellow beam against the black foliage. We didn't speak for what felt like an hour until we finally arrived at the clearing, where the lean-to was falling with age and the weight of nature.

"Isn't it beautiful?" Maggie cried out in her raspy voice. She flicked off the flashlight, leaving me standing in a shallow pool of murky moonlight. "You could forget all about stuff up here."

I nodded, but she couldn't see me.

"Let's get a fire going. What time have you got?"

I shined the small flashlight on my watch. "Nine forty-five."

"Good. The fireworks probably won't start until ten." She set down the backpack of beer and stale marshmallows I found in one of Gussy's cupboards. "There's some good kindling over there."

I followed the faint outline of her gesture to a pile of wood left, as if for us, in the lean-to.

"So why did you come back to Gormlaith?" she asked. "You moved all the way out to Seattle, didn't you?"

"Yeh," I said.

"I can't imagine you missed this place." She laughed. "There's got to be a hell of a lot more excitement there."

"Not really," I said.

"I think about moving every now and then," she said. "But

it's hard, with Alice. I don't want her to grow up in the city. I think it's important for a kid to feel safe. She can play outside without me worrying. Play in the woods, be around animals."

"I agree." I nodded.

"So why'd you come back then?"

My heart pounded. "To help Gussy with the camp. My grampa died last year, and it's hard for her to take care of it on her own." The relief of my excuse made me sigh.

"That's cool."

"Someone is bringing me presents," I said. My head was thick with beer.

"Yeah?"

"A robin's egg. Polliwogs. Plants."

"Who is it?" she asked.

"I don't know. At first I thought it was my neighbor, but now I'm pretty sure it isn't. I'm going to try to catch them tonight."

"Are you sure they're presents?"

"I think so," I said and spread out the blanket I had in my own backpack.

"What do you mean?"

"I mean, I think they're supposed to be presents. I guess they could be accidents."

"Accidents?"

"Like, something that's not for me. I don't know anybody here. Not anymore anyway. Except for you." I stumbled as I tried to sit.

"What are you going to do?"

"I don't know," I said. The blanket was warm on my bare legs. I should have worn pants.

"I say we camp out at your house and catch him," she said, shining the flashlight brightly on my hands as I spread out the blanket.

"I tried that, and then those kids broke in."

"I used to do that," she said, nodding her head as she built a pyramid of kindling.

"What?"

"Break in. Just twice. With Bugs. That's Alice's daddy. When we were in high school."

"You did that?" I asked, bewildered.

"Just to make out. I think Alice might've been conceived at that green camp at the north end of the lake. You know the one?"

"I think so," I said and took a sip of my new beer.

"We didn't take anything," she said. "And we only went to places that we knew belonged to people from outta town. New Yorkers. Flatlanders." She laughed.

"Where's Bugs now?" I asked, though I had no memory of anyone named Bugs.

"Florida." She sneered. "West Palm Beach or some other fucking place like that. It can't be far enough away from me."

"And Alice, she lives with you?"

Maggie softened. She lit a match and watched the quick flame reaching for the wood. "Um-hum."

I handed her a piece of newspaper.

"She doesn't talk," Maggie said and held the flame to the newspaper.

"Why?" I asked.

She looked at me and shrugged. "She just stopped, that's all. The doctor says she's a mute. I hate that word. I told 'em she's just being stubborn." She laughed. "Like her mama."

"Look," I said, pointing to a vague explosion of purple in the distant sky.

"That's probably the grand finale." Maggie snuffed, ripping open the bag of marshmallows and handing me another beer.

I twisted off the cap, despite the sharp sting in the soft skin of my palm, and drank deeply.

. . .

We held hands to keep from falling as we walked down what we thought was the path after the marshmallows were all burned and the beer was gone. Maggie's hands were big. Her fingers were thick but smooth; no rings separating her hand from mine.

"I'm hungry," Maggie said, holding a branch away from the path so that I could get by without getting scratched. "I could go for a skillet breakfast. Hash, eggs, biscuits, and gravy."

"Me too," I said, stepping over a rock.

"Yeh, right. I bet you haven't had a drop of gravy in your life."

"I have too." I argued.

"I don't know how I can eat that crap after working at the diner all day, but I can. My mama used to say I had a hollow leg. Somewhere along the line it filled up though, cause now all that gravy is in my ass." She moved the flashlight from the path to her butt. "See?"

"Maggie," I said, but I was laughing at her illuminated rear.

Miraculously we arrived at the road, and inside the camp, Maggie started searching through the cupboards for something resembling biscuits and gravy. She settled on an old box of pancake mix, and as I was changing into something warmer, she made the kitchen smell like breakfast.

The butter was warm and sweet. Gussy's real maple syrup tasted like angels dancing on my tongue. Maggie kept putting more soft pancakes on my plate, and I didn't have the energy or the heart to resist.

After we ate, Maggie yawned. "I'm pooped."

"Do you wanna stay here?" I asked.

"Sure," she said. "I'm too drunk to drive back home."

"I'll make you a bed."

I brought some quilts down and set her up in the daybed. I

climbed upstairs to the loft and laid down. I couldn't sleep. My head was spinning, and I couldn't stop thinking about the gifts. About the Hansel and Gretel house. Finally, I got out of bed and put my clothes back on. I knew that if I walked for a while I would get tired enough to sleep.

Outside, the sky was dark blue. Clouds moved across the moon like ghosts. I was still tipsy, but it felt like I was only sleepwalking as I walked toward the stained-glass cottage. But I began to feel sick as soon as I had snuck around the side of the small building next to the Hansel and Gretel cabin. I thought of Maggie and Bugs breaking into the camp across the lake. I had never broken in anywhere before. My head was spinning, my hands shaking. But there was no car parked in the driveway. There were no lights on in the house. There was an unfamiliar bicycle leaning against the tree, but no signs of life otherwise.

I was dizzy and spinning. But the door was unlocked and when I shone the flashlight into the open room, I caught my breath. There were wooden boxes everywhere, all shapes and sizes. All colors and hues. The shelves along the walls were littered with jars, and in each jar was something different. Broken glass. Silver beads. Shells. Rusty nails and brittle leaves. On the counter were unidentifiable tools, glue, stacks of sheet music, old magazines, and filmy pieces of colored plastic.

I aimed the light on a box near the back wall. There was a dollhouse made of wood painted red. But inside, instead of furniture and dolls, were small glass balls: pink, teal, orange, and blue. In every room there were what seemed like a hundred colored balls. Like a gum ball machine. Like a dream. I walked to the dollhouse and realized that there was a wall of glass keeping the balls inside. That in the dollhouse attic, all of the balls were shades of blue.

I ran my finger across the counter, touching the rusty coffee can filled with paintbrushes. It must be an artist's studio, I thought as I pulled a long feather from a crack in the wall. I felt suddenly at ease here as I ran the tip of the feather along the length of my arm.

Then I heard a noise. Like music, faint but definitely there. I clicked off the flashlight and stood perfectly still. I began to spin again without the sense of walls to keep me aligned with the world. I reached over and slowly closed the door, trying not to panic. I was startled, and quite suddenly sober.

I crawled along the floor to a window and peered out into the night. I could hear my own heart pounding. I put my palms on the floor and leaned my weight onto my arms until my wrists began to ache. Just as I was certain that no one was there, a light went on inside the house, and I could see the profile of a man behind the drawn curtains. He walked across the room and stopped by the window. He lit a pipe (I recognized the graceful bend of wood from my grandfather and Magoo) and began to smoke. I swore I could smell the heady scent of tobacco from my place there on the brick floor. All the old men in my memories had smoked pipes, and the smell was as familiar and welcome as that of coffee or soap. But there was something inconsistent. Something wrong. Because he didn't have the posture of an old man. His shoulders didn't slope in the severe way of a man carrying time. He was young, and tall. And I smelled hickory and cedar. Smoldering fireworks and sweet, sweet tobacco.

My tongue felt like a fuzzy caterpillar when I woke up the next morning. There was a dull thud in my head, a simple reminder of the smoky memory of the night before. Clarity only came when I opened the window to gray sky and slivers of cold rain. I pulled on my flannel robe and a pair of warm socks. I vaguely recollected giving Maggie a quilt and a pillow and motioning to the daybed before I stumbled up the stairs that seemed to wind forever the night before. My visit to the Hansel and Gretel cottage could have been a dream.

When I reached the porch, I found the daybed made carefully. The quilt was folded at the foot of the bed. There was a piece of Gussy's stationery on the desk with Maggie's careful cursive, "Thank you for the place to crash. I'll give you a call. Love, Maggie."

I was not expecting a gift. Not today; it was a holiday yesterday. Maggie's departure had prepared me for an empty doorstep. I didn't hold my breath when I looked out the window. I didn't even feel sad when I saw there was nothing there.

I had a new feeling about Colette coming to visit. Until then, I had felt remotely nauseous imagining how I might entertain my sister for an entire weekend. But now, as the small green shoots sprouted up through the dirt in the terra-cotta planters, I felt a bit of anticipation, almost happiness at the prospect of seeing my sister for the first time in all these years. I was glad she was coming alone. Yari had always made me feel itchy. I couldn't stand to watch the way he fawned over Colette while she trod her slippered feet softly across him.

I even imagined that I'd take her to the island, that we would pick berries and make a pie. Those were the kind of things we used to do. We always liked to do the same things, even if she was always telling me how to do them. *Not so much flour. Roll it thinner, Effie.* But it was those moments in the kitchen when I didn't mind so much that her hands pressed against mine as we fluted the edges and poured sugar on the leaky berries. Gussy would leave us alone in the kitchen, let us play the college station on the radio, close her eyes when we carried her the steaming plate.

• • •

"Effie," Colette smiled and walked gracefully toward me from the Subaru where Yari was unloading their bags from the trunk. My heart sank. I thought she was coming alone. She looked taller than I remembered her. Her black hair was braided and wound, suspended magically by two ornate enamel chopsticks. She was wearing camel-colored clothes: palazzo pants and a thin taupe shirt. Her earrings dangled to her chin. She looked beautiful.

"Hi," I said and hugged her. Her lips brushed my cheek in an almost kiss. She smelled like sandalwood.

She put her arm around my shoulder as we walked toward the camp. It felt almost right, this new affection. "The camp looks great," she said.

"I've still got one more side to do," I said.

"Still, it looks a thousand times better than the last time we were here."

"You want some iced tea?" I asked.

"Sure," she said and stretched her arms over her head. Her sleeves slipped down to her elbows revealing her thin arms.

The day before I had put a pickle jar filled with water and raspberry tea bags out on the sawhorse to brew in the sun all day. I got out Gussy's blender and ground up garbanzo beans and garlic to make hummus, Colette's favorite. I bought whole wheat pita pockets and sprouts at the natural foods store. Colette has always been careful with what she eats.

Yari opened up the door and struggled to squeeze through the doorway with all of Colette's bags. They were mismatched, but tastefully so. A hard leather suitcase, an antique, tapestried round train case. An Oriental-looking garment bag.

"You guys are only here for the weekend, right?"

"Relax, Effie," Colette said, squeezing a slice of lemon into her tea and lighting a cigarette. "We're going straight to Saratoga from here to stay at Justin's."

"How is he?" I asked.

"Great. He's started a landscaping business."

Justin was Colette's best friend from college. I loved him when I was in high school. When she brought him home on the weekends, I couldn't sleep for days before their arrival. But he adored Colette. Of course, she would never admit it. They were best friends. They held hands. They argued. They napped curled around each other in the hammock in our backyard. If she admitted that he loved her, she would also have to admit that she was breaking his heart. I imagined him now planting flowers, digging into the soil, making mazes of leaves and trees. Sometimes when I was with Max I would close my eyes and try to conjure Justin's gentle face.

"Congratulations on your promotion, Yari," I said.

"Thank you." He smiled. He seemed relieved that we weren't talking about Justin anymore. Colette is capable of great cruelty.

"Christopher broke his ankle in five places," Colette said, shaking her head. "A bad break for him, but a good one for Yari."

Yari looked down at his hands.

"I'm sure he would have made it anyway, Colette," I said reprimandingly.

"Of course." She smiled and reached for Yari's hand. "I didn't mean it like that."

I brought the hummus sandwiches to Yari and Colette, who had spread a blanket out in the front yard. They had a deck of cards and a bottle of wine. My hands smelled of lemon and cucumbers. I joined them and saw that Yari was letting Colette cheat. I concentrated on chewing so that I wouldn't have to bite my tongue. Someone roared across the lake on a jet ski.

"I hate that," Colette said. "Remember when it used to be quiet around here?"

"I remember when the only boats out there were rowboats and canoes." I smiled.

"Effie and I could swim all the way out to the island without seeing another soul," she said to Yari and wiped a bit of hummus from the corner of his mouth.

"Do you want to go swimming today?" Yari asked.

"I'd love to, but I didn't bring my suit," Colette said.

"You can use one of mine," I said.

"Do you want to, Effie?"

"Why not?"

I gave Colette my bikini, and I put on an old blue one-piece. I changed in the loft, and she changed in the bathroom. I don't think we have ever seen each other naked. I wrapped a towel around myself and found her and Yari kissing in the kitchen. His hand was across the small expanse of her butt, his fingers prying into the elastic of the bikini bottoms.

"Ready?" I said.

"Let's go!" Yari said, startled.

Yari dove from the edge of Gussy's dock. For a dancer, he lacked grace in the water. He popped up about thirty feet from the dock and shook his head like a dog. "Come in you chicken girls!" he hollered. I loved his terrible syntax.

I sat down on the edge of the dock and started to ease myself into the water. Colette ruffled my hair and dove perfectly, gracefully, into the water. Yari screamed when she reached him.

"I'm naked!" he said.

She surfaced holding Yari's trunks in her hands.

I lowered my body into the cold lake and dipped my head

backward until my hair was thick and heavy with water.

"Come out here!" Yari yelled.

I leaned forward and swam slowly toward them.

"Let's go to the island, Effie," Colette said. She had given Yari back his trunks.

"Nah," I said and rolled over onto my back.

"Come on." She pleaded. I could feel her fingers pulling at my suit.

"Stop it, Colette," I said. But her fingers kept tugging.

"I'll race you both," she said and released me.

I didn't want to do this, but I followed her. I swam without taking a breath until I had caught up with her. I looked at her arms moving through the water like air or sky, and I started to kick harder. I moved my arms, my legs, and my head in a strange and steady rhythm. I was aware that she was swimming next to me. I could hear the sound of her hands slicing through the water. My lungs felt as though they would burst. By the time I saw the island nearing, it felt like I was stuck in quicksand. I watched Colette as she continued to move forward. I watched her pulling away from me. I watched her winning.

I could barely stand when I felt the mucky bottom of the lake beneath me. My legs were shaking, and my arms felt numb and heavy.

"That wasn't so hard, was it?" She laughed and twisted her hair, the water dripping on the sand beneath her. She coughed a little then, to remind me that she had done this even with her weak lungs, and said, "I wonder where Yari is."

I sat down on the sand and tried not to let her see that I was dying.

"You okay?" she asked.

"I'm fine."

"Just out of breath, huh?"

"I said, I'm fine." I looked at her, but she was looking out at the lake toward Yari, who had found the sand bar. He was running across the sand, and it looked like he was running on top of the water. Like a water spider or a skipping stone.

Colette jumped back into the water and swam to him. She stood up on the sand bar and he picked her up. Their limbs were strong and similar. They fit each other perfectly. I was not out of breath anymore, but my heart was still pounding. I crawled back into the water and lay on my back. I didn't open my eyes until Colette's voice skipped across the water, calling me home.

At midnight, Yari went upstairs to the loft, which I had relinquished for the night. Colette kissed him and patted his behind. "I'll be up in a bit."

I was doing the dishes, scraping spinach and ricotta cheese off each plate, burning my hands in the hot water. Colette was sitting in the breakfast nook sipping hot tea and smoking cigarettes.

"I'm sorry about Max," she said.

"What's to be sorry about?"

"I mean, you were together for a long time. All through college."

"We've also been apart for a long time," I said and struggled with a sharp lasagna noodle that had stuck to the plate.

"I was just trying to be nice," she said. "Jesus, Effie."

"Well, don't try so hard." The noodle came loose and pierced the skin underneath my fingernail. "Shit."

"What?" she asked and stood up. "A knife?"

"No. It's nothing. I'm fine."

We sat on the porch with all of the lights off except for the oil lamp on Grampa's desk. We didn't speak for a long time. The loons were quiet tonight. The lake was still. I was growing uncomfortable with this silence. I looked at Colette running her fingers across books of Grampa's that were propped up on one of the windowsills.

"I miss Grampa," Colette said, turning to look at me. Her eyes were pleading.

"Me too," I said, happy that we were finally able to agree on something.

After Colette went to bed I could hear her and Yari making love. She didn't make any noise at all. Not even breathing. There was only the careful steady thud of bone meeting bone. Yari's loud breaths. The sounds of his hands bracing the iron headboard to keep from crushing her.

When they were gone, I felt lonely for a moment. As I gathered my dirty laundry and the soiled sheets, I missed their voices. But by the time I had driven into town and pulled into the parking lot of the Duds-N-Suds, I remembered how quiet and peaceful being alone can be. I watched my clothes tumble around, the sheets like arms intertwined with legs. Panties and bras revealed and then hidden. And the entire world smelled clean.

"Alice has to go to the doctor, wanna come into town with me?" Maggie asked. She was leaning out of the car, staring up at me on the ladder.

"Like this?" I asked, gesturing to my paint-splattered overalls.

"Quimby ain't no goddamn fashion capital." She laughed. "Get in."

I crawled down the ladder, careful not to spill any more paint on myself. I locked up the camp and crawled into the back of Maggie's station wagon. It smelled like a child in her car. Like dried apricots and crayons. Alice was sitting in the front seat playing with a headless Barbie.

"What happened to Barbie's head?" I asked.

Alice didn't look at me.

"The dog ate it and she won't let me buy her another one."

Alice looked back then and smiled. She was a beautiful child. She didn't look real. Her blond curls were like gossamer. Her cheeks were flushed the color of raspberries, her eyes disturbingly green, like pebbles under water. And she didn't speak.

"What's the doctor's appointment for?" I asked, leaning into the space between the two front seats so that I could hear Maggie better.

"Checkup."

"I need to get back before supper," I said. "Gussy's coming over."

"Your gramma?" she asked.

"Uh-huh."

"Why do you call her that?" Maggie asked, keeping one hand on the wheel and the other stroking Alice's hair.

"What?"

"Gussy."

"Oh," I say. "I dunno."

I'd called Gussy by her first name since I could remember. I used to think that everyone had a Gussy and a Grampa. No one told me otherwise until I called Tess's grandma Gussy.

"Why don't you and Alice come over too?"

"Yeh?" she asked, turning her head to check for sincerity.

"Sure. We can get something in town to make. Gussy's bringing salad."

When we pulled into the parking lot of the doctor's office Alice started to cry. She didn't make a sound, but her eyes welled up and she shook her head *no*. "I thought we talked about this, Alice," Maggie said. "Dr. Green is not going to hurt you. It's just a checkup.

"Rectal thermometer," she whispered to me. "Last flu."

"Oh." I smiled.

I went to the grocery store while Maggie and Alice were waiting for the doctor. I do love to go grocery shopping. I love the rows and rows of possibilities. The promise of each vegetable, each jar and can and bottle. Two people could buy exactly the same items and wind up with two entirely different meals. When I was in Arizona on my way to Seattle, I ate every meal at a small Mexican restaurant by the train tracks. I got something different every single night. But the basic ingredients were exactly the same: beans, tortillas, and chiles. Red tomato, green avocado, and white, white onions. But while the colors were the same, each entree was completely unique, the difference in the combination.

I pulled a cart out from the rusty stack by the door and decided to only buy things I never buy. It was liberating knowing that I didn't need to buy bagels or bread or eggs. I wanted to buy Chinese noodles and sauerkraut. Relish instead of mustard. Rhubarb and limes. It wasn't practical on my budget, but I wanted to make something that might make Alice smile. When Max and I were together, I didn't do the shopping. Because he cooked, he always went to the grocery store alone and would come home with things I had never heard of. He didn't ask me what I wanted. I would never have suggested tuna casserole with Ritz crackers on top like Gussy would make for me. I would never tell him that I loved maraschino cherry and cream cheese sandwiches. I never asked for dates to pry with sticky fingers from their white cardboard box.

I got to the checkout and realized that I hadn't bought anything that I could make anything out of. I decided to start over again and checked my watch to make sure I would still have time. I considered leaving the cart full of sardines and tomato sauce, frozen squash and potato puffs. But instead I went back through the aisles and put everything away. I left my cart where I found it. As I was leaning into the cold freezer to grab two frozen pizzas, I felt a tap on my shoulder. I jumped.

"You forgot your wallet in the cart," he said. He was so tall, I had to tilt my head back to see his face. It was the man from Hudson's, holding my wallet. I felt my ears get hot.

"Thank you," I said.

My arm was still in the freezer. I was trying to grab the pizza box without losing his glance, but soon all the boxes were tumbling down, pushing the door open into me. His arm reached past me and stopped the cascade of yellow cardboard. He was close to me. The whites of his eyes were bright against his dark skin. I could see flecks of green in his pupils. I could smell a familiar scent on his skin. Tobacco. Pipe tobacco. It was the man from the cottage. The man whose silhouette I saw through the window. It was that same sweet smell.

"Are you okay?" he asked.

"Fine," I said and held the cold pizza box to my chest. "Thank you again."

I started to turn away, but his hand touched my shoulder again. I didn't know if it was the pizza or his fingers that sent the chill through me.

"Your wallet," he said and handed me the billfold. "It seems we're neighbors, Effie Greer."

"How do you know my name?" I asked. I imagined that he had found me out. That he knew about my forays into his mailbox and his studio.

"And date of birth and address?" He smiled, gesturing to my wallet. "It's amazing all of the information you can get onto a tiny little piece of paper. And a picture too, even."

"Oh," I said, my ears growing red again.

"Have a good day."

"Thank you?" I said, wanting his name. If he had a name then he would be real.

"Devin Jackson." He nodded, winking. I had not been winked at in my whole life. Not once.

Alice loved the frozen pizza. Gussy picked the hard pieces of sausage off hers and set them at the edge of her plate. I felt so light and happy I couldn't seem to fill myself up. I ate four pieces for Maggie and Gussy's one. Alice and I had tomato sauce on our clothes, on our faces.

"Look at you two," Maggie said, grabbing a napkin from the holder on the table and wiping Alice's face.

"You're going to wipe her mouth right off her face," I said.

"Look out or I'll get you too," Maggie cackled.

"What are you so playful about tonight, Effie?" Gussy asked, drizzling some of her homemade honey mustard dressing on her salad.

"I'm not playful." I laughed.

Gussy left before the sun went down. She hated to drive at night. Her vision had gotten so much worse over the years. I watched the road until I couldn't see her headlights anymore and then went back into the living room where Alice had fallen asleep on the couch. She could have been a kitten, she was so small. Maggie was stroking her hair. When I came in, she stood up and walked quietly out to the porch.

"All right. What's going on?"

"What do you mean?"

"I mean that you've had the same stupid expression on your face since you came back from the grocery store. It's a guy, isn't it?"

I blushed. I hadn't felt like this since junior high. "I met him in the grocery store. I've seen him before. At Hudson's. But today, he found my wallet."

"Slow down," Maggie said, putting her hand on my knee to steady its shaking.

"He winked at me."

"Well, what are you going to do?" she asked.

"What do you mean?" I asked.

"Are you going to call him?" Maggie pulled her legs up under her like a kid and stared at me expectantly.

My heart dropped. "I can't," I said.

"Can't? I haven't seen nobody coming around here to take you out. Unless you're hiding a boyfriend under your bed."

"I haven't . . . I haven't seen anybody," I started, trembling a little. My throat constricted. My palms were sweating. "Since Max."

"So? You guys split. *Years* ago from what you've told me."

"You don't understand," I said, my voice quaking and louder than I intended.

"Don't you think it's about time you move on?"

"He's dead," I whispered.

"Who?" Maggie asked.

"Max. He died in May."

"Oh honey," Maggie said, moving next to me on the edge of the daybed. "I didn't know. How did he die?"

I stared at the lake. I could smell a storm in the air. There were whitecaps on the waves that were crashing against the dock. "Heroin." The word tasted like liquor on my tongue. Like liquid fire.

"Jesus," Maggie said and put her arm around me. I leaned into the scratchy warmth of her sweater. "I thought Alice was the only one who wasn't talking."

• • •

After Maggie carried Alice to the car, using one of Gussy's extra umbrellas to shield her from the rain coming down in hard pellets, I returned to the porch where the oil lamp made the room smell even more like a storm. Where the rain tapping at the glass sounded like a late-night visitor's knock, tentative but steady.

I decided to sleep there that night, to watch the storm shielded only by glass. I brought the quilts down from the loft and changed into a pair of Grampa's old flannel pajamas that Gussy kept for company. I hoped that they would smell like him, but they only smelled like mothballs and cedar. I closed my eyes and waited for thunder. When lightning flashed bright behind my closed eyelids, I thought *heroin, heroin, heroin*. An incantation or a prayer.

July 1991

∾ ∾ ∾ Blue bruise. I discover the blossom on the inside of my thigh and clench my legs together in shame even though I am alone. I am naked and bruised, and I can't breathe anymore. When Max finally fell asleep, I untangled myself from his legs and slipped through the fleshy noose of his arm. I crept quietly down the stairs into the living room.

Now, in the bathroom mirror, I turn to the side and stare at the sliver that is me. No soft curves. No yielding belly, slightly rounded. No breasts, no gentle curve of the spine. Everything is sharp. I am wearing an armor of bone. My hand moves from the pointy tip of my nose, down to the hollow of my throat, to the sharp hangers of my collarbone. I trace the faint blue of his fingerprints on my ribs. It is as if he dipped his fingers in India ink before he touched me. I cup my pelvic bone, touch the old bruises consistent from his bones. *This is drowning.*

I am so cold I can barely keep my teeth from chattering. I go to the closet and find one of Grampa's old coats and a pair of Gussy's rubber boots. The wool is scratchy against my bare skin, the rubber cold and clammy on my feet.

I don't turn on any lights. I don't make any noise. After the back door closes silently behind me I think for a moment that I could get away. I could, in only minutes, go to someone's door and say, *Help me.* In only moments I could be dialing a phone. Sitting in the backseat of my parents' old station wagon, Gussy's car, Tess's truck driving away from Max. I could (in less than an hour) begin to unravel the threads of the stories I've woven to keep myself safe.

But as my thoughts travel down the dirt road past Magoo's, as I dream-knock on a stranger's door, as I imagine arms around me as I unravel, my feet will not move. I stand by the door of the camp, naked beneath my grandfather's moth-eaten coat, and know that I will not leave. Because the neighbors are sleeping. Because I would never be able to articulate this never-place I have fallen into. And because I can't imagine how I could stare at the back of my mother's neck as they drove me home. How I would be able to watch the red of my mother's shame ascending, flushing the soft skin of her neck and the tender edges of her ears despite herself.

I am not cold anymore. I walk to the road and decide to walk around the lake. It will only take an hour or so. Max will still be sleeping when I get back. The lights are all out at the surrounding camps. Only a few scattered Chinese lanterns strung on weather-beaten porches glow in pink and orange and blue. The air is thick, and a small breeze winds its way through my bare legs. I can feel sharp stones through the bottom of Gussy's rubber boots.

The Forester's camp is two camps down from Magoo's. When I was little, it was only a one- or two-room cottage. But over the years it has grown, a room at a time with each new addition to the family. There was even an extra bedroom added for the yearly Fresh Air kid. It looks like a child's toy house, like a string of Legos put together in no particular order. To get to the bathroom from the kitchen you need to travel the length of three bedrooms, a living room, and a glass breezeway.

A flagstone path winds down from one of the porches to the water's edge. The broad wooden dock is straight and purposeful, anchored by invisible weights under the water. Every summer Mr. Forester paints it a different color. This summer it is bright red. It stretches out for almost a hundred feet, like a red carpet leading out to the middle of the lake.

I walk through the wet grass, my feet protected from the dampness but not from the cold. I am certain that the Foresters are sleeping. There are no reading lights or candles in the windows. I can almost hear the sounds of them sleeping. I wrap my arms around myself and step onto the dock. It sways beneath me, and my knees buckle instinctively. I walk slowly toward the end of the dock, balancing as if I were on a tightrope instead of a floating bridge. I kneel down and put my fingers in the water. It is cold, still. I feel the chill all the way up my arm. When I look up again, I see her pink bathing suit.

She is only about ten feet away, close enough that I can see the slight curve of her belly, her unruly hair heavy with the water. The ridiculous bathing suit threatening to slip away. I am paralyzed. I watch her silently, and after a few moments my heart begins to quicken. I am suddenly startled by the child lying motionless in the water. She has not stirred, has not moved.

I stand and begin to pull Grampa's coat from my body. The

night air finds my naked skin quickly and I shudder. I slip my arm from the heavy sleeve without moving my eyes from her. If she were to suddenly sink I could lose her.

Her name rises in my throat. But just as I am about to call out to her, her feet flutter. There is a splash of water and she is propelled backward, further away. My body sighs. And then I begin to panic. I quickly slip my arm back into the sleeve of Grampa's coat and watch to make sure that her eyes have not opened. I feel guilty, as if I have stumbled into my parents' bedroom or a stranger's house uninvited. I stand up slowly and walk as quickly and quietly as I can back to land. When I am on solid ground again, I can still feel the sway of the water beneath me.

And later, after I have put Grampa's coat and Gussy's boots back into the closet, after I lie down next to Max and his arms lock around me again, I can feel the water underneath me, my body rocking with its subtle motion.

July 1994

᭝ ᭝ ᭝ Tess came in the middle of the night. She snuck inside the camp and sat down on the edge of the couch where I had fallen asleep despite the half pot of coffee I drank with dinner to try to stay awake to greet her.

"Boo," she said.

Blurry-eyed and half-asleep, finding words that made sense took a minute as I pulled myself out of the strange thick dreaming. "Tess!" I said, amazed by how thrilled I was to see her, to smell the familiar scent of her shampoo.

"Get up!" she said, tugging at my shoulder. "We've got stuff to do."

I sat up and made room for her on the couch.

"First, hug me," she said, and I reached for her. This embrace was so familiar I began to ache.

"Now, apologize for not calling me," she said, punching my arm a little too hard.

"I'm sorry," I said. "I am."

None of what I expected had happened to Tess. No stuffy suits and stockings. She had on a pair of overalls I recognized from college. A black T-shirt that said *Fuck You* in tiny red letters. Her hair ran loose down her back like oil, only a small rhinestone barrette keeping it out of her face, unchanged by worry or pain in all these years.

There was a place deep in the woods behind Gussy and Grampa's camp that I had almost forgotten until now. But the next morning, as Tess led me by the hand through the velvet foliage, I recollected other mornings when Tess and I escaped. Said that we were going fishing, berry picking, elsewhere.

The woods smelled thick and green. The early morning sun was beginning to leak through the green ceiling. The ground was soft and yielding beneath my feet. I loved the small pricks of branches, the gentle reminders of burrs.

Tess let go of my hand but didn't go too far ahead. Her steps were steady, certain, and it felt like the first time.

It was quiet, only the songs of invisible birds, the strange music of waking in the still green. Tess's braid swung against her back like a tail. I half expected her to be transformed in this half-light. That she would disappear behind a tree and emerge as some sort of horse, her legs thick and strong. Muscles taut. I nearly tripped over a tangle of roots, and then I saw the clearing.

Sun spilled through like a spotlight illuminating the pool, reflecting off the blue surface making mirrors. I shielded my eyes and watched Tess skipping over rocks, now more nymph than horse, to get to the other side. She stood on a large flat stone and unhooked her overalls. She peeled off her *Fuck You* T-shirt.

She was wearing a holey bra and grandma underwear. I started to laugh.

She pointed at me, "Not a word. I'm on vacation."

And then she slipped out of those too and into the water. I watched her descend, her skin golden and flawless. Her hips were soft and round. Her small breasts floated to the surface of the water, and her hair glistened.

"You coming in?" she asked, splashing some water at me.

"Sure," I said. My throat constricted.

The first time. We were children. Skinned knees, spider arms and legs. I stared at the pink blossoms on her chest, at my own like a boy's. She didn't notice the thin wisps of hair like angel's wings between her legs. And when she dove from the flat rock into the pool, I felt longing deeper than water. Thicker than leaves.

The last time. I undressed slowly. I remember the feeling of soft denim moving slowly down my legs. I remember the tight neck of my T-shirt against the skin of my forehead, the moment when my hair was trapped. And then I remember the way she breathed. I remember the way her hand flew to her throat, like a timid bird. I didn't dive into the water. I only stood and let her look at the places he had ruined. But when her head began to shake, I stared at her body, blueless, bruiseless, and gold. I felt that longing again. Something greener and deeper than these woods.

Tess has always been the person I wanted to be.

Now, I was again afraid to show her the places he had destroyed. I removed my clothes and pretended that I wasn't small.

I breathed the thick summer morning sky and let my lungs fill my body. I was certain that she could see them expanding through the transparent place that was my chest. My ribs were like a fragile cage. I pulled my hair forward to hide the places where bone had begun to threaten flesh. Bruises from the inside this time. Tess closed her eyes.

The water, warmed by the rare spot of sun, covered my body quickly. I expected that the water, like a funhouse mirror, would make me appear whole instead of broken. But through the gray, my legs disappeared altogether.

We swam like this until the sun moved behind a tree. I scurried out of the water when she wasn't looking, and we didn't say a word as we walked through the woods back to the camp.

"I suck at this game," she said, trading in all of her wooden letters for new ones.

"Shut up," I said. "You got thirty-six points for the last one. Triple word score."

Tess contemplated her new letters. "Is *aloneness* a word?"

"*Alone-ness?*" I asked.

"Yeh. Like loneliness, but good. Like the state of being alone. As opposed to the state of being lonely?"

"You only have six letters," I said.

"I know." she said and made *escape* out of *cape*. "Fifteen points. Double word score."

"What about *aloneness*?" I asked.

"Oh, I was just asking." She winked.

"I'm not *alone*," I said. Suddenly I wished that I had told her earlier about Maggie. If I told her now, it would just seem like I made it up.

"I know," she said. "I didn't say you were."

109

"I mean it, Tess. Damn, I'm not some sort of hermit up here."
I reached for the box cover and stared at the directions so I
wouldn't have to look at her.

"Do you ever miss Max, Effie?" she asked, staring me down
behind the box cover.

"No," I said.

"You don't have to pretend for me, Effie."

"I'm not pretending," I said. "I don't miss him. I don't want
to talk about him."

She reached out for my wrist, and I pulled my hand away.

"You're different."

"What are you talking about?" I asked.

"When you were still with him, at least it felt like you were
here."

"What do you mean?" I challenged. I stared at her eyes, which
were small and certain. Brown and deep set.

"I mean, I feel like you're a sliver. Like you are a piece of
Effie. At least when you were still with Max you knew you were
alive. Damaged, and I hate to sound like a goddamn sociology
textbook, *abused*, but alive." Her expression was purposeful. "But
now that he's not leaving handprints on you, you're fading away."

I couldn't look at her eyes anymore. The game we played as
children I always lost. When you look at something for too long,
too closely, it stops looking like what it is. And her eyes didn't
look like eyes anymore. She didn't look like Tess.

"I don't know what you're talking about," I said. It was easy
to lie to Tess, because eventually she would stop fighting. Eventually, she would nod her head and agree. When she saw how
much I needed her to believe, no matter how absurd the lie, she
would nod and punch me in the arm. She would nod and her
skin would come in contact with my skin and she would pretend
for me.

"Max is gone. And I am here. And I am happy," I said. Each

sentence like a strange mantra to keep from drowning in this warm sunlit pool of Tess.

"I don't believe you," she said.

I willed her to stop.

"It's been three years, Effie."

I wasn't ready for this.

"You're wasting away for nothing. He's dead."

"Stop," I said softly, tears rolling hot down my cheeks.

"I miss you, Effie. I miss you so much. I want you to come back to me. I thought that when he was finally gone I could have you back." She grabbed my wrists, enclosed them in her hands. "It's not fair. To *me*."

"I'm fine," I said, pulling my hands away and wiping furiously to remove the evidence of my tears. "I swear. I'm getting better. I am."

I struggled to catch her eyes again, but she was already nodding. Giving me what I thought I needed. "I'm sorry, Effie. I know you are. I didn't mean it."

Tess has always had the power to convince me that I am telling the truth. If I told her that I drank stars, she would make me believe they tasted like cheap champagne. It's why I love Tess, and why I hate her sometimes too.

Tess and I slept curled around each other like children. I could feel the faint prickle of the hair on her bare legs. The smell of her perfume clung to her T-shirt. It was three o'clock in the morning, and I couldn't sleep. Tess and I never fought, but the conversation earlier kept running through my head. Tess and I had only really argued once. In twenty years, we had raised our voices, our fists, only one time.

The summer Billy Moffett and I discovered making out and destroying household appliances, Tess went to summer camp. She made the decision before school got out, and broke the news to me as we walked home, our backpacks heavy with locker contents, our steps light with summer.

Art camp. In the white mountains. Colette had gone there every summer since she was six years old. Every August we made the three-hour trip to watch her dance in the amphitheater, and then took her back home. It seemed then that it took forever to get to the campus, anticipation nagging me like bug bites. As much as we bickered and picked at each other, I always missed Colette when she went away to camp. I would sit in the seats after the theater emptied out, while Colette gathered flowers from all the friends she'd made that summer. I would watch them in their diaphanous skirts, fussing over Colette's blisters or torn toe shoe ribbons. By the time she finally noticed me, the anticipation was all leaked out of me. The ride home was even longer than the ride there. Colette would sit in the backseat with me, her head leaning against the window, her eyes closed. She pretended that she was tired, but I knew she was pouting. Coming home for Colette was always the worst part of the summer.

"You don't even dance," I whined to Tess, throwing my heavy bag to the ground so I could tie my shoe.

"I'm going there to study poetry. Writing. They have all sorts of programs—drama, music—" she started, defensively.

"What do you know about poetry?" I demanded. "You haven't written a single poem in your whole life."

"Shows how well you know me," she said and kept walking.

"What's that supposed to mean?" I asked, scurrying to catch up to her.

"What it means is that there are things about me that nobody, not even *you*, knows."

She only wrote one letter that summer, a poem. I don't remember what it said. I do remember that I read it out loud to Billy, and we both laughed, and then I threw it into the fire we'd made out of a bunch of old doors we'd found in the woods. When the fire burned out, we picked up the brass numbers, still too hot to touch with bare hands, and put them in our pockets like prizes.

Since Colette was in college, we didn't make the trek to see her perform at the end of the summer. And because I was so busy with Billy, I almost forgot that it was time for Tess to come home. It took her three days after she got back to call. It was my birthday, and she wanted to come see me. I told her I had plans.

When Billy and I got back from the double feature at the drive-in, Tess was sitting on the front steps to the camp. Her parents' car wasn't there, so I figured she must have gotten dropped off.

"I'll just go back home," Billy said. "She looks pissed off."

"She is," I said. "But don't go. That's what she wants."

I opened up his father's station wagon door and closed it softly so I wouldn't wake up my parents.

"Hi," I said. I took Billy's hand and said, "Tess, this is Billy."

"I *know*," she said. "We had homeroom together in seventh grade."

"Hey," Billy nodded.

Tess put her hands on her hips. "Happy birthday."

"Thanks."

"Listen, I gotta get back home," Billy said, his hands stuck deep in the pockets of his jeans.

I looked at Tess and then Billy. "Let me walk you to your car."

I walked back to the car with Billy, leaving Tess standing stubbornly on the front lawn. He reached for the door handle, but I stopped him before he could open the door. Then I reached for his face with both of my hands, gently touching his sharp jaw, pulling him close to me, and kissing him the way we usually reserved for the woods. I could feel Tess's hard stare on my back. I squeezed my eyes shut.

When I left Billy and turned back toward the camp, Tess was gone. I watched Billy's car slow down and saw the faint silhouette of Tess on the road near the access area. I assumed she would get in and accept a ride home, but after just a few moments Billy drove away, and she was still walking.

My temptation was to let her walk home. She'd abandoned *me*, after all. But I knew that Tess was afraid of the dark. That she never went outside alone at night. So I started walking toward her, quickly, to catch up.

"Hey," I said, breathing heavily by the time I reached her.

"What do you want?" she said.

"Slow down," I said. Her legs were long, her strides nearly twice mine.

"I thought I'd do something nice for your birthday, you know," she said. "But I guess you don't have time for me anymore."

"Time for *you*? You're the one who took off to camp all summer."

Tess stopped and turned around. I stopped too, relieved to finally catch my breath. She stared at me, and I jutted my chin out as defiantly as I could.

"You're just jealous," I said.

"Oh, is that right?" she asked.

"Yeh. You went off to your damn poetry camp, and I got a boyfriend."

"At least the people I spent the summer with were *intelligent*."

"What the hell is that supposed to mean?" I asked, kicking a giant rock, stubbing my toe. I winced softly.

"I mean, that Billy Moffett is one of those boys who'll wind up working at the Cumberland Farms. Pumping gas, if he can figure out how to read the numbers."

"Shut up," I said.

"I mean, think about it. He's seventeen and a sophomore. Even *he* could do that math."

And then it felt like all the times with Billy in the woods, swinging sticks at ovens and washing machines. I hurled my body toward her, pushing her shoulders until she fell backward into the middle of the road.

I waited for her to get up, to come back at me with greater force. I braced myself for her. But instead, she blinked and looked down at her hands, studded with dirt and small stones. The shorts she was wearing were the ones she saved all of her babysitting money for. When I saw the tear in the soft fabric, my throat felt thick.

"I'm sorry." I stumbled, reaching to help her up.

She didn't take my hand. She stood up on her own and said, "No problem."

"I didn't mean—"

"It's okay," she said. "Don't worry about it."

We walked back to the camp quietly. I handed her a rusty spray can of Bactene when she went into the bathroom to get ready for bed. And later, when her breaths had finally slowed into the rhythms of sleep, I buried my face in her hair.

Now, the last night before she returned to Boston, I realized that I'd never gotten over that. Not that she left me to go to camp or the things she said about Billy. Not that she was able to sleep that night while I stayed awake. But that she wouldn't let me help. That rather than take my hand, she used her own bloody ones to raise herself up. I could never forgive her for her independence.

"I'm coming back, you know," Tess said as she brushed her teeth the next morning. "And you could come to Boston."

"I will," I said. "I promise."

"I don't believe you." She scowled at me in the mirror over the sink.

"I *will*," I said and started to braid her hair.

"I'm sorry about yesterday, Effie," she said and wiped her mouth on one of Gussy's hand towels.

"That's okay," I said. I looked at her reflection in the mirror. We had always looked similar, Tess and I. But not anymore. I looked tired.

She left later that day and I felt strangely happy, not because she was gone but because I had survived her visit. It wasn't so terrible, I thought. She'd come see me again.

When I was six years old, I didn't sleep for an entire year. Of course, I must have slept, but my memories of that year are of lying in my bed awake watching the glowing hands of my Cinderella clock spin slowly. Of watching headlights coming down the road until they flashed across my ceiling in strange shadows. I watched ice form on my windows that winter. I watched the moon acquiesce to the sun. But what I remember the most about my childhood bout with insomnia is the terrible loneliness of being awake in the middle of the night. It didn't matter that I could hear my parents as they tossed and turned on the other side of the wall. It didn't matter that Colette was sleeping beneath me on the bottom bunk and I could hear her breathing.

Tonight, I wandered from the comfort of the featherbed and quilts in the loft to the lumpy daybed on the porch to read myself to sleep, and I felt lonely. Perhaps that is why I could sleep in Seattle. My apartments were on busy streets where there was always someone awake. Even at four o'clock in the morning I could hear people stirring beneath my window. I could hear people walking purposefully through the rain. There were always passengers inside the glowing buses. There was always someone lonelier than me.

I love my grandfather's books. I believe that he is the sole reason why I wound up first in the university's libraries as a student and later in another library as an employee. But it wasn't for the same reason most people become librarians. It was never the order of the library that I loved. It was never about the categorizing and alphabetizing. It was never the Dewey Decimal system. It has always been because of the books. The weight of a book in my hands, the gentle yielding of a new spine, the sound of the pages meeting callused fingers.

My grandfather's books took up almost the entire living room of the camp. At my grandparents' house in Quimby, they spilled from shelves onto floors. Gussy gave up trying to keep them contained years ago. She said she had come to respect their reckless behavior.

At the camp, the characters were not the only inhabitants of my grandfather's books. For more than twenty years, the books have housed a family of bookworms. Generations of them. When I first learned to read, my grandfather showed me the pencil-sized holes like tunnels through all those words.

I pulled down two books from the top shelf and ran my fingers across the dusty covers. Tom Sawyer. Huckleberry Finn. I imagined that the childhood friends I read about to keep me company might come alive again tonight and make me feel not quite so alone. I lit the oil lamp on Grampa's desk and curled up on the daybed. I had learned how to lose myself in other people's words. I had taught myself how to burrow tunnels and crawl into the pages.

Suddenly I heard someone walking down the road. The sound was faint but familiar. It pulled me from the storybook river back to my tired shoulders. The shades were still up, making me visible, I'm sure, to whomever was coming. I had almost forgotten about the gifts while Tess was here. But now, someone was coming toward the camp again, in the middle of the night. I reached over to the oil lamp and turned the brass key, extinguishing the flame and making the room completely dark. I set the book on the floor without marking my page.

The footsteps were coming closer. I held my breath. I strained to see out the window, but the clouds had obscured the faint sliver of moon, and I couldn't see anything. Soon, though, I could make out the outline of someone. A man, I thought. The shadow was too tall and thick to be a woman. He was illuminated by very tiny bright lights, four or five of them like pinpricks of sun swimming in front of him. I struggled to see what he was carrying, how he was managing to hold the stars.

When the sound of pebbles and gravel crushing disappeared, I felt a drop of sweat trickle down my side. He was on the lawn in front of the camp. I slithered off of the bed and onto the floor. It was him, the night visitor. I had finally caught him. The window was open. When he knelt down to leave the gift, I leaned against the unused door. We were so close now, separated only by the door, by darkness. I was afraid that he would hear me breathing. I was afraid I was only dreaming and that when I saw his face, it would belong to Max. I was afraid it wouldn't be who I hoped it would.

But the familiar scent I was waiting for found me, and I was intoxicated by its incense sweetness. He must have carried that smell in his skin, that sweet tobacco darkness, the smell of smoke. Of ash and fire.

Fireflies' luminescence is saved for the night. To communicate, to attract. I imagine they must gather light from the sun, from the moon, from a candle's flame, until they have enough to glow through the night. But when morning comes, they look like any other insect. Like any other winged creature: a gnat or a fly. I found the jar sitting on the doorstep, cheesecloth stretched carefully over the top and fastened tightly with a rubber band.

PART

TWO

Each hand that has touched me has made me who I am. In your hands, I am something new entirely. I allow this. I can even forget for a moment that there was before. That there is cruelty. That I am capable of terrible negligence. I can forget. But while I am reborn in your palms, it is the remembrance of hands that haunts me.

If you insist that I recollect, that I collect again and again the gestures, I will. (The single curve of thumb, the flick of a wrist, hands cradling, or fist, fist, fist.) But you must remember that touches linger, and it often becomes difficult to tell them apart. I may mistake tenderness for malice, your fingers for knives. I may misunderstand the stroke of my cheek for dismissal, turn grasp into gasping for air, wonder what differentiates this hand from that hand.

I can only truly know my own hands and the power they have to hold or to break. I can only offer you this and ask that you trust. I may hold you for too long. I may crush you. I may seem gentle and then turn on you in a moment and leave you desperate and longing for something that I can't give you, or won't give you. Or shouldn't.

Do not ask me for haunted. Please, do not ask me to collect the gestures like stones or shells or bits of colored glass and try to make sense of this. Because fragments and slivers are not what you are looking for. I watch and listen to your hands and know that there is something beyond wanting here, something beyond need.

Breathe. And trust. And try. Because all that matters for now is your hands on my spine.

July 1994

    I searched the antique shop for a gift. I wandered through the cluttered rows of the converted barn, looking for something to leave on his doorstep. There was no order to these items: red wooden-handled egg beater, cigar box, rusty stamp dispenser, and rhinestone-studded eyeglasses. I let my fingers run across the kitsch and the dusty treasures, the trash and the discarded remnants of someone else's history.

"What are you looking for honey?" Gussy asked. She was studying the underside of a Blue Willow plate.

"I'm not sure. I guess I'll know when I find it."

"Do you still have the tea set?" she asked.

"I think so," I said. It was probably in one of my boxes. I used to throw tea parties for my collection of stuffed dogs. Colette buried the creamer in the backyard once when I broke her Etch-a-Sketch. She denied it until the end and blamed it on Blink, the German shepherd with a missing eye.

I peered into a glass case at the dizzying patterns of costume jewels and silver cigarette cases. A Tiffany lamp rained pink and orange across a white velvet clutch.

"Would you like to start collecting these dishes?" she asked. "I'll help you get started if you like them."

"Sure," I said. I have never owned matching dishes. I have rarely owned more than two dishes at a time. Everyone in my family collects things. Colette has a collection of toe shoes that

125

used to belong to famous ballerinas, my mother a collection of tea kettles. My father has a shelf in his office at school filled with Buddhas of all shapes and sizes. Gussy has her clocks, and Grampa his books.

Gussy smiled. "Well, let's get you started. I think I can talk 'em down on this one. It's a little scuffed." As she gathered four plates and carried them to the woman at the register, I found an aisle I hadn't traveled down yet.

I walked around a rusty birdcage to find a box spilling over with *Life* magazines. I moved it carefully and pushed aside a yellowed wedding dress hanging from a shelf to find a small box. It was a shallow wooden box, and when I turned it over I found the butterflies. Three perfect butterflies, behind glass, fragile wings pierced gently by silver push pins. The glass was smudged, and the parchment behind the butterflies yellowed and old. *Erynnis baptisiae. Aptura iris. Glaucopsyche malanops.* Wild Indigo. Dusky Wing. Black-Eyed Blue. I lifted it carefully from behind the stack of suitcases and held it to my chest, imagining I might somehow feel the beating of their wings. The last flutters of their short lives.

While Gussy and I ate lunch at Dunphy's Pub near the mountain, I kept touching the wooden box under the table. Gussy ordered homemade turkey pot pie. I order baked Brie with transparent slices of Granny Smith apples and perfect cubes of sourdough bread.

"My mother used to have a whole set of these dishes," Gussy said, pulling one of the pretty plates from the bag. "We lost them in the fire."

"How old were you then?" I asked.

"Twelve," she said, examining the delicate blue bridge in the center of the plate.

I remembered her stories of the fire. I imagined her helplessly watching her mother as she hung precariously from the red hot fire escape of their apartment. I thought about her mother's blackened palms and the scars on Gussy's own legs from the metal steps. No one in her family died in the fire, but nothing was left. They lost everything they had ever owned or loved: china dishes, photographs, love letters. Even her mother's fingerprints were lost.

"How did you start over after that?" I asked.

"What do you mean?" she asked.

"I mean it must have been so terrible. How did you go back to work or school after that?"

"We didn't have a choice. Sophie was a baby. Your Uncle Whiskers was supposed to start college that fall. You just go on, I suppose. That's all you can do. It certainly could have been worse," she laughed. "I do miss those dishes though."

I filled my mouth with warm Brie and bread.

"Your mother is worried about you," Gussy said, spearing a steaming carrot with her fork. "I'm supposed to tell you that."

"Tell her not to be," I said.

"I already did." Gussy smiled.

We sat eating silently. Celtic music floated to us from an unknown source.

The pub was new. Since the new ski resort was built, the town had metamorphosed. In an effort to make Quimby more appealing to the ski tourists, the entire downtown was renovated to look more like Burlington. A street blocked off to traffic, storefronts filled with expensive ski equipment, folk art galleries. The five and dime of my childhood was gone. Frisky's Stationers where I bought construction paper and pens had become a coffee shop that looked more like Seattle than Quimby, Vermont. This was the first time I had been to Dunphy's. I was used to the menu at the diner. Maggie and the other waitresses knew what to bring you before you sat down. Here, the waitresses were disinterested. Faces I didn't recognize behind perfect haircuts. Mostly daughters of the summer people, too old now to spend their days playing in the lake or woods.

"Do you mind going to the library with me before I bring you back to the camp?" she asked.

"Not at all. I'll pick up some books. I think I've read the ones at camp at least two times each."

"Your Grampa's granddaughter," she said.

"Do you ever dream about him?" I asked.

She looked at me and frowned, shaking her head. "No."

"Really?"

"I wish I did."

I thought about the ways Max invaded my dreams. He'd tap me on my shoulder when I wasn't expecting him. He'd surprise me by being gentle again. In my dreams he didn't hurt, and I even felt longing. Longing for something and I didn't know if it was for him or for something I never had.

"I miss him," I said.

"I know." She nodded.

Through the window, I could see the gondola rising up the mountain, the ski trails like fresh scars.

The Quimby Athenaeum smelled like Christmas trees. Pine floors warped with time, five generations of feet had traveled across them. It was the oldest building in Quimby, one of the few that remained untouched by developers. It was attached to the Quimby Museum by a marble-floored walkway. The displays never changed at the museum. The same moose and nearly naked Cree Indian have stood in the entrance since my third-grade field trips. The same spectrum of birds (ruby-throated, yellow-bellied, and bluebird) has remained perched on the shelves gathering dust. Grampa used to take me to the library on Sunday afternoons to gather as many books as I could hold, and then up the winding staircase where we would sit down in the planetarium theater seats and stare at the ceiling as a recorded voice boomed: *Andromeda. Cassiopeia. Orion.*

Gussy returned her mysteries, the brightly colored paperbacks that looked more like candy than books, and I wandered downstairs to the children's room. Mr. Woods, the children's librarian, sat behind his desk like one of the museum displays next door. Preserved, intact, dusty.

"Well hello, Effie." He smiled, standing to greet me. He was smaller than I was and gray like a mouse.

"Hi, Mr. Woods," I said, offering him my hand.

His skin was cold, his hand small inside mine.

"You got your degree in English literature, I hear from your grandmother," he said, nodding his head knowingly. Little white tufts of hair sprouted from his ears like cotton.

"Quite a while ago, actually," I said. My life seemed frozen here since the last time I lived at the lake. "I've been working at a library in Seattle."

"Wonderful." He sighed.

I used to rely on Mr. Woods to help me choose my books. I could depend on him to fill my days, to find the books that would pull me inside until the date on the red stamps arrived. Now, we stood awkwardly next to the rolling cart of returned books for a minute. He was looking at me sadly. He had nothing to offer to fill my days anymore.

"It was nice seeing you," I said.

"And you. Please stop by and visit us again."

"I will."

Gussy had run into a friend and was talking quietly in the reference room, so I wandered into the museum and found the stairs to the planetarium. There was a faded velvet rope stretched across the entrance. It didn't look as though anyone had been there for years. It smelled old. The air was thick and stale.

I peered into the darkness and then ducked quickly under the rope. I sat down in one of the uncomfortable seats and leaned my head back. In the darkness, I soon lost my sense of direction and depth, and waited. But there were no artificial stars, no sonorous voice to explain the cosmos. There was only darkness and the sound of mice stirring in the old walls.

It took Maggie and I almost an hour to blow up the plastic swimming pool that I had bought for Alice's birthday. Alice was afraid of the lake, but I thought that in this terrible heat she might be persuaded to cool off in the safety of a swimming pool.

My cheeks were sore from blowing. I put my finger over the hole and exhaled.

"It's not filling up," I said, exasperated.

Maggie was spread out on a big green blanket on the grass in front of her house. Her bikini strap was undone, revealing a thin white line of skin on her back. The ice had melted in her glass, and her shoulders were turning pink.

"You just don't have good lungs. You need to smoke more," she laughed. "Watch." She retied her bikini and sat up, motioning for me to hand her the lifeless swimming pool. She blew and blew, and slowly the pool began to take shape. She covered the plug and gathered air. When the pool was solid and standing, she laughed. "What doesn't kill you will only make you stronger. Even cigarettes."

"Where's your hose?" I asked.

"Around the side of the house," she said.

There were toys all over the yard. Alice's rusty tricycle sat abandoned by the gas tank. Headless Barbies, plastic romper stompers. Maggie's Siamese, Angel, slithered out from underneath the porch and wound her tail around my legs as I crouched to find the hose in the overgrown grass. I pet her and she purred like a small motor, pleading for more with her persistent head. I struggled to uncoil the hose. It was knotted and bent. I finally got it untangled, and stood up.

"Alice!" I said loudly, startled.

She was standing next to the gas tank in her ballet costume and cowboy boots, holding Angel like a baby. Her face began to crumble.

"No, honey. It's okay. You just scared me. I didn't know you were there." I reached for her, but she shrank away.

My stomach sank. "Can you help me?" I asked. "You probably know how to turn this on, don't you?"

She looked at me, waiting it seemed to make sure I could be trusted, and then let Angel wriggle free from her arms. She found the rusty spigot and turned the knob with both hands. The hose came to life, spitting water on the thick grass at our feet. As the water sprayed across her toes, she ran around the side of the house, nearly tripping on boots that were at least three sizes too big for her.

As I filled up the pool, Maggie tried to convince Alice to change out of her tutu into her bathing suit.

"Come on, Alice. Effie bought this swimming pool just for you. For your birthday. Don't you want to get your toes wet?

Alice shook her head.

"I'll get in there *with* you," Maggie suggested and stepped into the pool. She looked silly standing in the tiny pool, and I stifled a laugh.

"I'll teach you how to do the doggie paddle," she said. "The crawl?"

Alice stood stubbornly by the front door.

Maggie squatted down in the pool and then eased herself onto her stomach. Her legs were sticking out of the back. Her chin was resting on the edge of the pool. "The back stroke?" She flipped onto her back.

Alice bowed her head to her chin to hide her smile. I couldn't hold back my giggles anymore, and I laughed and pointed at Maggie like an elementary school bully.

"Thanks a lot." She scowled. "This was your idea."

Later, Alice reluctantly put on the silver paper hat that strapped under her chin. The six candles on the Cookie Monster cake made Maggie's kitchen feel warm, the small glow made me feel sleepy and safe. Maggie sang off-key, and I couldn't find my own voice as we sang the happy birthday song.

Alice's face was illuminated, and for a moment I thought, *This is all I need.* All I need in the world is this child's face, full of light, contemplating her one wish. Knowing that she was the one who would not tell, would not give away her secret. That her silence would make the wish come true. Her eyelashes flickered and she extinguished the light, and then Maggie was cutting the cake and my mouth was full of the sweetness of blue coconut.

When Maggie carried Alice up the stairs to her room, I went outside onto Maggie's porch and stared out at the lake. It's funny how this lake could have been an entirely different lake than the one I saw when I looked out of Gussy's windows. From here, the water was veiled in intricate lacy patterns of leaves. Black and complicated, obscuring everything familiar. I couldn't see the island from here. I couldn't see the Forester's dock or the Hansel and Gretel cottage with the lonely red swing. I could have been in an another country altogether tonight. I could have been further away from home than ever before.

I didn't bring the butterflies to show Maggie. I didn't even show them to Gussy earlier. Like a birthday wish, I was afraid that if I talked about them their magic would disappear. I put them in the top drawer of the bureau, burying them underneath a nightgown.

"Out like a light. Even without a swim," Maggie said, handing me a beer.

"No thanks."

"You're quiet tonight," Maggie said. She sat down in the wicker rocking chair. The caning was coming apart, sticking out in places. Its lap was hazardous if you didn't understand its weaknesses.

"I guess," I said.

"Thanks for the swimming pool. I'm sorry she didn't want to swim. She's terrified of the water."

I noticed the unconscious rhythm of a bullfrog's moans against Maggie's slow rocking. I noticed the rhythm of my own breaths struggling to catch up with theirs.

"She wasn't always afraid. I used to give her baths in the sink when she was a baby. I used to take her in the lake with me too. But when she got older, she wouldn't go near it. I even had to take her in the shower with me and tell her that it was only rain. Imagine that. Trying to convince a bright kid that it's raining from the ceiling." Maggie paused and took a drink. "It didn't matter to her father though. No sir, he wouldn't have it. Hell, his brothers were practically *born* in Gormlaith, he said. No child of his was gonna be scared of no goddamn lake. He liked to tease her. He'd hold her over the water, pretend he was going to drop her in. He never would have, of course, but it still wasn't right. Lots of things about that man weren't right."

"Why doesn't she talk?" I asked. My voice was so quiet, I wasn't sure if I had said anything at all.

Maggie looked at me and then looked out at the lake. "He used to go to this place in Quimby after work. Damn, what was it called? Remember that bar near the old roller rink?" She turned back toward me.

"I don't know," I said.

"Anyway that's where he used to go after work sometimes.

I'd be at home trying to put something decent together for supper, trying to get Alice cleaned up. I'd get so pissed that I was doing all this work just to make his life easier when he got home from work, and all the while he was getting loaded in town. On top of it all, we only had the one car, so if I needed anything from the store I had to wait until he got back before I could get it. Most of the time even Hudson's was closed by the time he got home. Half the time the food was cold and Alice was already in bed. Know what I mean?"

I nodded.

Maggie's face looked tired. She pulled her hair up off her neck and wound it into a knot on the top of her head. She pulled a cigarette out and lit it, breathing in the smoke and letting it out in one graceful motion.

"One night, he comes home late from 'work', and he's stinking like the bar. I remember when he pulled into the driveway I took his plate out and put it in the microwave. When he came stumbling in the kitchen, I was standing there watching it go around and around. That's how I used to deal with him, you know? I'd stare at something. Didn't matter what it was. It could have been laundry or a crack in the linoleum. Just something to take my mind off of him. That night it was that plate, spinning around and around. Shepherd's pie. That's Alice's favorite next to macaroni and cheese with hot dogs," she rocked quietly, and I pulled my knees up under my chin.

"So anyways, he says, *What's that crap?* Or somethin' to that effect. And all I do is watch it spin. *I said, what's that shit that's stinkin' up my house?* he says and comes up behind me. But still I'm staring at that plate like it's the most fascinating thing I've ever seen. Like it's the goddamn Mona Lisa or something. And then I can feel him pushin' up against me. That same feeling you'd get in junior high when you're dancing with some stupid boy and his stupid eighth-grade hard-on. *It smells like pussy,* he says, cackling like he's made about the funniest joke ever, like he's fucking *Seinfeld* or something. And all the while, he's pushing me into the counter."

She leaned forward in the rocking chair and offered me the cigarette. I took it from her and took a small drag. My knees felt weak.

"Funny thing is, I must've known. I must've known that night when I picked the shepherd's pie instead of the laundry or the linoleum. I must've known that the blue numbers on the microwave were counting down for a reason."

I looked at Maggie's hands bracing the edge of the rocking chair, and I started to feel sick.

"*Come on, honey, he says. Let me taste that nasty pussy food.* And then all them blue numbers turned to zeros. It took a long time. Ten whole minutes I was watching that damn casserole go around. And when it beeped, I could barely believe it. It was like a frickin' movie or something. I mean, he kept on pushing into me, drooling down my neck, and I was reaching for the potholder like nothing was wrong. And for a second, when I pulled the plate out, I actually thought that it was over. That he'd take his hands off of me, and he'd go to the table and pick up his fork. That I'd set the food in front of him and he'd forget all about pushing me."

Maggie exhaled a cloud of silvery smoke. "But he didn't stop. He kept on licking my neck, scraping my skin with his beard. And no matter how hard I tried, I couldn't get him to stop. So I reached my hand up and touched his head. I did it so gentle, it was almost like the way we used to touch each other." Maggie's voice broke.

"I burned him so bad his whole face blistered. The plate shattered into a zillion pieces and he was sobbing and yelling. The neighbors finally called nine-one-one. Ironic, isn't it? Just a week before, he pushed me into the screen door so hard I sprained my wrist. I fell right out onto the front yard in the middle of the afternoon, and it takes his howling to get the cops to come."

"What happened to him?" I asked.

"He came home later on that night, all bandaged up. I slept in Alice's bed. He didn't bother me no more that night."

"I mean, when did he leave for good?"

Maggie rubbed her eyes with the back of her hand like a sleepy child. "About a year later."

I didn't ask any more questions. I didn't want to know.

Maggie got out of the rocking chair and sat down next to me on the steps. She put her arms across my shoulders and squeezed. She smelled like dish soap.

"How 'bout you?" she asked softly.

"What?" I asked, my eyes stinging.

"What did you watch?"

This was not the conversation I wanted to have. This was not the way I wanted to feel. I shivered and shook my head.

"I'm sorry," Maggie said.

"For what?" I asked, blinking furiously.

"For not answering your question," she said. "About why Alice doesn't talk."

Fall 1989

∾ ∾ ∾ Candle wax. Blue candle wax that drips in hot pools, solidifying as soon as the blue rains onto my skin. In the other room, he drinks his mother's face. He imbibes her face with too much mascara and too little patience, crow's feet etched into her eyes as if into stone. Her hands like a man's only painted and bobbled, nails chipping dime-store red petals.

I sit on the bare mattress in our first apartment, our first night, and wonder why I am here. I look at a pale brown stain on the Goodwill mattress and feel sick. I press my ear against the wall and listen to someone else's dinner. Forks and knives like wind chimes. Chairs pushed away from the table. Sighs and water running hot and soapy, hands washing and drying. I imagine two pairs of feet side by side at the sink. Wool socks to ward off the cold of wooden floors.

I am startled by the sound of the radiator next to the bed. I didn't realize that they breathe like animals instead of machines, that their insides rumble like hungry beasts, that they spit and cuss like angry old men.

I move slowly away from the wall and peer into an open box filled with blankets and sheets. It seems important suddenly to cover the bare mattress. Touching the flannel daisies, too large and too symmetrical, transports me to my mother and father's bed. Childhood Saturday mornings when the whole house smelled like coffee and fresh-squeezed orange juice thick with pulp. When my mother refused to get dressed until long after noon and she would read to us in that bed (the one that looked like the Princess and the pea's).

His mother's fingernails were like broken rose petals, rotting black and falling away from their stems. Stems of martini glasses as thin and fragile as blades of grass. While she waited for his father who never came home, she tapped her fingernails against the glass. Speared the salty olive with her sharp pinky nail and offered it to him.

I take the sheets out of the box and begin to make the bed. I tug at the bottom sheet, pulling it tightly under the edges of the filthy mattress. In the other room, I can hear the radiators clanking, the bottom of his empty bottle clanking against the kitchen table my mother gave us.

When the pillows are covered, and the comforter is resting tidily, prettily on top of the bed, I start to unpack the other things. Books and borrowed dishes. Plastic tumblers from the back of my mother's cupboard. Mismatched plates and a rusty can opener. I am beginning my life with him with borrowed things. Even the candles are ones I found in the junk drawer in my mother's kitchen.

I put the brass candleholder on the windowsill next to the bed. There are no dangerous curtains threatening fire. I can see the neighbors' television glowing blue through Venetian blinds.

In the other room, he drinks his mother's face. Too much mascara and too little patience. *When she cried,* he says, *the makeup made black rivers, black pools on everything white:* pillow covers, her cheeks, his fingers.

I hold the burning match for a moment too long. Long enough to burn the very tips of my fingers, but not long enough to blister.

The phone call came after he had taken my clothes off. After he pressed me into the old mattress so hard I thought I might be swallowed by the ticking. When the phone rang, he pulled himself out of me like a cork, letting the insides of me spill warmly onto the bare mattress.

Hello? A pause. *I'm not coming there.*

Naked and spilling on the bare mattress I imagined that I was glass. That he could see through me, at the empty places inside.

Mom, don't do this to me.

I reached for something to cover my body. I didn't want him to see through me now. But he wasn't looking at me, he was walking away with the phone, the cord curling into the kitchen where I could still hear him. A child's voice. A boy pleading.

And then he was lying down with his head in my lap like an infant, burying his face in my hair. His body trembled. I stroked his hair out of his eyes, ringed red.

"It's okay," I said. "She won't do it. She never does."

He sat up, blinking the tears out his eyes, his facing changing from a child's into something else. Something angry and cruel. "What the fuck do you know?"

"I only meant, don't worry," I said, shrinking away from him.

"Now you're an expert at convincing someone not to swallow the medicine cabinet? How many times did your mother hold a razor blade to her wrists while she was on the phone with you? *How is school honey? Getting straight As? By the way my wrists are bleeding all over the fucking carpet.*"

"Max, you're not being fair." I tried holding my hand out to him.

He reached toward me and grabbed my shoulders. It startled me, and my body turned to wood. "I'll tell you what's not fair. It's not fair that my mother is a fucking lunatic. It's not fair that my father took off and left me with her to fend for myself. It's not *fair* that people like you walk around in a haze of happiness. That you live your life oblivious."

"Oblivious to *what*?" I asked. His fingers were pressing into my shoulders like pins. "I'm here aren't I? I'm here with you."

"What an angel you are, Effie. What a kindhearted soul to offer yourself up to someone as troubled as myself. You're on your way to heaven, Effie. There's no stopping you now," he said, his teeth clenched together.

In the other room, he drinks his mother's face. Mascara puddles and hands trembling too much to hold a cigarette. Nails red with the blood of his back when she clung to him asking him when his father was coming home.

I pull my shirt off and touch the blue fingerprints on my shoulders; I am pinned still to this stinking mattress, hidden in my mother's sheets. I take the candle and let the blue wax drip hot onto my skin. It burns at first, but then it doesn't hurt anymore. I can get used to this pain. I can understand.

July 1994

꙳ ꙳ ꙳ I took the butterfly box out of the drawer and carried it down to the kitchen. I used a sponge to clean the glass and polished the wood with lemony oil. Outside the sun was falling swiftly behind Franklin. Suddenly there was a knock on the door, and I jumped.

"Hello there," Magoo said. He was standing in the doorway holding a bucket.

"Hi, Mr. Tucker," I said. "Whatcha got there?"

"Birdseed."

"Birdseed?"

"I noticed your Grampa's birds haven't been around this summer. Thought they might be hungry." Magoo set the bucket down on the kitchen floor and motioned to the breakfast nook. "May I? An old man's legs don't hold up so long as a young man's."

"Oh sure, I'm sorry," I said. "Can I get you something?"

"You got any coffee?" he asked and started to fill his pipe.

"Just instant," I said. "I used the last of the beans this morning. That okay?"

"Um-hum," he said and puffed on his pipe. "So Gussy's thinking of selling this old place, I hear."

"Maybe," I said. "I hope not, but the property taxes are so high now that they've built the ski resort. That and it's hard to take care of without Grampa."

"Your Grampa took care of most things." He nodded. "Did you know the first time I met your Grampa he saved my life?" Magoo puffed on his pipe, and the smoke made strange halos around his head.

"I don't think I've heard this one." I laughed.

"Back in thirty-six. We were just kids then, fifteen, sixteen, I think. He and your great-grandfather had just built the camp. We didn't know each other then. My folks and I were living up here for the summer, and of course I knew who he was. He was a year ahead of me at school. But he didn't play sports, so I didn't know him *too* well. Quiet kid. Spent most of his time at the library if I recall, nose in a book, that sort. I was an athlete. Track and field. Football. But up to Gormlaith there weren't any other kids my age. Just a bunch of old people, and I wasn't looking forward to spending a whole summer wandering around by myself. I suppose my parents thought it would keep me out of trouble to be away from my friends in town.

"Well anyways, I was bored one day and I decided to introduce myself. He and his dad were finishing up, putting on the shutters or some such thing. I walked over and said, 'Hey, Mc-Innes, you wanna row out to the island with me?' Well, he looks about startled out of his skin, but he goes inside the house and comes out in a couple of minutes with his shoes on.

"We didn't say more than a couple of words the whole way out to the island. He sure was a quiet fellow," Magoo puffed on his pipe. "So there we are in the middle of the lake not talking. Finally, I decide to tell him I got some liquor I stole from my daddy's liquor cabinet. I figure maybe that'll loosen him up some. Well, when I pull the bottle out of my bag, his face lights up like Christmas.

"We spent the rest of the afternoon drinking that nasty booze, smoking cigarettes, and diving off the rocks into the lake. It's a wonder we didn't break our necks. I was so drunk by the time it started to get dark, I could barely remember where I'd put the boat. Finally we found it and managed to get headed back toward our camps.

"It must've taken us an hour and a half to maneuver our way back to shore. It was pitch black and neither one of us was in any condition to be operating any kind of vehicle. Your grampa could handle his liquor a lot better than I could though; I must have announced to the entire lake that I was crocked off my ass.

"I was hooting and hollering so much, drunk so blind, that I didn't even notice my mama's shoes standing at the landing. Your grampa noticed though. He must've known that she'd be there to meet us. Because before I laid down in the back of the boat to take a little nap, I heard him fabricating about the best story I ever heard.

"He told her that we'd gone out to the island to go fishing. He said that he'd asked me to come along because he'd heard that I was a damn good swimmer and seeing's how he himself couldn't swim too well, he thought it would be a good safety measure to have me with him. And then he told her that while we were fishing I stumbled into a hornet's nest. That I got stung about fifty times. A hundred. And that no matter how many times I got in the water I still couldn't make the sting go away. That's when he got the brilliant idea to look in his father's fishing box. He knew that his daddy kept a bottle of whiskey in there for just such emergencies. What he didn't know was how little it took to heal a man. That sooner than he could say *bottom's up*, I was drunk as a skunk and falling all over myself.

"My mama stood at the edge of the lake with her arms crossed, her face not flinching or giving show of whether or not she was buying this fib at all. Now, my mama was never one to let her leg be pulled. But your grampa was so earnest, so sincerely concerned about my impaired condition that my mama never asked why there weren't any fishing poles in the boat. Never asked why not a single sting left a welt on my skin. She just left me in the bottom of that boat to sleep it off. And your grampa brought me three aspirin and a soda pop in the morning."

"How did he save your life?" I asked, smiling.

"You'd have needed to see my mama mad to understand."

"I'll make sure to feed the birds," I said, pointing to the bucket of seed. "Grampa never told me he fed the birds."

"He was a man of few words. But all his words were good ones." He grinned.

After Magoo left, I went outside to put the birdseed in the feeders. It was chilly for a midsummer night. I went back inside to get my sweater and the butterfly box. The sweater came down over my hips, enclosing me in the warmth of wool and the faint smell of mothballs. Everything on my body was soft tonight. Grampa's flannel pajama bottoms held up with a safety pin. Soft socks and tennis shoes worn to the exact shape of my feet.

My heart was thudding in my throat as I approached the Hansel and Gretel house. The air was still. The sky was streaked with the brightness of moon-illuminated clouds. My hands were cold. There were no lights on in the cottage, and the bicycle was missing. Relief rushed through me like a breath of warm air. I stood in the road looking at the house for a long time before I moved toward the door. The shingled roof pointed up sharply into the night sky. The front door was bright blue with a knocker shaped like some sort of night creature. There were tulip stalks standing like silent guards at either side of the door. Ivy climbing bravely up the side of the house, clinging like a lover to the trellis.

I could barely feel my feet when I walked across the yard, aware only of the winding flagstone path leading to his door. When I got to the door, I saw that there was a chalkboard for messages, clean and bare. A piece of chalk still sharp and white cradled in the tray.

I set the box down, turning it this way and that. Upside down, right side up. On its side, turned face down. I finally left it right side up, the butterflies facing the door. It was hard to walk away from this, hard to leave this gift behind.

As I was about to run back to the safety of the camp, I spotted the swing. I looked again at the dark cottage. The bicycle was missing; no one was home. I walked slowly to the swing and touched the wooden seat. I sat down carefully, afraid that it would crumble beneath me. I forgot that I was the size of a child now. I was lighter than air.

I pumped my legs underneath me, remembering other swings. Remembering how to go so high I could see the tops of trees. But this swing was made of wood, not the iron of elementary school playgrounds, so I swung gently.

I leaned back, letting my hair drag on the ground below, and closed my eyes. When I opened them again, I heard something behind me. Startled, I stopped swinging.

"Evening, Miss Greer," he said.

I didn't speak or turn around in the swing.

"You need a push?" he asked softly. His voice was as deep as pockets.

I felt myself nodding, my shoulders trembling as he touched them. And then I let his hands push, and I flew higher. His hands were there each time I swung backward toward earth, catching and then pushing gently until I was flying again. When I wanted to slow down, when I was ready to land, his hands caught me and resisted the pull of gravity for me.

When I stood from the swing my knees were weak. I moved into the safety of the shadows of a tree. I could barely see him in the darkness.

"Do you often swing in stranger's swings at night?"

"No." I smiled. "Not often."

"Are you cold?"

I shook my head, but I was shivering.

"Would you like to come inside and warm up? I could make some tea." He was standing only a few feet in front of me; I could smell the sweet tobacco smell of him. His head was cocked slightly, his hands in his pockets.

"I really need to be getting home," I said softly. "But thank you."

"Any time." When he reached his hand out to me in the darkness it looked like a giant's hand. I accepted it tentatively. His skin was warm. He covered my hand with both of his larger ones, and I shivered again.

"You sure you don't want to borrow a jacket at least?"

"No thanks," I said, drawing my hand back quickly and folding my arms across my chest.

"Okay then, you have a good night," he said and put his hands back in his pockets. He smiled and the turned to walk back toward the cottage.

I walked quickly back to the camp, pulling the sweater over my hands to make them warm. The clouds moved across the sky, thin white dresses on an invisible line. I dreamed his hands the color of night. Warm on my shoulders.

In the morning, I woke early and made a huge breakfast. Leaving the kitchen a mess, I carried two plates of bacon and eggs and toast out to the picnic table and skipped over to Magoo's to invite him to join me. I knocked on his door and listened to his dog, Policeman, yipping and scratching at the screen.

"Mr. Tucker?" I said loudly. I didn't hear the shower running, but his Fairlane was in the driveway so I knew he was home.

Policeman yipped inside.

"Mr. Tucker!"

My palms were sweaty. I opened the screen door and peered through the window. His kitchen has looked the same since I was little. Yellow curtains, Formica table, and red vinyl chairs. I knocked again and then opened the door gently. "Mr. Tucker?"

Then I saw Magoo's shoes, his body curled up on the floor.

"Mr. Tucker, it's okay. I'm calling nine-one-one. Just hang in there."

The last time I was in an emergency room was with Max when his mother took a half a bottle of tranquilizers. We spent twenty-four hours holding hands in the fluorescent waiting room. There is no day or night in a hospital, there is only *now*.

"He's going to be fine, thanks to you," Gussy said, emerging from the ICU room where Magoo was hooked up to wires monitoring every beat and breath.

She sat down next to me and held my hand. "He's a lucky man." She smiled. "To have such a good neighbor."

"God, Gussy. We almost lost him too," I said and suddenly I was crying so hard that a nurse came out from behind her station and offered to get the doctor to give me something to calm me down.

My heart thudded dully in my chest, and I took the two pills with some lukewarm water in a paper cone-shaped cup she offered me. Soon I felt the pounding in my head and chest subside, and I curled up in the plastic seat and slept with my head in Gussy's lap.

Gussy drove me back to the camp and tucked me into my bed like a child. My tongue felt thick and my head woozy.

"He'll be fine, Effie. You get some rest."

She kissed my forehead, and I fell asleep before she even got to her car.

I woke up disoriented and confused. I sat straight up in bed, an awareness of everything that had happened like a buzzing alarm. I thought at first that it was morning, but the clock said 4:30 P.M. The sun was bright outside.

I went downstairs and outside for some fresh air. I went to

the backyard and saw that the breakfast plates on the picnic table had been licked clean. *Policeman.* I forgot about making sure he stayed inside when the paramedics came.

"Policeman!" I hollered. "Police!"

I walked to the water and to see if he had gone for a swim. He, like Grampa, could float for hours without being disturbed. I started walking toward the Foresters'. "Police!"

Nothing.

"Are you okay?"

I jumped. Devin was on his bicycle coming toward me.

"Excuse me?" I asked.

"You were hollering for the police," he said, stepping off the bike. "Are you in trouble?"

"Oh God, no. I was looking for my friend's dog, Policeman. He's named that because he yelps like a police siren. Mr. Tucker had to go to the hospital and Policeman got out. I'm looking for him."

"Maybe I can help," he said.

"Sure," I said. "Sometimes he likes to go into the woods."

We walked along the edge of the lake whistling and shouting "Police" until we got to the Foresters' camp. Suddenly Policeman's siren went off behind some bushes. It sounded horrible.

"Stay here. He might be hurt," Devin said and walked into the woods. I stood in the road and listened for their return.

Just as I was beginning to fear that he too had disappeared, they emerged. Devin was holding Policeman in his arms. Policeman's front leg was twisted and bloody. "Looks like he got in a bit of trouble," he said. "We need to get him to a vet."

"I'll take him," I said. "I should go check on Mr. Tucker anyway."

"You want me to take you?" he asked as I got into the car.

"That's okay. I'll be fine."

147

My hands were shaking as I started the ignition. Devin helped put Policeman in the backseat on an old blanket.

"Good luck," he said, waving as I backed out of the driveway.

My brain was still a little fuzzy as I drove into town again. The day felt divided into halves. The first half, with Magoo and the hospital, seemed far away. The second half, of Devin and Policeman, felt sharp and new.

The Animal Hospital in Quimby was just like the emergency room except that it smelled wilder. It was noisier too. The vet's assistant took Policeman in to be examined, and they came out an hour later, his leg bandaged and one of those ridiculous cones on his head to keep him from chewing on his leg.

I put Policeman in the front seat; the cone was too big to fit him in the back. He was sedated and sleepy next to me. By the time we got back to the camp, it was dark outside. I felt even more disoriented, as if I had spent a whole day inside a room without windows.

I carried Policeman into the camp and made a bed for him out of more old blankets. I took the cone off, trying to give him some dignity, and fell asleep on the couch, listening to the gentle whistle of his doggie snores.

The next day, I finished painting the shutters and window boxes. The geraniums from Devin had opened their red palms to the light, so I transferred them from the terra-cotta planters to the window boxes on the front of the camp. Gussy came with news of Magoo's progress and a box of Grampa's things for me to go through. She said it was a box she didn't know what to do with. It had taken her a year to whittle it down to this. That I was welcome to anything inside.

When she left, I stared at the box for almost an hour before

I could bring myself to open it. At dusk, when the public radio station started to fade like it did every night, I decided to go through the box. I sat down cross-legged on the living room floor, petted Policeman's sleeping head, and peeled back the lid. Inside, on top, was Grampa's wool suit. Suede patches on the elbows. When I lifted it out of the box, a red bow tie unfurled like a ribbon. A pair of black wing tip shoes, the bottoms scuffed. Three ivory chess pieces: queen, pawn, rook. A fountain pen. Two unlabeled cassette tapes. His pipe.

When the sun was almost gone behind the hills, I turned on the oil lamp on Grampa's desk. Inside the soft wool suit, I felt safe and warm. From the deep front pocket, I pulled out a grocery list in Gussy's careful cursive and a half roll of wintergreen Life Savers. A rusty tin with some loose tobacco inside. I packed the bowl of the pipe with my fingers, trembling despite the warmth of his clothes. I found a box of kitchen matches in a drawer and lit the pipe. It made me cough, and I didn't know how to put it out. As I tried to regain my breath, I tossed the pipe in the sink and ran water into the smoldering embers. I went back into the living room and looked at the pile of my grandfather's things. I pulled up the pants, which had fallen down, and reached into the jacket pocket, loosening a Life Saver from the roll. It was familiar and cool on my tongue.

"Hello?" The screen door creaked open.

I froze, the Life Saver numbing my tongue. "Hello?" I asked back.

"Effie? It's me, Devin."

I looked down at the pants that were threatening to make a puddle of gray flannel at my feet.

"Hi," I said, still not moving.

"Can I come in?" he asked.

"Sure," I said.

And then he was standing there, filling the doorway. The kitchen light behind him made him into a strange silhouette.

"I . . ." I stumbled.

"Oh, I'm sorry, sir. I'm looking for Effie Greer. Little tiny thing, have you seen her?"

"These aren't my clothes." I laughed nervously. "They're my grandfather's."

"Quite flattering," he said. "You could use a good tailor, though."

And then he was sitting on the love seat, holding the fountain pen that I handed to him to keep him busy as I changed back into my own clothes.

"I'll be down in a second," I said from upstairs as I struggled to put my jeans on. "Just a minute!" I looked at my frazzled reflection in the cracked mirror over the bureau.

When I came down the stairs he was still there. I was afraid I'd imagined him.

"Hi." I smiled.

"Hi."

"I didn't hear you coming," I said. "Did you drive?"

"Not tonight," he said. "There's a truck in the garage at the house. Part of the rental, I guess. But I can get just about everywhere on my bike," he motioned for me to sit down.

"I am terrible at riding a bike," I said, my hands fluttering in front of me. I wished for pockets, a cigarette, something to keep them occupied. "I fall. I mean, I used to fall a lot. When I was a kid."

He smiled.

"Do you want something to drink?" I asked.

"No thanks," he said and set the fountain pen down gently on the coffee table. "Listen," he said and I listened so closely I could hear him swallowing. I could hear the brush of his fingertips on the cotton of his shirt. "Thank you for the butterflies."

"Thank *you*," I said.

We were both silent. I looked out the window, trying not to seem so nervous.

"Do you want to see the frogs?" I asked.

"Sure," he said and followed me to the porch where Lenny and George were paddling about in the aquarium.

"The others died."

"Hey little ones," he said, bending over and tapping on the glass. Lenny hopped quickly away to his hiding place by a large piece of slate I found in the lake.

"I made you something," he said.

"Why?" I asked. My voice sounded like an accusation. I didn't mean to sound so angry. I looked at his eyes for the first time since he came in. The flame from the oil lamp leaped across the dark pools. "I mean, you didn't have to do that. Already, you've done so much, and I don't understand why. You don't even know me."

"That's not true." He smiled and touched my arm so gently I could have imagined it. "I know that you're here this summer because you've come home. That you haven't been home in a long time."

I looked at him for an explanation.

"It's a small town, Effie." He grinned.

I blushed. And then I worried about all the other things he might know. It didn't seem fair that I didn't know a thing about him.

"I know the way the sun looks when it touches your hair in the morning," he said. "I know that you're left-handed, that your back hurts when you paint for too long without taking a break. I know that when you swim, you like to lie on your back."

I looked at him and watched the fire travel across the whites of his eyes.

"That's not the same as knowing someone. That's just knowing somebody's habits, somebody's characteristics," I said. I sat down on the edge of the daybed and he walked to the window.

"Our habits can be pretty revealing." He grinned.

I scowled.

"Well, then I should probably really get to know you," he said, clapping his large hands together decisively. "What's your first memory?"

"Excuse me?"

"Your first memory. The first thing you remember. It's a very important question."

"I don't know," I said, trying to remember. "I guess it would have to be the time my sister Colette shut the car door on my hand."

"Do you have a scar?"

"Uh-huh," I said and pulled my hand out of the sleeve where I had been hiding it. The scar was small. It looked like a sliver of moon across my knuckles. He traced the scar with his finger. His nails were clean and dark pink, his cuticles white against the dark charcoal of his skin. He moved his fingers tentatively to my face and touched that place by the corner of my eye that was still tender in my dreams. "And this one?"

As his fingers touched the old scar, I recoiled, shaking my head.

"I'm sorry," he said and took his hand away.

I nodded.

"What is *your* first memory?" I asked, eager for him to stop looking at the scar on my face.

"I think it's probably of my mama washing my hair. When we lived in Virginia she used to collect rainwater during storms to wash our hair with. I remember being inside some sort of washtub and her pouring cold water over my head. It was so hot in the summers then. I remember it felt so good, like it was raining all over me. That was the best thing about living in the country. Nobody thought anything of a woman washing her babies outside in a bucket." His laughter was as deep and full as a washtub filled with cool water.

We sat for a while, watching the clouds move across the dark sky, listening to the sound of the loons. When he went to the kitchen, I thought that he was going to leave me there without saying good-bye. I suddenly wanted to do something to make him stay. I wanted to hear his voice again. I wanted him to keep startling me with his fingers. I started to get up and follow him, but then he was walking back out onto the porch.

"This is for you," he said, handing me a small wooden box.

I took it from him, and looked at him for an explanation.

"Just open it," he said.

The lid was attached by two brass hinges, a delicate clasp holding it shut. The wood was stained dark. Cherry, I thought. The color of trees at night. There was a glass window to the inside protecting the contents from careless fingers. But it was so clear, it seemed as though you could reach inside.

The Dusky Wing was flying against a backdrop of a thousand blues. The inside walls of the box were lined with bits of paper (metallic, slightly patterned, textured, torn) made into a sky. I couldn't see how the butterfly was suspended. It was like a magician's box. Like an illusion. And no matter how close I looked, I couldn't see where its wings had been pierced by the two push-pins.

August 1991

ᘯ ᘯ ᘯ Every day I meet the mailman at the mailbox in front of the camp. Today it is raining, but as Max sleeps, I stand barefoot in the rain waiting for the postman to drive up and deliver me my future. I can see Mrs. Forester struggling to get all of her children into the station wagon, to go into Quimby for swimming lessons. I don't understand why she insists on taking them to the public pool when we have a perfectly good lake right here. But every morning at nine she piles them all into the car, fussing and arguing, and drives past me standing at the mailbox. Today when the Forester clan drives by, I wave. Keisha sits in the backseat with her face pressed to the glass. Mrs. Forester has put bright pink ribbons around her two pigtails. One of them has come loose and curls against her dark cheek. She smiles a small smile at me.

Magoo walks by with Policeman about ten minutes later, puffing smoke into the dewy morning air. He nods his head at me, but keeps walking purposefully down the road. It's understood that we can't converse while Magoo is walking Policeman. He doesn't allow Policeman to converse with other dogs. It's only fair that he shows some restraint as well.

I am shivering and think about going inside for my shoes. I decide to wait a bit longer rather than risk waking Max up. When I left him this morning, he was sleeping deeply, his arms across his eyes to shield them from the bright white sky pressing against the windows.

I shift my weight from one foot to the next, trying to keep my feet from going numb in the cold grass. Every morning since the middle of July I have waited for the letters that come for me. Of course Max knows that I have been accepted into graduate school in New York for the fall semester. He knows that I will be leaving. But he doesn't know that I have already found an apartment, a roommate with a name that sounds like an exotic flower. He doesn't know that she has written to me about the plants she keeps in her rooftop garden, about the small room with big windows that will be mine, about the coffee shop on the first floor of the building. He doesn't know that her thick creamy stationery looks like paper buttermilk. He doesn't know that I've been hiding the letters in my grandfather's books after I bring them inside each morning.

Today I stand shivering in the rain cursing the sky. *Rain, sleet, or snow, my foot,* I think. After a half an hour, I run back inside, my hair dripping puddles onto the kitchen floor.

"Hey," he says. He is sitting in the breakfast nook drinking coffee. His hair is disheveled, covering one of his eyes now, his hair uncut since we arrived at the beginning of the summer. "What're you doing out there in the rain?"

"Waiting for the mail," I say.

"What's coming in the mail?" he asks.

"Stuff from school," I say, testing him.

He raises his eyebrow but doesn't say a word. He sets his coffee cup down and stands up. He opens the refrigerator and grabs three eggs in one hand, pulls out cheese, mushrooms, fresh green chilies from Gussy's garden, a bright red bell pepper. I pick up yesterday's newspaper, sit down in the breakfast nook, and pretend to read.

He quietly makes the omelettes. The sweet smell of onions and peppers and chilis makes me feel nauseous. He grates the cheese and sprinkles it on the runny eggs. I stare at the paper, but I don't comprehend the pictures or headlines.

"Here," he says, setting the plate down in front of me. "Breakfast." He starts to eat, and I hold the paper in front of me like a wall.

"No thanks," I say and push the plate toward the edge of the table.

"Why don't you fucking eat? You look like a goddamn skeleton," he says, looking up from his own plate.

"I'm not hungry," I say. "I don't feel good."

"That's bullshit," he says softly.

"What do you mean?" I ask.

"This is your way of punishing me. Turning away everything I offer you. Am I right?"

"No," I say, staring at the mountain of eggs and vegetables on my plate. "I'm not hungry!"

"You're fucked up, Effie. It's not normal to starve yourself. Especially just because I'm not playing Mr. Enthusiastic about you leaving me."

"I'm not leaving you," I say. "I'm going to school."

"Same thing," he says, spearing a slippery brown mushroom.

"It's not the same thing at all," I say.

"Jesus, Effie. You're pathetic."

"Fine," I say, bile rising up the back of my throat in a familiar tang of grief and anger. I grab my fork and scoop up a heap of eggs and cheese. "I'll eat."

I begin to shovel the food into my mouth, swallowing the salty forkful despite the now instinctual gag reflex. "Is this what you want? Are you happy now?" Tears are running hotly down my cheeks into my mouth. Everything is salty. Everything is blurred.

When he grabs my wrist, the fork scrapes the roof of my mouth and I can feel the salt of my own blood. Metallic.

I pull the fork out of my mouth, but he doesn't let go of my wrist.

"I'll stay!" I scream. "I'll forget about school. I'll stay here with you. I'll give it all up to be with you. To do *this*," I say, motioning to his hand, which has completely enclosed my wrist.

And then I feel the thrust of his releasing me and the fork tines piercing my skin. Blood runs into my eye, and I stare at him, blurry and emotionless, through all the liquid in my eyes.

Later, when I walk to the water, the Foresters return from the public pool. I am sitting on the big rock at the boat access area in the pouring rain. Mrs. Forester slows down and rolls down her window.

"Effie, you look like a drowned rat. Let me give you a ride back to the camp," she says. Her chubby elbow hangs out the window, her children sulk in the backseat, towels wrapped around their wet, chlorine-saturated bodies.

"That's okay. I'm just enjoying the rain," I say and wave her on. I concentrate on the circles each drop of rain makes in the lake. Circle upon circle, widening and disappearing.

"Suit yourself." She shrugs. "Tell Gussy I've got a new recipe for all that zucchini she's got growing in her backyard."

"I will." I promise.

And Keisha is still looking at me through the back window as they drive away. Her hair is wet too. The bright pink ribbons are wilted, and her face softens when I don't return her smile. I touch the butterfly tape at the corner of my eye and she waves at me, pressing her pink palm against the glass.

I stay on the rock until my clothes have soaked through and my hair is flat against my face and arms. It is not raining hard, but steadily. I don't hear her until she is standing next to me.

"What are you doing?" she asks. She is wearing a yellow rain poncho with a hood.

I shrug.

She bends down and picks up a rock.

"Swimming lessons got canceled," she says.

"The rain?" I ask.

She nods and rolls the stone in her small hands.

"I hate swimming lessons," she says and throws the rock into the water. It splashes and sinks.

"I didn't like them either," I say. "What level are you?"

"Dolphin," she frowns and looks at the sandy shore for another rock.

"I didn't even make it past Frogs," I say. "I couldn't tread water."

"Yesterday they made us do the dead man's float for almost a whole minute. It's so stupid." She finds another rock and chucks it into the water.

I crawl down off the boulder and join her on the shore. I search for a rock to throw and settle on a good-size chunk of quartz. I throw it hard, but it doesn't go far.

"At home nobody goes to swimming lessons," she says. "You just cool off with a hose or something. I learned how to swim already at my gramma's. Me and my brothers would go swimming there all the time. Then she died. That's why they sent me here."

"Who?" I ask.

"My mama and daddy. Mama's got my little brothers to take care of and Daddy's at work. He brings me with him sometimes and sometimes I stay with my big brother in his apartment. I like that. He makes stuff with me."

"What kind of stuff?" I ask.

Her eyes light up and she stands up with a new rock. "All kinds of stuff. Like this rock," she says, holding it out in her hand. "It looks just like a stupid rock, but he could make it into something else. He might paint it or glue stuff to it or smash it up so the insides are showing. He can turn all sorts of old junk into something pretty."

"That sounds neat," I say and inspect the rock she is holding. "What do you think he'd do with this one?"

She peers at it for a long time and then closes her hand around it. "I dunno." She hurls the rock into the water. "I can't do that kind of stuff. I'm not like him that way. I don't know how to make something good out of something stupid."

Quietly we stand at the edge of the water throwing rocks into the water until my arm is sore and all of the good rocks are gone.

"I gotta go back now," she says. "Mrs. Forester's gonna have my hide."

"You tell her that you were with me." I smile. "She can have *my* hide then."

I watch her walk away, a small duck waddling through the rain in her yellow slicker. I wait until the sky is dark before I find my own way home. I stay until the cut by my eye doesn't sting anymore.

July 1994

∾ ∾ ∾ In the Quimby Atheneum I searched the card catalog for the books Magoo had requested. They were mostly history books. More bricks than books. I made a pile at the circulation desk. World War II, biographies of kings and soldiers, ancient Roman myths. It took me two trips to the car to carry them all. He was bored, stuck in bed; this was my second trip in the last week.

"For Mr. Tucker?" the librarian asked. I didn't recognize her. She was young and tall.

"Uh-huh." I nodded. "He can't get enough."

"He's becoming a reader now, huh? More like your grandfather than himself. He's lucky to have a delivery driver. Like meals-on-wheels, huh?" Her laughter surprised me. It was high and nervous, too loud for a library.

"I don't mind," I said.

. . .

I pulled into the parking lot at the diner and had a hard time finding a parking place. I finally squeezed in between an RV and a little sports car with New Jersey plates. I got out of the car feeling a little pissed off by the tourists. It would only get worse, I imagined. When autumn came, they would come in throngs, causing accidents on the freeway as they gawked at the leaves. And now, with the new ski resort, they would never leave.

"Hey Maggie," I said, sitting down at the only empty seat at the counter. It was lunchtime, the diner was full of demanding and hungry people, but she handled each of their requests and gripes with the grace and poise of a great diplomat. "Tuna melt on sourdough, extra mustard, and a diet Coke with lemon?" she asked the man sitting next to me at the counter. He nodded and within minutes she was back with his lunch. She sat down next to me and lay her head on the counter.

"Just a little nap." She sighed. "That's all I need. You can handle things for a minute?"

"Get back to work Maggie." I laughed and poked her side.

"Sure thing, boss." She said and got up.

"Come over tonight?" I asked. "I have something to show you."

"Can I bring Alice?" she asked, clearing someone else's dishes, scooping change into her apron pocket.

"Of course."

On my way back to Gormlaith, I took the long way, so that I could pass Devin's house. The bicycle was gone. The grass in the front lawn needed to be mowed. I longed to go inside, to see how he lived.

Policeman greeted me at Magoo's door. I had brought him over to visit with Magoo before I went into town. The cone made him look like an alien dog. Like a Shakespearean character. Elizabethan. Regal.

"Here's your weekly allotment, Mr. Tucker," I said, stacking the books next to his bed. "I'm going to have to limit you to fifty pounds a week."

"My library angel. She brings books on wings of silver and gold," he said. His skin was pale now. All the summer sun disappeared in the hospital. I couldn't help imagining the doctors syphoning it and capturing it in a jar.

"How are you feeling today?" I asked.

"I'd feel a lot better if I could eat meatloaf. You know that's my sustenance. I don't even know how to cook some of the things they've prescribed for me. *Vegetables. Whole grains.* Phooey. I know how to make meatloaf. So does Gussy. And now even she's refusing to give it to me." He eased himself to an upright position and opened one of the books I had brought.

As he checked to make sure I had fulfilled his requests, I glanced at the clock on his nightstand. The table was littered with orange prescription bottles, tissues, and fingernail clippings.

"What's your hurry, Effie? Have you got a date? Bet some fellow's on his way to take you out for dinner. I bet you'll be eating meatloaf and gravy as soon as you leave."

"No, Tuck. Just a friend. *Maggie.* She's coming over for dinner."

"Meatloaf?" he asked.

"Nope. Salad. With whole grain bread. Lentil soup. I'll bring you some leftovers if you'd like."

"Nah, I'll stick to my dreams of meatloaf. Now you run along then."

As I skipped back to the camp, I felt twelve years old.

• • •

Maggie was sitting on a tree stump, smoking a cigarette. Her hair was a mess of curls, and she had her happy shoes on. She only wore the Mickey Mouse tennis shoes when she was feeling particularly glum.

"Where's Alice?" I asked.

"At my mother's. Ma's taking her to a movie in Quimby. Something Disney, I think."

"Come in," I said and pushed the door open.

"I had to call Bugs's mother today. He's six months behind with his child support." Maggie put her cigarette out in an ant hill and then put the butt in her pocket. "She called me a whore and then hung up on me."

"You're kidding," I said.

"I used to call her *Mom*, can you believe it?" She laughed and ran her fingers through her tangled curls. "Anyway, I needed a break from Alice. Enough of that. Whatcha want to show me?"

"Come see," I said, grinning so broadly my cheeks hurt. I felt bad being so simply thrilled, but she didn't seem to mind. I led her out onto the front porch and up the stairs to the loft.

"How do you fit in here?" she said, stooping to keep from hitting her head on the ceiling.

"Look," I said, pointing to the box. It was sitting on the bureau where the sun could shine through the glass.

"That's amazing," Maggie said, holding the box up to the light. "He *made* this?"

I nodded. "He goes to an art school in New York."

"What do you call it?" she asked. "Sculpture?"

"It's a shadow box, I think. I don't know."

"Art school, huh?" she asked. Then, setting the box down on the nightstand, "How on earth can he afford to live up here for the summer?"

"He's a carpenter too," I explained. "He's working on some of those houses up by the mountain."

"The condos they're building by the ski resort?" she asked, disgusted.

"No, the old ones. The railroad houses. Once they're fixed up they're going to be low-income housing. It'll keep the new development down, if they can save some of those houses."

Maggie held the box up to the light and peered in at the impossible flight. She set it down carefully and sat down on my bed. It yielded to her weight and she put her hands on the iron bed frame.

"When do I get to meet him?" she asked.

"I don't know," I said.

"You can't keep him to yourself forever." She laughed. "Not in a place like Gormlaith."

But she was wrong. It was easy to hide things here. For as much as people are prone to gossip, they also have a certain quiet respect for closed doors. You could keep secrets in Gormlaith. Maggie knew that as well as I did.

The tree house needed a lot of work, and I wasn't sure how to go about repairing the leaky roof, the crumbling deck, or even the weathered ladder. I assessed time's damage and made notes about what I would need to re-create at least a semblance of what it used to be. I called Gussy and told her my plans and then headed into town to get the things I would need. Two by fours from the lumberyard. Nails. Tar paper. I didn't know the first thing about how to put this broken place back together.

I got in the Bug and headed for town. About halfway around the lake I realized that I would never be able to fit the boards into the car. Not even with the window rolled down. I drove nearly all the way to Hudson's before I decided to ask Devin. He said he had a truck in his garage. I turned around in someone's driveway and headed back toward the lake.

163

Devin's bicycle was leaning against the garage door. There was a bright red wheelbarrow in the front yard. His door was propped open with a couple of dusty bricks. I stepped up to the door and knocked gently.

Through the front door, I could see the open back door, sunlight streaming through, making dusty rays. I squinted and leaned in, "Devin?"

I could hear the scratchy radio. Miles Davis inside the hollow metal box.

"Devin?"

"Effie?" His voice swam to me through all of that dust and sunlight. "I'm out back. Come on through."

I stepped hesitantly into his home for the first time. It was dark, but I could see the faint shadows of a couch and a worktable. The back door led to a huge backyard bordered by woods. He was kneeling in the garden. He was wearing jeans the color of sky and a T-shirt that said *Georgetown*. The letters were cracked. He stood up and brushed soil from his hands. The corn was taller than he was. There were tomatoes bigger than my fist growing on the vines. This was a giant's garden.

"Wow," I said, looking at him dwarfed by all these living things.

"It's great, isn't it?" He smiled. "Try this." He held out a peapod that looked like a small green purse.

I took the peapod and snapped it open. It cracked sharply and the tender skin bled green on my hands. I coaxed the peas out and popped them in my mouth. They were hard and sweet.

"You don't have to work today?" I asked.

"I only go in a couple of days a week. By the end of July we should be done," he said and stepped carefully out of the garden.

"That's good," I said.

"That would be *great* if I had some money saved. At least I won't starve." He laughed and motioned to the garden. "We start work in May, so I usually have August free."

"You've been to Gormlaith before?" I said.

"For a few years now," he nodded. "Never had a garden until this year though."

"I have a favor to ask," I said and tossed the peapod into the compost pile.

"What's that?"

"I need a truck."

"Well, I just happen to have a truck in my garage. A nineteen seventy-four Chevy, a fine automobile. And what, little one, do you need with a truck?"

"Wood."

"Ah, wood," he said, scratching his chin. I noticed for the first time the faint shadow of his unshaven cheeks. "A truck of any other caliber might not be able to help you. But the Chevy? I think she can handle it. And would you also need a driver, miss?"

"I think so." I smiled.

He had to boost me up into the cab of the truck, a rusty green thing that smelled like french fries inside. Inside the cab, I felt like a kid. Tess and I used to sit in her father's truck and pretend that we were truckers. We smoked rhubarb cigarettes and talked on shoebox CB radios. There was an 8-track stuck inside Devin's truck playing "Ring of Fire" over and over. I could barely see over the dashboard. My feet didn't even touch the trash-littered floor.

"Sorry about the mess," he said.

He stopped at Hudson's and filled the tank with gas. I sat in the cab and looked out at the hills, which were glowing green on this rare cloudless day. He went in to pay and came out with two giant-sized Cokes and a bag of Reese's cups.

"Breakfast," he said and handed me the treats.

All the way into town I sucked on the sweet chocolate and peanut butter, crumpling the gold wrappers and putting them in the ashtray. It felt good riding high above the road in the truck, sitting next to him. It felt right.

We went to the lumberyard and he selected the boards that I would need to repair the tree house. He threw them in the back of the truck and chatted with Mr. LaFevre, who owned the lumberyard. Devin was so friendly with everyone here, more at home than I was even, it seemed. Meanwhile, I sat in the front seat of the truck trying to check my teeth for chocolate in the side-view mirror. Devin's elbow rested on his open window. His arms were thick and strong. My heart stuttered at the involuntary twitch of a muscle as he opened the door.

"You need to go anywhere else?" he asked as we left the lumberyard.

I thought about going to the diner to see Maggie. To show her that he was real. I thought about the way it would feel to say, *Maggie, this is Devin. Devin, Maggie.* I thought about walking through the doors into the busy diner, the smell of gravy and biscuits. I thought about his hand spreading fire across the small of my back as we walked to a booth near the window. I imagined watching each stool at the counter turn, each head turn, as Effie Greer walked in with this big black man. I imagined the whispers like beestings.

"No," I said.

"Sure?" he asked at the intersection.

"Yes." I nodded. I could handle the stares. I could even withstand the hushed disbelief at my *audacity*. What I couldn't stand were the rumors that would spread like an infectious disease. That would mutate as they spread, reaching my parents eventually. It was inevitable. At the lake, I didn't have to share him with anyone. He belonged to me.

When we pulled into my driveway, I opened the door and jumped down out of the cab. I could feel the blow of the hard ground in my knees. He helped me unload the wood and tar paper. He handed me the crinkled brown paper bag of nails like a gift.

"Thank you," I said.

"You're welcome."

We stood in front of the camp not speaking for a forever-moment.

"Well I should get back to the house," he said.

"Me too," I said. "I mean, back to the camp. I've got a tree house to build."

He stretched his arms over his head. "Let me know if you need any help."

"I will," I said.

"Well then." He smiled and got into the truck. My heart sank. I couldn't think of a single thing to say.

"Hey," he said and leaned across the huge expanse of the truck's front seat and rolled down the passenger's window. "I've got more Swiss chard and zucchini than I know what to do with. You want to come over for dinner tonight?"

"Sure," I said, heart rising to the surface again, bobbing. A pulsing buoy.

"Sure." He smiled. "It'll have to be a late dinner. I have some work to do. Come on over at nine or so. If you like."

"I like," I said. "See you at nine."

I looked at everything I had brought with me to wear and hated it all. Moth-eaten sweaters. Torn jeans. Dingy T-shirts and thermal underwear. When Maggie got home from the diner she opened up her closet doors and said, "Have at it. And good luck. You'll swim in most of it."

Alice sat on her mother's bed, dressing and undressing her headless Barbie.

I pulled dresses out of her closet and pulled them over my head. They were all at least six inches too long. The shoulders hung wrong. I felt like a kid playing dress up.

"What do you think, Alice?" I asked in one particularly ridiculous purple dress.

Her face scrunched up and she pointed to her pile of Barbie clothes.

"Those are probably a little *too* small." I sighed.

"Wait a minute," Maggie said. "I may have something." She disappeared into the other room and came back with something black. As it unfolded from her hands, my heart jumped. "I found it in my grandmother's closet a long time ago. I thought it would be fun for Alice to play dress-up with."

The dress was beautiful. It looked as though it was from the twenties or thirties, black beaded sleeves and a thin layer of black lace spilling like night across my knees when I tried it on. Alice clapped her hands together and Maggie nodded. "Yep."

"You can borrow it if you promise to let me meet him."

"Fine," I said. "Soon."

I felt silly walking down this country road, dressed like this. I had to walk slowly in Maggie's shoes. They were two sizes too big; I had stuffed cotton in the toes to make them fit. I was glad when I arrived at his door without bumping into anyone on the way.

The door was still propped open, but now I could see the inside of his house illuminated by several lamps glowing green and pink and blue from stained glass shades. I knocked.

"Come in," he said. I stepped into the room and saw that it was much bigger than it looked that afternoon. There was a big blue couch against one wall, a coffee table under a mountain of books. A worktable with rolls and rolls of butcher paper and jars of tempura: red, blue, and yellow. The floor was covered in newspaper. There were piles of sawdust like anthills underneath the table.

"I'm in the kitchen," he said, and I followed the scent of sweet tomatoes to the kitchen entrance. "Give me a hand?" he asked. He was leaning over the tiny stove, stirring something.

"Okay," I said.

When he turned around, I felt ridiculous in this dress.

"Wow," he said.

My hands fluttered around the beads at my hips.

"You look so pretty."

The steam coming from the pot on the stove, the heat of the fire spreading to my ears was almost stifling. I was sure I was turning as red as the tomato sauce.

"Go out there. I don't want you anywhere near this mess, dressed like that," he said. "Go on, scoot. I'll bring you something to drink as soon as I calm this thing down."

I stumbled in my oversized shoes back into the living room. I stood there awkwardly until I saw the shelves. All along one wall of the room were floor-to-ceiling shelves filled with boxes. Boxes of every shape, size, and color. In each box was a small world. Like my butterfly box, each of these boxes could have been an illusion. Wings suspended in air. Shells in an ocean made of green glass. There were worlds made of paper cutouts, layer upon layer making dimensions you could only dream. An antique perfume dispenser from some long-gone hotel bathroom labeled HOPE, REQUITED LOVE, PURE AND UTTER JOY. When I pressed the lever that said HOPE, purple sand spilled into my hands like slivers of violets or grains of tonight's sky.

"I'm afraid this is not going so well," he said, startling me.

"Are you sure you don't want some help?"

"Not so sure," he said. "I've got an apron. If you don't mind."

I returned to the kitchen, and he was leaning into the oven now, trying to retrieve a lasagna that had fallen off the back of the oven rack onto the orange coils of the electric stove. "I think I can save some of it," he said, turning to look at me from the mess that was our dinner. "Grab that bowl."

I pulled an apron over my head to protect Maggie's dress and reached for a big silver bowl on the small counter, holding it for him as he scooped big messy spoonfuls of lasagna from the wreckage. Soon there was enough to make a meal and he sent me back into the living room. "Get comfortable, Effie," he said. "Take off your shoes. Please." He smiled, pointing at my feet. A bit of cotton was sticking out from one of my shoes.

While he finished in the kitchen, I hurried out of my shoes and stuffed the cotton back into the toes. "I put a table in the backyard," he said. "Not much room inside."

I opened the door to the backyard and saw that he had put a small round table near a window that illuminated the makeshift tablecloth. When I looked closely at the table, I could see the paint-stiffened spots. A drop cloth. A canvas of spills. He had arranged two chipped china plates and the silverware was all there, but wrong. Fork and knife on the left. Lonely spoon on the right of each plate. One fat candle. One thin, stuck into an old wine bottle.

"I never promised it'd be intact," he said, stepping out into the backyard with the bowl of lasagna and a Tupperware container of salad. "I've only got one bowl," he explained, motioning to the Tupperware.

I sat down in the chair and realized that it was so short that my chin was practically resting on the table. He laughed when he saw me. "The Quimby phonebook isn't thick enough to make much of a difference. How about a pillow?"

The lasagna noodles were blackened and stiff. The cheese was brown at the edges and stringy. But the sauce was sweet. The lettuce and Swiss chard were greener than earth itself. I piled vegetables onto my plate, helped myself to seconds and thirds of the lasagna until I felt like I would burst through the seams of this delicate dress.

"Easy there, truck driver," Devin said, handing me a paper towel to wipe the bright red sauce from my chin.

"I'm sorry," I said, my mouth filled with his garden. "It's so good."

"I'm not much of a cook. *Obviously*. My mama and sisters never let me into the kitchen. I'm not sure how they expected me to woo a girl without learning how to cook."

I felt *woo* like a thousand butterfly kisses on my bare arms. I looked at him, waiting to hear it again. He rested his elbows on the edge of the table and looked at me.

"You grew up in Virginia?" I asked.

"Um-hum. Until I was thirteen. Then we had to move to the city because my dad got a job working for the Smithsonian. He's a preparator."

"What's that?"

"It's sort of like a curator's assistant. The curator makes the plans, and the preparator puts the displays together."

I thought of the Quimby museum with its ancient displays and untended artifacts.

"What does your mother do?" I asked. I had stopped eating. Suddenly full, sated.

"She's a mom. Seven children," he said. "I was number two."

"Wow. My mother almost went crazy just raising me and Colette," I said. I folded up my soiled paper towel and laid it across my plate. "She had to come up here sometimes to get away from us. Even in the middle of winter, she'd drive up here. I remember I loved that. It was like a vacation for us too. My dad would play Mom for a week. He'd let us do all sorts of stuff Mom wouldn't. Like sledding on the garage roof. Eating dinner at midnight. Skipping school to go ice skating." I hadn't thought about my mother's vacations for years.

"My mama should have had a lake of her own," Devin said, pouring me another glass of wine. "Maybe her own ocean."

"Are you close to your brothers and sisters?"

"Yeh." He nodded.

I thought about Colette, about how much I wanted to adore her, to look up to her. But she had ruined that for me a long time ago.

I was a bit drunk when I walked away from the Hansel and Gretel house, thinking I should have brought breadcrumbs to find my way back home. I carried the enormous shoes, and stepped carefully to avoid the sharp pebbles and stones lurking in the darkness. When I got back to the camp, I laid down on the daybed and stared at the ceiling. I felt so full I was ready to hibernate. I could sleep and sleep and sleep with all that was inside of me at that moment.

Maggie and Alice came with me to the library to return the mountain of books that had been accumulating at Magoo's bedside. He was strong enough now to make himself breakfast (to slice peaches, to pour the thin skim milk his doctor has mandated), but he still needed me to make the trips into town for his weekly fix of history. Today the load was particularly burdensome: World War I and World War II. Alice pulled most of the books in her Radio Flyer wagon, along with every baby doll she owned, while Maggie and I struggled with our own armloads. We must have looked like a strange parade walking down Main Street on this hot hazy summer afternoon.

The *clack clack* of Alice's cowboy boots stopped at the steps to the library. She relinquished the wagon to Maggie, who slowly dragged it up the steps. She was red and wheezing by the time we got to the door. Mrs. LaCroix, the Wednesday/Thursday librarian, greeted us at the heavy wooden door.

"Mr. Tucker certainly has you working," she said. She took the wagon handle and pulled it to the front desk. Her hips probably used to sway, I thought. But now they were lumpy under the stretched polyester roses of her dress, and she waddled away from us, chattering all the while. As she started to lift the books out of the wagon, Alice tended to her dolls, smoothing synthetic curls, peeking into the backs of imaginary diapers.

"Would you mind doing me a favor?" Mrs. LaCroix asked.

"Not at all," I said and rested my own books on the counter.

"My Aunt Bethany lives up to the lake. She doesn't come into town much, but she loves the books on tape. *Cataracts.*" She shook her head. "Would you mind dropping some off to her house?"

"No problem," I said. "Which camp does she live in?"

"You know where the Foresters used to live?"

I nod.

"Next camp down. The one with the dwarves out front."

I thought of the eyesore that Gussy complained about each and every summer. The yard looked more and more like a miniature golf course than a yard: lawn jockeys, devilish dwarves, elaborate butterflies stuck to the house midflight.

"I know the one." I smiled. "I'll drop them off on my way home."

Maggie had found a seat at one of the long wooden tables

near the cold fireplace. In the winter, when I was a child, Grampa would bring me to the library on days that school was canceled because of too much ice and snow, and I would sit on the floor in front of the fire until my cheeks glowed red as embers while he wandered through the rows and rows of books.

"Whatcha reading?" I asked. She had one of the enormous ancient yellow newspapers spread out like a map in front of her.

"Things were easier then, you know? I mean, look." She motioned to one of the old-fashioned ads. "Hair cream, whatever that is, thirteen cents. This girdle thing is only a buck."

"It looks cruel," I said, staring at the illustrated woman smiling despite the contraption turning her body into an hourglass, or a dumbbell.

"Look what the headline is," she said. " 'Quimby to Hold First Annual Fourth of July Parade.' Damn. When was the last time you saw something like that?"

"I guess bad things didn't happen so much then," I said, sitting down next to her at the table. "Either that or nobody wanted to read about them."

"Bugs called last night," Maggie said, closing the paper and looking at me.

"Are you serious?" I asked.

"He wants to see Alice," she said.

"What did you say?" I asked.

"I said over my dead and rotting body."

"Good. Where is he?"

"Still in Florida somewhere, I imagine," Maggie said. She smoothed the crinkly paper down flat, her fingers stopping at the woman's small waist. Her careful nail polish had chipped away a little, leaving her pink nails exposed. I felt like I had seen something I wasn't supposed to. "Where's Alice?" she asked.

We found Alice sitting in a purple beanbag chair in the children's room. Her baby dolls were tucked around her, and she was holding a book close to her face. I could see her lips moving silently as she read.

"Hey, baby," Maggie said, dragging a big orange beanbag chair from across the room, putting it next to her chair.

"I've got to get some books for Magoo," I said.

Maggie sunk into the chair and leaned her head back. As Alice continued reading, Maggie stroked her hair.

I loved that there was still a card catalog in this library. I pulled the long drawer out and looked for the books that Magoo had requested. Each card had been typed, the letters not always even or clear. I imagined the person who organized things here. I imagined her sore back and eyes straining in the dim light of the library. I imagined the way the metal keys must have felt under her fingers and the quick rhythms of typing.

After I had scratched down the call numbers with the stubby yellow pencil tied to the card catalog with a string, I browsed through the catalog for something to bring Devin. I found Magoo's books easily. The library's history shelves were as familiar to me now as my grandfather's. I had to search a little for a book for Devin. I wanted to find something perfect. Finally I found one in the shelves for oversized books. I knelt down, the bare skin of my knees pressing into the ornate black grate in the floor.

The photos inside were deceiving. At first, the rooms didn't look out of the ordinary at all. Kitchens with gingham curtains, loaves of bread on wooden cutting boards. Beds with lace canopies and books tossed carelessly on blue nightstands. But then, in the corner, you could see the giant's hand, reaching in toward the Christmas tree laced with tiny white candles. Miniature palaces with marble floors and chandeliers with pinpricks of light. I thought about his boxes, the small worlds inside.

I carried the books to Mrs. LaCroix. She stamped each book and I signed the dog-eared card. No computer magnets or anonymity. The list of names on the sign-out card revealed the books' histories, the names of the hands that had held them were there for anyone to see in careful cursive.

I found Maggie and Alice in their respective beanbag chairs, both asleep. I sat down with my books and read three paragraphs about Alexander Hamilton before my eyes grew heavy too.

I dropped Maggie and Alice and the Radio Flyer full of babies off at Maggie's house and headed around to the other side of the lake to drop off the tapes to Mrs. LaCroix's aunt. I pulled into the driveway and noticed for the first time that the yard was not only littered with inanimate plastic critters, but with live and frantic chickens as well. I closed the door to the Bug loudly to let Mrs. LaCroix's aunt know that I was there.

I walked tentatively toward the camp, watching my feet so that I didn't step on any of the squawking birds. I knocked on the screen door, which was hanging by one rusty hinge. The storm door was shut tightly, curtains drawn.

"Who is it?" A voice cracked loudly, startling me.

"It's Effie Greer." I struggled to remember Mrs. LaCroix's first name. "Evelyn, your niece, asked me to stop by with some books on tape from the library."

"Evelyn?"

"No, this is Effie Greer. Gussy McInnes's granddaughter." I stepped back from the door. A chicken ruffled its feathers at my audacity.

"Don't know her," the voice said definitively.

"Evelyn, your niece, sent me with books on tape for you. From the library."

"Books on tape?" The door opened slowly. "You got Grisham?"

"I do." I smiled at the sliver of a face behind the door. "His newest one."

She opened the door and looked toward me suspiciously. Her eyes were milky, like a newborn kitten's instead of a woman's. Her hair was wrapped up in elaborate silver braids. She was wearing a loose green floral housedress and leather men's shoes with nylon stockings.

"Well, come in then," she said angrily and motioned vaguely to the center of the kitchen.

I walked into the kitchen, following her slow and blind lead. Immediately, I recoiled at the smell and sight of the kitchen. There were cats everywhere, crawling across the filthy counter tops, crouching in the corners retching and scratching. I covered my mouth with my hand and squeezed my eyes shut against the ammonia smell.

"You want something to drink?" she asked, shuffling toward an old refrigerator.

"No," I said. "I really need to be going. I'm dropping some books at Mr. Tucker's place as well."

"Blind as a bat, that Tucker." She laughed and opened the refrigerator door. The light was out.

"It was nice meeting you." I stumbled, realizing that I had no idea what her name was.

"Mrs. Olsen," she answered me, turning on her heel. "Can you help me with something before you go?"

"Sure," I said, trying hard not to gag as a dingy white cat retched in the corner.

She reached for me with a thin cold hand riddled with liver spots and touched my bare shoulder. She was waiting for me to lead her now.

"In the living room is my tape recorder."

I walked in front of her through her house, looking for what might be the living room. I stopped when I saw a battered couch and a coffee table with a bouquet of dusty plastic tulips in the center. She eased herself down onto the couch and motioned toward an end table where I found a bulky tape recorder with sticky buttons.

"Can you put it in please?" she asked, reaching for a nylon stocking that had slipped like transparent skin down to her ankle.

I slipped the cassette into the tape deck and listened as the story began. I sat with her until the voice on the tape became part of the room, as at home in this dirty room as the cat gently purring beneath her fingers and the giant fan in the window spinning the stench of all these cats. I sat with her, waiting for her to motion again for me to leave. I waited for her to become lost in the story until I slowly left the room and went back into the yard filled with chickens and futile ornaments.

As I opened the door to the car, she poked her head out the window and said, "I'll be done with these by next Wednesday."

"I'll see you next week then, Mrs. Olsen."

"Do you know Mrs. Olsen?" I asked Gussy and Magoo as Magoo double-checked to make sure I had gotten all of his books.

"Bethany?" Magoo asked. "Sure. Crazy old bat."

"Tucker," Gussy reprimanded.

"I brought her some tapes from the library today."

"That's sweet, honey," Gussy said. "Evelyn ask you?"

I nodded. "Why do you say she's crazy, Tuck?"

"Killed her husband."

"Shush," Gussy said, gently hitting his arm. "Everyone knows it was a heart attack."

"She killed her husband?" I asked in disbelief.

"Effie, really. It's ancient history. And it was a *heart attack*." Gussy stood over Magoo's sink as comfortable as if it were her own, peeling carrots. She can do this, make a home in anyone's kitchen.

"Rat poison," Magoo insisted. "Arsenic. Put it in his tea."

"Why?" I asked. Gussy stopped peeling, frowned at us both, and then resumed peeling the thin slivers of orange.

"He was a lady's man. Had six or seven girlfriends from what I understand. Of course, they were the girls that nobody else wanted or knew what to do with, but he didn't seem to mind. One for every day of the week. One of each: blonde, brunette, redhead, fat, skinny, short, and tall. Story goes that when Bethany lost her sight—it happened real quick, when she was only forty or so—that he started bringing them around the house, right up underneath her nose."

"I'm sure she couldn't have smelled them in that house." I laughed.

"Story is that he'd invite them to dinner, dinner that Bethany spent all day making, let them sit on his lap the whole time. It was like a game to him or somethin'. Your Grampa used to deliver the paper there. He always showed up around dinnertime with the Olsen's paper. Anyways, one night Mr. Olsen brings over his Tuesday girl, what was her name, Gussy?" Magoo scratched his head and Gussy shook hers. "Doesn't matter. She was the short redhead. Terrible skin, I remember.

"So, he brings her to the house, and she's not so bright and she thinks that Bethany is deaf too and sits there on Olsen's lap during dinner, giggling. He keeps trying to shut her up, putting his hand over her mouth, whispering in her ear.

"That's when Bethany does it. Stares right at the girl as she pours her husband a cup of tea. Doesn't spill a drop."

"What did the girl do?" I asked.

"Some say she was so spooked just by that that she ran out of the house before he keeled over. But your Grampa told me that she stayed there on his lap, his hand halfway up her skirt when he started to pitch—"

"Enough, Tucker," Gussy said, slamming down the peeler.

"That the rigor mortis set in and she couldn't get her panties loose from his fingers."

I started to laugh, and Magoo shrugged. "That's what your Grampa told me, anyway."

Gussy grinned a little and handed me a peeler from the drawer. "Help me out here, Effie."

"Here is little Effie's head, whose brains are made of gingerbread." Magoo smiled, lighting his pipe.

Before Grampa died, he used to read me an e.e. cummings poem, tapping his fingers gently on my head, ". . . God will find six crumbs. . . ."

Devin came for me just as the sun had gone down. I hadn't been to the drive-in since I was in high school. I didn't think it was even open anymore, but Devin showed me the newspaper advertising the double feature: two movies I didn't recognize the names of.

He came to the door as I was pouring the hot popcorn into a brown paper grocery bag. The metal foil from the popper was hot on my fingers. "Ow!"

"Need some help?" he asked, as I struggled to shake the burn away.

He held open the bag and I managed to get all of the popped kernels in without burning myself again. "Thanks," I said. "Is it cold outside?"

"Um-hum." He nodded. He was wearing a thick corduroy barn jacket the color of chocolate. The inside was lined with flannel.

"Let me get some warm clothes," I said. I went to the closet to look for something warm to wear. All I could find was Grampa's black wool coat. I found a pair of gray mittens and a moth-eaten scarf. "July, huh?"

"You got any boots in there?"

"Shush," I said and threw the coat over my shoulders.

"Ready?"

"Uh-huh." I nodded.

In the truck, he pulled his pipe out of one of his deep pockets. "Do you mind?" he asked.

I shook my head. I didn't tell him the way the thick sweet smell of his pipe made me dizzy with remembrance and longing. I leaned my head back when he lit the pipe and puffed. When he rolled his window down and the smoke escaped, my heart plunged just a bit.

The sign for the Moonlight Drive-In Theatre was the original one, from a time when girls swooned and boys' hair was thick and hopeful with grease. Thigh-high weeds sprouted up through the entrance. We payed the bored teenage girl in the fluorescent booth and drove into the empty lot. It looked like a graveyard, the microphone stands like silent silver monuments.

"Where do you want to park?" he asked, scanning the rows seriously.

"How about that one?" I said, selecting a spot in the center of the dirt lot.

"Are you sure?" He looked at me, intent.

"Positive." I nodded.

He backed into the space so that the bed of the truck was facing the enormous white screen in the distance. He opened the door for me and helped me down out of the truck. We climbed into the back where he had created a virtual living room with an air mattress and thick army blankets. As I got settled, plumping pillows, and pulling the black wool coat around me, Devin struggled with the microphone.

"It's supposed to hook onto the window," I said. I got out of the truck and rolled the window down, attaching the microphone to the inside of the truck so that the microphone faced outward. "There."

"Perfect," he said. He fiddled with the knob and found the station that had been lulling me to sleep every night this summer. The reception was full of static. The horns of old music filtered through the mute of this metal box.

A few cars arrived, shining their headlights across our laps. The popcorn was gone before the first movie started.

"I'm going to get some french fries," Devin said, licking the salt from his fingers as the previews flashed blue across the screen. "Want anything?"

"Um-hum." I nodded. "A hot dog and an Orange Crush." I hadn't had an Orange Crush, in the ten-ounce glass bottles they still had here, since before I could drive to the drive-in myself.

When he was gone, I stared at the screen, at the ramshackle playground beneath it. Seesaw, merry-go-round, and monkey bars. Colette and I were never allowed to play there when we were small. My mother was afraid of tetanus, as well as of the hot dogs at the snack bar.

He handed me the hot dog, smothered in onions and mustard. The first bite was like breaking skin, but the insides were hot and sweet.

"Come here," he said, wiping roughly at my cheek. "Where'd you learn your manners, anyway?"

"*You* try to eat this thing without making a mess," I said.

"No, thanks," he said. "I'll stick with these." The french fries smelled hot and familiar. I wanted one.

"Can I?" I asked.

"I suppose." He frowned playfully as I grabbed four or five of the hot french fries and stuffed them into my mouth.

"Thank you," I said and crumpled the mustard-stained napkins into a tidy ball.

"I've been thinking about the book you gave me," he said, plumping a big pillow and putting it behind his head. He leaned back and turned to look at me.

"Really?" I asked.

"It's strange. I mean, there's no way you could know, but in D.C., I spent every Saturday wandering around the Smithsonian. I mean *all* day. I'd ride the Metro in with my dad, he'd give me a dollar or something for lunch, and then he'd set me loose. And the exhibit I loved the most was the miniature exhibit. Some days that was the only place I went all day. My friends would have teased me something fierce if they'd known I was spending my weekends hanging around looking at dollhouses, so I always went by myself. Told them I had to help my dad or something."

He shrugged. "But there was something so peaceful about it. You know, I felt so big there. Standing over all those small things . . . nothing could hurt me there, you know? I was looking down on the entire world. Little streetlamps and windows, door-ways too small to fit your fist through. I felt like God there," he looked straight ahead at the movie.

I nodded.

"That's why I make the boxes, I think. I mean, I've tried to paint, sculpt. All that stuff you go through to find what it is you do best. But I keep coming back to them. They take me back, you know? Give me that Saturday feeling of a dollar in my pocket and the whole world at my feet. In my hands."

His hands were like dark birds in his lap.

"I do that too," I said.

"What's that?" he asked.

"I'll read the same books twenty times looking for that too. Books let you do that, you know what I mean? You can go back to the same place over and over. Maybe the first time you read a book you were lying in a hammock in the spring. But you can pick up that book in the middle of December on a bus to San

Francisco and you'll be back there again. It's like making your own déjà vu."

He nodded. "I guess that's why I do a lot of things I do. Even building things, working on houses. I do it because I remember the way pine smelled the first time I took a saw to a board, the feel of a hammer in my hand."

"Is that why you come to Gormlaith?" I asked. I could not figure out why he would want to return here again and again. People here can be unforgiving, cruel to strangers like Devin.

"Partly." He nodded. "Every summer when I arrive I'm looking for the exact shade of blue I saw the first time. In the mornings I wake up because the birds are predictable. Because I know that when I fill the basket in the percolator with coffee that it will smell like morning. I know the way the sun will feel when I sit in the window."

"That's nice." I nodded. "Having a routine. Being able to count on something."

"But it's more than that. By coming to Gormlaith, it's better than just remembering. Your books, my boxes. That's just imagination. Nostalgia. Some places you can't ever return to except in your head. But Gormlaith will always be here. That's nice."

I shivered.

"Are you cold?" he asked.

"A little," I said and his raven hand flew out and landed tentatively on my shoulder.

"The best thing though is when you find a new one."

"A new what?" I asked. His arm had created a warm half circle around me.

"A new feeling. Like the way the sky looks from the back of a pickup truck at a drive-in movie in late summer. Like now. It's original. And we can come back whenever we want to."

The sound went out of the microphone during the beginning of the second movie. No static, no anything.

"There's no sound," I said.

"That's okay," he said. "Let's make it up."

"What do you mean?"

"My brother and I used to do this with the TV. Turn the sound down and make it up. You be that girl with the big hair. I'll be the mean old lady."

I looked at him.

"Here, I'll go first. *Damn, my skin itches. I wanna scratch so bad I can barely stand it. I might kill somebody if I can't scratch myself soon.* See? Now you." He laughed.

"I can't," I said.

"Oh, come on, play with me." He pleaded.

I shook my head. "Let's just listen," I said.

"Okay," he said. "I can listen." He leaned toward me, slowly, and pressed his ear against my head. "It's so quiet I can almost hear what you're thinking."

"Yeh?" I asked. "What am I thinking?"

"You're thinking about something sad," he said.

"I am?"

"Yep."

I looked at him and wondered how he could hear my recollections. Of Max and me and the games we played at movies, not so different at all from the one Devin played with his brother. How he could hear my thought that at one time everything was normal, that Max wasn't always a monster. Wasn't always so full of hate.

"And now you're thinking about Chinese food," he said, nodding.

"How did you know?" I asked.

"Actually, I heard your stomach growl," he said. "What do you say? There's that twenty-four hour place at the mall in St. Johnsbury. It's a long drive, but I could really go for a big bucket of beef and broccoli."

"Just a couple minutes longer?" I asked.

"Sure," he said and pulled his pipe out of his pocket.

The smoke swirled around me in my grandfather's coat and up into the night sky. There was something new and something old here. Longing for something gone and the anticipation of something I had never felt, intertwined. Silent lovers on the screen intertwined, breasts and thighs as large as trees. Quiet as wind.

It began to rain Sunday morning. The rain fingers tapped their secrets on the roof just above my head. The sky through filmy curtains was dark like night. I raised my hand and touched the rough wood of the ceiling over my bed and felt the tap-tapping. Insistent and certain.

All I wanted this morning was a Sunday paper from a city I didn't live in and warm bagels with thick cream cheese. I hurried out of bed and pulled on my softest sweater and jeans. I ran a brush through my tangled hair and noticed that it was now touching the waistband of my jeans. I pulled it up and fastened it with the silver moon barrette.

The Bug sputtered and coughed and roared. I drove all the way to the bakery in Quimby, where I got a half-dozen bagels, still hot and smelling of yeast. At the Shop-N-Save I bought bright red smoked salmon and cream cheese. A thick Sunday *Burlington Free Press* and real cream for coffee.

The dirt road had turned into a river of mud by the time I got back to Gormlaith. There would be no trips into town again until the sun returned. I liked this feeling of being trapped. I drove past the Foresters' and noticed that the dock was under water; the pale red of the wood surfaced and disappeared again. No one had painted it since the Foresters had lived there. I pulled into Devin's driveway and covered my head with my sweater before I opened the door to the storm.

"Get in here," he said. "You'll catch your death out there!"

"Okay, Mom." I laughed and handed him the wet paper bag with the steaming bagels inside.

I took off my sweater and sat down on his overstuffed couch. He brought a cutting board and plates and knives into the living room and cleared a place on the coffee table for breakfast. "Effie, the patron saint of Sunday mornings." He laughed.

He brought two mugs of bitter coffee and sat down next to me on the couch.

"I didn't know if you would be awake," I said. It was only eight-thirty.

"I get up early usually."

"Your studio light was on. Did I interrupt you?"

"No, I work in the afternoons, but I like to have a few hours to get to know the day." He took a plump salt bagel from the bag and split it open with his hands. A burst of steam escaped from the bread.

"What are you working on now?" I asked, cutting into a cinnamon raisin bagel.

"Another box. I've been working on it all summer. I'm just having a hard time finishing it."

"How come?"

"I dunno. Sometimes that happens. Usually I just wait it out and it comes together. I can be patient."

"Can I see it when you're done?" I asked, spreading cream cheese on the bagel.

"Of course," he said, peeling a thin sliver of salmon from the package.

"Great."

"Cheers," he said and touched his bagel to mine.

"Cheers," I said. The cream cheese was sweet and messy. The raisins were plump and hot inside. I swallowed the creamy coffee and I felt warm.

"I need to do something about the garden," he said, reaching for another bagel. "I'm not quite sure what to do with all that food. It's like a vegetable jungle out there."

"Can you freeze it?"

"My studio in New York is about the size of a freezer. Why do you think I had to bring all this stuff with me?" he said, motioning to the rows and rows of boxes.

"Maybe Gussy can keep it for you. I think there's a freezer in the shed. Grampa used to fish."

"I'll figure something out. Maybe invite all the neighborhood animals over for a feast."

"I'll talk to Gussy," I said, wiping the corners of my mouth.

Devin finished his second bagel, stretched, patted his stomach. "You are going to be the death of me," he said, "you keep feeding me like this. Damn."

I drank the last few drops of sweet, now cold coffee and set my cup down. "Will you be back next summer?" I asked.

"Oh, yeh. This is home now. *Summer* home anyway. You?"

"I don't know," I said, my heart quickening. "I mean, I haven't thought much about it."

"Are you going back to Seattle?" he asked.

"No, no." I shook my head. Seattle seemed as far away now as a dream. A liquid memory. "Too much rain." I smirked.

Suddenly the clouds split open and an opaque blue sky emerged. Sun struggled through the murky sky and found us looking through a box of objects Devin had been collecting for his boxes. There were gum ball–machine rubber balls, Cracker Jack prizes. I pulled out a handful of jacks. "Do you play?" I asked.

"My little sister's," he said. "She could play all day long. I never had the patience for it."

The cracked window of the studio let in the sun, and I shielded my eyes.

He pulled something else from the box. "Fool's gold," he said, gently touching the surface of the rock.

I touched the rock and squinted. "The sun is out. Let's go outside." I opened up the door and stepped onto the wet grass. The garden was shimmering in the new light. Every leaf was sparkling, speckled with pure shimmering light.

Devin pointed to a metal bucket accidentally left at the edge of the garden. "I was going to start picking the beans before it started raining. I hate picking beans. My mama used to send me and my brothers out to the garden when all we wanted to do was play baseball."

"It's full of rain," I said. "Guess you'll have to wait 'til it dries up."

"Guess so," he said.

Suddenly the sky rumbled and the clouds closed around the sun like a fist.

"Fool's gold," I said, motioning to the disappearing sun.

"Let's get inside," he said. "I have an idea." He grabbed the bucket of rain and carried it to the door of the cabin. It sloshed and spilled.

"What are you doing?" I asked.

"You'll see."

Inside, I sat on the couch, curling my knees under me while Devin disappeared into the garage. He came back with an armload of fire wood.

"Oh, let me help," I said. "I can make a great fire."

"Go for it," he said and dropped the wood on the floor.

I went through the motions, my grandfather's hands helping me build the pyramid of twisted newspaper and kindling inside the woodstove, igniting the careful construction. And then the fire was roaring inside, and the room smelled of wood and flames.

Devin lifted the bucket of rain up and set it on top of the woodstove. Soon the water was hissing and steaming. "Don't want it too hot," he said, checking the water with a careful finger. "Just warm."

I watched him watching the rain, listened to the rain tapping secrets on his roof.

"I have a present for you," he said when the water was warm.

"Again?" I asked.

"I'll be right back," he said and disappeared into the closet. He came out with a thick white towel. "Here."

I took the towel from him and looked for an explanation.

"Come with me," he said and led me toward the door. "You have to do this outside," he said apologetically.

I stepped out into the misty morning air and shivered.

"Now sit down on the bottom step here," he said. He went back into the house and came out with the bucket.

"Ready?" he asked.

I nodded.

He sat on the step behind me, circling my body with his legs. And then his fingers were prying loose the silver barrette. He set it down on the step next to him and said, "Okay, now I need you to bend over at your waist." He stood up and I put my head between my knees.

The water was warm as he poured it slowly onto my hair. I could feel it seeping into the tangles, warm on my neck and scalp. When my hair was completely wet, I could see his dark hands disappear into the ends of my hair. His fingers were tentative, cautiously working the lemon-smelling soap into the ends. Slowly, his hands moved toward my head, making quiet circles. When his fingers touched my scalp, I shivered. My eyes grew heavy, and

I concentrated on the calluses of his fingers and the soapy circles they made in my hair. I could have stayed like this forever.

"Okay, this may be a little colder than before," he said, and I felt the warm rain coming again. I opened my eyes and watched the soap swirl onto the grass beneath my feet. And his hands were working so slowly, so gently, coaxing the soap from my hair. His hands were making prisms of light, glass bubbles from my hair. Finally, when the water ran clear, turned from glass into rain again, he twisted my hair, wringing out the rain. And then the towel was enclosing me, soft and warm on my head. He wrapped the towel like a turban; when I sat up my head was heavy.

His hands were wet. He reached to adjust the towel that was leaning with the weight of my hair. He left his hands on the sides of my head and crouched down, facing me, and peered into my face. Curious.

I caught my breath.

His hands moved slowly down from the sides of the towel, pressing against my temples, my ears. The sound of rain and birds and the lake were muffled by the darkness and thickness and warmth of his hands pressed against my ears. I closed my eyes.

And his hands found the sharp bones of my face. Lingered at the bones beneath my eyes, grazed the straight short plane of my nose, the sharp corners of my jaw.

I could smell the incense sweetness of him, the breath of him not so familiar this close, new and stronger. Less subtle than before. And then I could taste the sweet incense of him. The thick dark sweet incense of him. And soon I was not sure if it is his lips or the kiss of rain saved and warmed by fire. Or just his hands, dark birds, that were redefining my lips, softening the angles, the sharp edges of me.

Late Summer, 1991

～ ～ ～ She was always there.

My head is pounding, my heart is pounding, my feet are pounding against the sharp ground as I run to the night water. She knows that I am coming. She expects me now. When I reach the edge of the water, I will see her floating under the moon or moonless sky. When I walk down the red dock, away from land and solid ground, she will feel me, feel the way the water yields and responds to my weight. Then she will paddle slowly toward me, motioning with her small hand for me to join her. Then I will lower myself into the water, roll onto my back, let the water hold me. And knowing that she is there will be enough to make me feel not so alone.

Max doesn't hear me anymore. I could sing or cry as I rise from the bed where he lies like a dead man. He doesn't stir when I escape. *He might not know that I am gone. He might not notice.*

It is warm tonight. After rain. The air is electric and humming. My legs are humming, new bruises like beestings. I run to the edge of the water. But she is not here tonight. I look to the Foresters' house, frantic, buzzing. The house is dark and still as water. I stop walking, and my legs become dead currents.

I opened the door tonight. I opened the door and looked at the car sitting in the driveway. I even peered into the window and stared at the torn vinyl upholstery, at the crushed shoebox on the floor, the Coke can and the ashtray filled with gum wrappers and coins. I imagined my hands on the wheel, the way my fingers might feel curving around the wheel, on the cold key. His breath did not change when I moved away from his body. The uninterrupted rhythm of his almost-death. *He might not know that*

I am gone. He might not notice. I am transparent. I do not need the car to carry me. I can throw myself into the wind and be lifted by the breezes. I can lay myself in the water, be carried by the current to somewhere safe.

She and I don't speak in the water. What would there be to say? Instead, we lie on our backs in the water's hands and stare at the sky. I note the differing shades of summer, the patchwork of blue and yellow and green of my body is really no different from the changing sky. When I am cold and tired, I swim back to the dock. She returns to land too. And I help her out of the water. Then I pull my grandfather's coat around me and she grabs a threadbare towel from the clothesline and pulls it over her shoulders like a cape. When she walks back to her window, cracked open ever so slightly to the night, she turns sometimes to see if I have left. She doesn't wave. She only watches to make sure I am safe.

But tonight the lake is empty, the surface unbroken by a child's arms or legs or breath. I take off the coat and lay it on the edge of the dock. I pull my T-shirt over my head and cringe at the tender blue bruises that once were breasts. I pull my hair over my shoulders to hide the colors of my skin. But no matter how hard I try to hide the shades his hands have made of me, I always find another blossom. I tug at my curls, pulling the long dark strands, making a futile costume of hair. I am anxious without her. I am terrified of the water.

But I lower myself to my knees, allow the pain of bone against wood. And then I lower myself into the lake, the water dark enough to hide even the most purple of my ribs and vertebrae.

When I lean back my hair becomes heavy with water. It falls under me, reaching for the bottom of the lake. Water fills my ears until all I hear is the sound of Gormlaith. The strange watery, thick sound of bagpipes. The sound of a thousand nights like these. The sound of drowning. My hair reaches like wet fingers to the bottom of the lake, finds the weeds that sometimes wind themselves around my legs. My hair grows as it reaches, tangles with the beckoning weeds. Conspires and intertwines. Soon there is no difference between my hair and the dank weeds. And I am being pulled under.

The sound comes from somewhere older than this lake. Deeper than this water. I open my mouth to let it out, a bird trapped in a concrete room. Its wings beat and smash against the walls. It is the sound of bagpipes. Strange siren. It moves the water. It shifts the earth beneath the lake. It loosens the weeds and roots, *my hair, my hair, my hair.*

In Gussy's kitchen I pull the drawers open frantically. I can no longer remember where to find things. The drawers slam and creak. Nothing wakes him. Finally I find what I am looking for. I take the scissors and close the bathroom door loudly. I am suddenly capable of making terrible sounds. *Nothing wakes him.*

The blades are dull. The roots are thick. But soon the first one falls to the floor and curls around the pedestal of the sink. Each one is reluctant. Strong and unwilling. I make a forest of the bathroom floor. I cut until there is nothing to hold on to. I cut until I am standing in a lake of my hair. Until I am lighter than air. Until I am nothing but a canvas covered with the colors of his hands.

My shoulders are cold, bare. The sink is laced with dark strands. I blow the small hairs from my arms and chest and legs. In the mirror, I see the reflection of something blue. Transparent.

Like this, exposed, I walk through the brightly lit kitchen. There is a long-legged mosquito on the wall. A box of cereal on the counter, an empty carton of milk. I walk naked across the cold wood floors of the living room, up the twisting staircase to the loft where he is sleeping. And at the foot of the bed I stand and look at him.

He doesn't move.

I turn on the small lamp on the nightstand, filling the dark room with artificial warmth and light. I pull the covers off his body. Motionless, his pale soft skin doesn't seem to rise or fall. He could be dead tonight. I could have dream-wished him dead this time. I open up the window, old paint chipping from the sill like dead skin. The window is heavy, tired, but finally I am able to get it open and use his shoe to keep it propped it open. The late summer cold wind battles against the curtains. I am freezing. Nothing. I stare at him in the bed and hate him. I look at my hands and wonder what sort of damage they could do. I wonder what they are capable of. If they could save me after all.

For a long time (*minutes, hours, years?*) I stand waiting for him. My back aches. My hands wish. But it is not until nearly dawn that he stirs. Liquor like quicksilver when the sun breaks. His eyes flutter open and he rolls over, confused by the light, by my absence. Then he is awake, awake and aware.

"What the fuck?" he says. His voice sounds like a crumpled paper bag. "Jesus. Are you insane? What are you doing?"

The curtains blow into the room, wrap my legs in their lacy arms. I do not say a word. I am learning silence. His eyes grow wide with something that looks like fear.

"What's wrong with you? What did you do to your hair?"

And I don't speak. I don't answer. I don't cry. I only stand there, looking at his confusion.

When his hands come, when they grab my shoulders, and his fingers fall into the holes they have made over time, I am silent. When his voice crawls into my ear, *no, no, no,* I am leaving this place. And when his mouth tries to breathe me back, tries to fill me with breath instead of water, I am already gone.

There *was* a child in that swing. In the red swing. And it was her.

I find her when I am looking for something else. For the woods, I think. For the safety of trees. At first, I think she is the dream child, the one whose mother was dead. The one that I imagined for Max. But she is real. I can see the swing moving, her legs pushing it higher and higher. When I get closer, I can see that her knees are bloody. Her knuckles are skinned, her hands wrapped tightly around the rope on either side of her. Her hair is a mess of dark curls, wild and sure. I stop at the edge of the lawn in front of the Hansel and Gretel house and watch her. She doesn't see me; I am invisible without my hair. She is looking at the lake behind me, through me. But it must just be the sun in her eyes, because when she descends from the tree line she looks startled.

"Hey!" she says. "Whatcha doin?"

I look for a way to escape, but the woods are not welcoming me today.

She keeps swinging and I stare at my feet.

"You wanna swing?" she asks. Her voice is raspy, as if she were fighting off a cold.

I shake my head.

"Sure?" She rises again then, and leans back, opening her mouth to the sky.

I nod.

She slows the swing down. The dirt under her feet makes small brown clouds. When she jumps out of the swing, she could be walking on air.

"You cut your hair off," she says. "Why'd you cut your hair off? It was pretty."

I shrug my shoulders and motion to the new cuts on her knees.

"Some kids in town," she explains, kicking at a stone in the driveway.

My voice comes from somewhere outside of me, as if I caught the words in a gust of wind. "What happened?" I ask.

"Swimming lessons," she says, reaching to touch the open wound. "None of them kids like me."

"That can't be true," I say, my words coming back to me. I can feel them in my throat.

"No, I mean none of them *like* me. They all *different*."

"Oh," I say.

"It's okay, I don't need none of them. I'm going back home in a week. I got plenty of friends back home. I got you too, right?" she asks me then, taking my hand. Holding my hand like it's something fragile and real.

We start walking together back toward the camp. Her hand is small inside mine. I can feel the bones of her fingers, the bones of a small dark bird. In front of the camp we stop. A motorboat hums across the lake.

"You goin' swimmin' tonight?" she asks.

I nod my head, as I see Max behind the porch window.

"Promise?" she asks, raising her eyebrow.

"I promise," I say. Max moves from the porch into the living room. I can see his silhouette moving through the camp like a ghost.

I recollect this day, all of the small details of this day. I remember stubbing my toe on the threshold as I went back inside to him. I remember the thick waffle batter in a glass bowl, teetering on the counter. Eggs running yellow across the griddle. The earthy smell of potatoes and onions. The sweetness of peppers. I remember walking past him in the kitchen, through the stench of the air that circled him in a liquor cloud. I remember the mug he used for coffee, the chipped handle, the ring of orange flowers around the rim. Memory serves this day like a fancy cocktail, the clarity of water and ice. But drunken somehow, slow-moving-hazy.

As Keisha returns to the Foresters, I walk past Max pouring coffee into the chipped mug with orange flowers. Through the vodka cloud, the scotch haze of his breath.

"What'd she want?" he asks, sitting down at the table with a plate covered with leaden waffles and runny eggs.

"Who?" I ask, touching the bristles of hair at the base of my neck.

"That kid, the Fresh Air kid I saw you talking to outside," he says, and cuts into the waffle flesh with his knife.

"Oh," I say. "Nothing. Wanted to know if I'd seen her base-ball." *I imagine the ball lost in a game of catch or throw, rolling down the dirt road, across lawns, through the woods. I imagine the pursuit.*

"Did you?" he asks.

"What?"

"Find the ball," he says annoyed.

"Yes," I say. "I found it." *I bend over in the tall grass and hold the baseball in the palm of my hand. I hand it to her and a smile spreads across her face.*

"I hope you're planning to go to a hairdresser and fix that mess you've made," he says.

I touch the sharp points of hair that frame my face like black razors.

"If you were trying to shock me, it worked," he says. There is a bit of yellow egg stuck in the corner of his mouth.

Instead of staying, instead of defending the sharp edges of my hair, of my bones, instead of searching for the words that will soften him, I stand up and move away. He moves toward me and I turn away. He reaches for me and I recoil. He asks me questions and I pretend that his words are only air. All day, I practice. He doesn't know what I am planning. That each successful parry brings me one step closer. I move from room to room, each doorway one doorway closer to the last door. I am so close now. Close.

August 1994

෮ ෮ ෮ Mrs. Olsen stared through the milky veils past me toward the forest.

"I finished them books on tape you brought three days ago."

"I'm sorry, I've been very busy. I'm delivering to a couple more people now," I said. This morning the library had sent me away with an entire box of books to bring to three different people at Gormlaith. As I was lugging the heavy box down the library steps, Mr. Woods came running after me.

"For your troubles, Effie," he said, pressing a twenty-dollar bill into my hand. "You've been so generous."

"Oh, no," I said, shaking my head. I felt like I did when Colette and I shared a paper route and some of the old ladies would try to give us money for bringing their papers up difficult stairs or past vicious dogs.

"Please." He smiled.

I had been running around all morning. Books for Magoo. Books on tape for Mrs. Olsen. Food for the frogs. I found an old book of Grampa's about reptiles and amphibians and went to Hudson's looking for something to feed them. *Bait*, was what the pimply sales boy suggested. *We got lots of bait.* Then to the lumberyard with the list of materials in Devin's handwriting for the tree house. I handed it to the man and he nodded, smiling, chewing on a thick wad of tobacco, spitting on the ground next to my feet. "Ayup. This is a tall order, ya know. A tall order."

"Can you come in for a while," Mrs. Olsen said, "to help me with the tape recorder?"

"For a minute," I said. I wanted to get to work on the tree house that afternoon.

Inside the cats were sleeping. It was the strangest thing. Sunlight streamed through in hot pools onto the floor and the arms of chairs and tabletops. And in each and every spot of sun was a cat.

I tried to imagine what it must have been like when a man lived here. When Mr. Olsen must have come home from work and thrown his coat across the back of a chair. Before Mrs. Olsen couldn't see. Before he started bringing his girlfriends home with him. When there was the smell of a man's cologne and sweat and breath in this air. I thought now, as the smell of litter boxes and musty heat began to overwhelm and burn in my nose, that maybe after he died she couldn't bare the absence of his smell. Maybe she even missed the scent of the women he brought home. Unbearable, the way the scent of him disappeared after time. Even the clothes she couldn't bear to take out of his drawers must have faded after a while. And so perhaps at first she filled the house with flowers to replace the smell of him. Perhaps she even sprayed the air with a bit of his cologne. But in the end she must have chosen the cats. Because they, at least, were alive.

Every time I went to Mrs. Olsen's house now, she would sit down on the ratty couch as I put the first tape in the tape recorder. And as the voice crackled and began each story, I would watch her close her eyes. There were usually two tapes for a book, sometimes three. I knew that she listened all the way through because she complained often about the endings. Too sad, she'd say. Cheap, as if I were somehow at fault for the contents. She didn't need me to flip the tape for her, or to find the second one.

I think she liked having someone there with her. A real voice before the recorded one. I left her sitting upright on the couch, her eyes closed, and a cat on the spot of sunlight on her lap.

The water was choppy. A lone canoe in the center of the lake bobbed and drifted with the current. When I got to the camp I could see Gussy's car in the driveway as well as a car I didn't recognize. I pulled in behind the car, noticing Connecticut plates.

I didn't know anybody in Connecticut. I walked into the kitchen tentatively, as if I didn't live here. "Gussy?"

I heard voices above me, the ceiling creaking. I walked to the stairs and looked up, "Gussy?"

"Oh, hi, honey." Her voice floated down to me. "We'll be right down."

"Okay," I said, wondering who was in my bedroom.

Gussy led the way down the stairs. Following her was a man wearing a flannel shirt so new it was still creased from being folded inside a package. Behind him was a small woman with perfectly straight blond hair, sharp features like a bird's, and brand-new hiking boots.

"Effie, these are the Kings. From *Connecticut*," Gussy said as if that explained everything.

I stared at her outstretched hand.

"They're interested in the camp," Gussy said.

"Oh," I said, my throat thick.

"Effie is my granddaughter." Gussy smiled and touched my shoulder. "She's living here for the summer."

"Oh, how nice," the bird woman said. "Where do you normally live?"

I looked to Gussy for an answer. She looked at her hands, busying themselves with the Formica top of the kitchen table.

"I just moved home from Seattle," I said.

"Oh, I love Seattle," the woman squawked and bobbed her head. "We used to go sailing on Lake Washington every summer."

I hated her.

"Can we take a look at the plumbing?" the man asked.

I busied myself with the books for Magoo and the groceries I had picked up on my way back to Gormlaith. After everything was put away, I went outside and sat on a lawn chair in front of the camp and watched them. The woman walked on the man's heels. The man ignored her. He motioned vaguely to things like the roof, the forest surrounding the camp, the lake. I couldn't hear their voices but I could imagine them. *We plan to put a sun room on, a Jacuzzi maybe. Of course we'll have to build a larger dock. We've got jet skis. A power boat. Our daughter will be with us too. She's a sophomore at Boston College. Pre-law. Or Political Science. Gawd, we never know what it'll be next. She changes majors like she changes shoes.* And I pictured her, thin and pale, perched on the edge of the dock like a bird herself. Wishing she were back in Boston. Wishing her mother didn't talk so loudly.

When they drove away in their silver car, I found Gussy inside inspecting the windows.

"We could really use some new windows," she said, leaning down to look at the warped windowsill.

"Gussy, I don't want them to live here."

"Honey, I can't keep this place up. And they were just looking. I've had about a zillion calls. It doesn't mean they're going to buy it."

Tears were welling up in the corners of my eyes, hot and thick.

"It's okay, Effie," she said, offering me the warm circle of her arms.

"It's not okay," I said, shaking my head hard. "Nothing about this is okay."

The graveyard where my grandfather is buried is next to Quimby High. I expected the school to be deserted now, but the football field was dotted with field hockey players. Knee pads and sticks, listless girls stretching their skinny legs, lounging on the grass, dreaming, perhaps, of anyplace but here. It was still too hot for summer to be coming to an end. The first few weeks of school, they knew, would be torturous. The arms and legs, no matter how much they ran and swang and stretched, would still belong to summer.

I parked in the cafeteria parking lot rather than trying to maneuver the Bug through the hilly cemetery. I locked my door and smiled at two red-faced girls who had escaped from the athletic field and were leaning against the brick wall of the cafeteria in their plaid skirts, smoking, their hockey sticks discarded on the grass. I thought of all of the generations of field hockey players, the girls summer after summer who traded in their cutoffs for kilts. Tess and I were not these kinds of girls. We were not legends here. We were not even ghosts in the halls.

The gate to the cemetery swung open without resistance, its spring sprung long ago. I closed it gently behind me. The cemetery was the first thing they built in Quimby. Before houses and roads, shops or churches, the settlers of this town needed to take care of their dead. From the stones it seemed that most of the dead were infants and mothers. Most of the babies didn't even have names. They were lined up and numbered next to their mothers, most younger than me.

Tess and I would escape here. We weren't running from field hockey practice or cheerleading practice or anything in particular for that matter. But when school let out for the day, this was the first place we came. Mostly just to linger a while before we had to go home. But sometimes to find others like us who were dead.

At fifteen, we found a girl, Mary Elizabeth Miller, loving daughter. Child of God. And perched above her name was a stone angel that looked blind, her eyes the same gray stone as her wings and hands. At seventeen we found Katherine Blake, loving mother and wife. Next to her were twin babies without names.

I grazed the granite stones with my fingertips as I went to where I had been told my grandfather was resting. But when I get to the spot that Gussy had described, I couldn't find him anywhere. I walked the crooked rows of stones, stepping over the crumbling monuments, trying to find him. Desperate and certain that I had looked at every stone, I saw a small granite block that was glossy and new. I was alarmed when I peered at the cutout words and could see my face reflected in the polished stone.

I was also alarmed to find that I was not the only visitor Grampa had had recently. There were bunches of freshly cut daisies in jelly jars, jelly jars from my grandmother's cupboard, lined up neatly in front of the stone. And next to the jelly jars was what appeared to be a dominoes game in progress, the familiar ivory pieces aligned according to the rules I only vaguely remembered. Magoo.

When I pulled the pipe from my pocket, it seemed that he was not alone. That there were conversations still to he had. Dominoes games to be played still, if only in Magoo's imagination. I set the pipe down on the stone and sat down in the tall grass.

When Grampa died, Gussy threw the party he had requested reluctantly. He did not want a funeral. He did want guests, music, people dancing and drinking. She must not have known how to do this. She had buried sisters, her parents, a child. She understood the rhythm of gathering the clothes, of choosing words, of nodding and hugging and tears. But true to his wish, she did none of that at all. She ordered a hundred blue balloons, cheese and fruit plates, and champagne. She called his friends from the Quimby Pipers and sent invitations to the party to celebrate the life of my grandfather.

She insisted, though, on this stone. Because balloons set free over the lake and the music and dancing did not give her a place to go back to to cry when she needed it. It didn't give her a place to set her best daisies. And below his name, she insisted, *True*. A word uttered between them once so long ago they might not have remembered when it began at all. And muttered again so many times that it grew to mean more between them than *mine*, or *stay*, or *love*.

In the distance I could hear the field hockey coach's whistle and the hot breath of running girls. When I laid down and pressed my ear to the ground, I could hear the sound of their feet like hooves. I listened for something beyond the pounding, but there was nothing to hear. And when I whispered into the grass, I was certain that my words were lost in the pounding of their feet.

I kept the key to the safe deposit box in a locket my sister gave me when she went away to college. I knew she would have liked for me to put a picture of her inside (a small one from the photo booth at McCarthy's drugstore), but instead I left it empty, waiting for the right thing to hide inside. When Gussy gave me the key, I thought immediately of the locket, the funny silver heart that lay twisted in a jewelry box I rarely opened.

"There's not much in there, honey," she had said. "But he wanted you to have it. And, of course the money, and the books. Whenever you want them, you can have them."

The cold silver of the necklace felt strange on my chest underneath my shirt. It hit the bone between my breasts as I walked from my car across the street to the bank. The teller looked annoyed when I told her that I would like to open my safe deposit box. She found the file and the twin key and motioned for me to follow her down the stairs.

Together, we fit the keys and turned, pulling the long metal box from the wall.

"You can take it in there if you like. Press that buzzer when you're ready to come up."

"Thanks," I said and took the box from her. It was heavy. I had to struggle to keep my wrists from folding in on themselves.

There was a small table in the room. A lock on the door and a hard wooden chair. I set the box on the table and shook the pain from my wrists.

Inside the box were some savings bonds, a bundle of letters with names I didn't recognize on the return address. There was a sock filled with old coins. I poured them out onto the table and sorted them by size. They were mostly pennies, wheat pennies grown green with age. Some of them looked foreign. *Some coins,* Gussy had said. *Nothing terribly valuable. You might be able to get a little something for them. He seemed to think they were some sort of treasure just because they were so old.* There were also some documents rolled and held together with a rubber band that crumbled when I started to slip it off the end. I scooped the coins into my hand and poured them back into the sock, knotting the end tightly and putting it back in the box. I put the savings bonds back too and unrolled the papers.

The paper was fragile, yellowed, and the blue ink was faint. I smoothed the paper out on the table and reached for the bag of coins to hold the corner down. I traced the outline of the camp. I touched the blue walls, the windows, and doors. I let my fingers linger in the kitchen, the closet, the loft bedroom above. Imaginary walls then. *Here?* My great-grandfather must have asked Grampa. *A sun porch here in the back?* And my grandfather, still a child, must have said, *Dad, why don't we put the porch on the front so we can look at the lake?*

Your mother would love that, he might have said, ruffling his hair.

A tree house, Dad? You said we could build a tree house?

Easy there, one thing at a time, he must have chuckled.

And there will be blueberries? And a boat for the lake?

There will be more blueberries than you'll know what to do with. Yes, yes. All in good time. And then he must have leaned over in the half-light to erase the porch he had sketched on the back of the imagined camp. And as Grampa rested his chin on his father's shoulder, he must have moved the porch to where my grandfather could watch the water. And he could watch my great-grandmother gathering stones for the garden she planned.

Before I realized that I was crying, my eyes had already rained one drop that blurred the blue ink of the front door. The front door where my great-grandmother must have wiped her muddy feet before she brought the stones inside to inspect. The front door that later was ignored and blocked by the end of Gussy's daybed. The front door where Devin left a robin's egg, cracked and blue as this line.

I didn't want to go into town that night, but it was Maggie's birthday, and she wanted to go out dancing. I knew the only live music we'd find anywhere near Quimby would be country western music or some high school band with acne and bad rhythm, but she pleaded with me, and it was her birthday.

I was balancing on the ladder below the tree house, tearing a rotten board off the deck, when I heard Devin below me.

"Effie!"

"Yeh?" I said through the trees.

"You up there?"

"Yeh," I said louder, and braced my foot against the side of the tree house as I yanked an old nail out of the board. The force of it nearly sent me falling down the ladder, but I got my balance just as Devin made his way through the marshy woods below me.

"Look out," I said, tossing the board down. It landed close to him on the soft ground.

"Easy." He laughed.

"Hey, you wanna come up?" I asked.

"Sure." He smiled and started to climb up the ladder. I knelt on the remainder of the deck and held the ladder steady for him.

"Hi," I said, reaching for his hand to help him the rest of the way.

"How's it coming?" he asked.

"Okay. I really just started. I think I just need to replace the deck and the roof. The rest of it seems okay. Some paint. Redo the inside."

"Can I?" he asked, motioning to the door.

I unlocked the padlock and let him in. He ducked and went inside.

"I used to have forts." He smiled, still ducking. The ceiling was a good six inches shorter than him. "In Virginia. My brothers and I would build them out of cardboard boxes. Twigs and stuff. They didn't hold up so well. I think I know how we can fix the deck."

"Really?"

"Yeh. I think the answer might be to make it wrap around the whole tree house. It'll make it sturdier, brace it."

"That seems a bit elaborate, don't you think?"

"It wouldn't be too hard."

"Sure." I shrugged. "I'll try anything at this point."

"Great." He smiled.

"My grandfather built this. He and his dad," I said.

"Little people?" he asked.

"Nope. I'm the only small one. My mom's almost six feet."

He sat down on the rusty bottom-bunk frame, and looked around the room. "I feel like Alice." He smiled.

"You know Alice?" I asked, wondering how he would know Alice if he didn't know Maggie.

"In Wonderland?" He laughed. "*Eat me, drink me.* I don't remember which one made her big though, do you?"

"Oh, I thought you meant . . . this little girl. Alice, her mom is a friend of mine. They live up here too," I said. "It's her birthday today."

"Alice?"

"No, Maggie, Alice's mom. We're going to the Lodge tonight. She wants to go dancing, and I don't really think we're going to find any good music, but it might be fun anyway." And then, remembering my promise to Maggie, I asked, "You wanna come?"

"Sure." He nodded, peering out the child-sized window.

"Really?" I asked, suddenly regretting asking him. "I mean, you don't have to. It will probably be a bunch of, you know, rednecks. Big trucks. Bad music. Fighting."

"I have a friend who bartends there," he said. "I'd love to go. If it's okay with your friend."

Maggie pulled off her jeans and waddled toward her closet to grab another pair. "These are my *lucky* jeans."

"Lucky jeans?" I asked.

"Maybe I should say my *get lucky* jeans." She laughed. "I haven't worn them in a long time, though."

"When was the last time you wore your jeans?" I asked, smiling.

"About six months ago," she said. She changed into the jeans and admired her butt in the full-length mirror on her bathroom door. "You got any lucky pants?" she asked, raising her left eyebrow.

"I haven't bought jeans in years." I smirk. "*Years.*"

"Bugs called last night," she said.

"Again?" I asked, the stars fading slowly.

"At fucking *midnight*," she said. "He was wasted, I think."

"What did he want?" I asked.

"Who the hell knows. I could barely understand him. Going on and on about Alice mostly. And a little bit about me."

"What about you?"

"Oh, the same old shit. *Maybe we can get back together some day.* He misses me. He didn't ever treat me right." She frowned. "*No shit, Sherlock, I say.*"

Alice came into the room then, holding her headless Barbie. She crawled up onto Maggie's bed and leaned to turn on the TV. She turned the knob until she found a tennis match. The reception was terrible, but she seemed fascinated by the game.

"Would it be okay if I brought a friend along tonight?" I asked, sitting down next to Alice, starting to braid her hair.

"You don't *have* any other friends," Maggie said, and then she said, "Shit, you mean him, don't you?"

I nodded. Alice's hair was soft between my fingers.

"Of course that's fine. It's more than fine. I was beginning to think you'd made him up."

"He's real," I said.

"I thought for a while there might be something wrong with him or something. Is he a midget? Have two heads?"

"No," I said.

"Well, what's he look like?"

"He's big. Six four or so." I tried to think of a way to describe the color of his eyes, the deep water that was his voice.

"Damn," she said.

"He's black."

"A black guy in Gormlaith? That's pretty damn close to finding a needle in a haystack."

"He lives in New York," I said.

"Flatlander." She nodded and unzipped her jeans.

"He's not like that."

"He's not pushy and obnoxious? Doesn't stop his car in the middle of the road to look at trees?" She peeled off her jeans and folded them neatly.

"No. He comes here every summer."

"I've been curious myself." She smiled. "I mean, about black guys."

She looked at my expression of disbelief and punched my arm. "I don't mean that. It's just out of the ordinary. It's not like we exactly see them all the time up here. There was what? *One* black guy at Quimby High? Terrence. Terrence Williams. And he only lasted a year. I think his folks moved back to wherever they came from when nobody would hire them. Hell, I wouldn't want to live here either. Don't blame 'em at all."

I smiled.

"Of course, there's always the Fresh Air kids," she said.

My heart sank. I stared at my hands, which became blurry and strange in my lap.

"Remember that little girl at the Foresters'? The one that drowned? You were here that summer weren't you? Jesus, black folks don't fare too well up in these parts."

My throat was thick, my palms sticky. I needed to sit down, but Maggie was spread out across the bed.

"Bugs always said 'Once you go black, you never go back.' Stupid motherfucker, wasn't he? Like he's so wise about what black men have to offer. I don't think he ever even *met* a black man before. Except maybe at the fair. One of the carnies he always managed to piss off every year. I say they're probably *all*

211

bad. Black, white, or green. They're still men." She thought for a minute, "But he's nice to look at, huh?"

"Yeh." I nodded, my stomach turning, bile rising acidic in my throat.

"You all right?" she asked, touching my arm.

"I'm fine." I smiled.

Devin picked me and Maggie up at nine. She, like everyone else, seemed to take to him immediately. We crawled into his truck, and she did all of the talking. I was grateful for her ability to make conversation about anything. Radial tires. Cheese. The new zoning laws.

I liked the way Johnny Cash's voice sounded inside the warm cab of the truck tonight. I loved the way Maggie's Designer Imposter perfume smelled mixed with the strange sweet tobacco scent of Devin. But when we pulled into the dirt parking lot of the Lodge, I was suddenly terribly uncomfortable. The parking lot was full of trucks, small groups of people standing around, girls sitting on open tailgates, blue clouds of smoke in the dark night. I didn't want to get out of the warm cab. I wanted to go home. But Maggie jumped out of the truck and said, "Okay kids. Let's get drunk and make some trouble."

Maggie led the way to the front door. I followed her, and Devin followed behind, touching the small of my back with his hand.

Maggie asked the bouncer what the cover was. He was a skinny guy with a beard and a John Deere baseball hat. "Five bucks," he said. "And I need to see some ID."

He read her ID and she said, "You probably noticed it's my birthday today."

He looked at her and winked. "You go on in then, honey. Your girlfriend too." And then to Devin, he said, "ID?"

Inside I relaxed a little. The music was loud, the lights were flashing, and no one seemed to be paying attention to us. Devin seemed comfortable here, at home. He found an empty booth and said, "I'll go get us something to drink. What do you ladies want?"

"Beam me up." Maggie smiled, pounding the rhythm of the music on the table, looking around to see who else was there. "The Reverend Jim Beam and diet Coke. With a lemon, if you please."

"Effie?" he asked.

"I don't care," I said. "Beer?"

"She'll have a shot of Cuervo and a Corona. With a lime," Maggie said.

"I'll be right back," Devin said and walked up to the bar.

"He's beautiful," Maggie said, leaning to watch him walk to the bar.

"Maggie." I blushed.

"I mean it. And *sweet*. So polite. I bet he's good to his mother too."

"You think so?" I asked. I watched him kiss the curly-haired bartender on the cheek. I could almost see her blush and I got a strange twang of jealousy. It felt good though, sharp. Real.

"And he likes you, too," Maggie said.

"*Shh*," I said, as he started walking back towards the table.

"I don't think you even *need* lucky jeans."

He sat down with us, and I scooted into the booth to make room for him. From here we had a perfect view of the dance floor. There was one drunk woman dancing alone, twirling around in her cowboy boots, orange makeup, and a tight, low-cut velvet top. Her chest was covered with freckles.

Maggie got the next round of drinks. I passed her my shot of tequila this time, and she chased it with her cocktail. "I'm going to dance," she said. She walked to the front of the bar, stopped at a booth full of guys, and dragged one of them onto the dance floor. His friends hooted and whistled, and he shuffled his feet all the way to the dance floor. But soon they were dancing, two-stepping, and Maggie was good. Really good. For a few minutes there was something nagging at me as I watched her. Like a word at the tip of my tongue. And then I realized that it was like watching Colette. It was the same feeling that I used to get watching Colette dance. Grace. Getting lost in the music. An ability to completely forget your body.

"Cheers," Devin said, raising his beer to mine.

"To Maggie's birthday."

"To Wonderland." He smiled.

"Hm?"

"*Drink me.*" He grinned.

Maggie came back to the table, breathless and smiling. "That was Billy Moffett's brother, Ted," she said. "Do you remember Billy?"

I looked towards the booth where the guy's friends were slapping his back and high-fiving each other. I looked for Billy in his faraway face.

"Sure," I said. "I knew Billy." I sipped my beer, and Maggie grabbed Devin's wrist. "You two-step?"

"I can give it a shot," he said.

They walked together to the dance floor, and I watched Billy Moffett's brother, Ted, watching them. I felt a chill. I pulled my sweater around me and watched Maggie teach Devin the simple steps. Soon they were dancing like some strange hillbilly version of Fred and Ginger. And Ted Moffett watched them. When he stood up, tripping on his friend's outstretched leg, I looked to see if the bartender was watching. She wasn't.

Ted walked slowly onto the dance floor, dancing alone, holding the rim of his cowboy hat, tipping it to no one. I sat paralyzed and watched as he tapped Devin's shoulder, as Devin turned around and saw Ted. Heard Ted's friends egging him on.

Devin let go of Maggie's hand and leaned to her, asking if she would like to be relinquished, I imagined. Maggie was drunk but not stupid, and I watched her shake her head no. And then I could hear his pleas, his friends' juvenile whistles and slurs, and the sound of the bartender opening the bar gate and slamming it down again behind her.

Soon she was standing next to Ted, putting her hand on his shoulder, trying to convince him to sit down again. When he threw her arm off of him, the bouncer was on top of him, twisting his arm behind his back. Within minutes he and his friends were gone. Outside at least, and Devin and Maggie were laughing at the table with me.

"I need another drink," Maggie said. "Motherfuckers. Quite the pickings in this town, huh?"

"You okay?" I asked. "Do you think they're really gone?"

"Oh, I dunno. They'll get bored with the parking lot eventually. Do you think Maggie's having a good birthday?" Devin said.

I smiled. "Yeh. I do. I really do."

When Maggie came back to the table she had a basket of french fries and another round of drinks. "Compensation for all the trouble," she said. "She's cool."

"Her husband works with me," Devin said. "A super carpenter. He built half of the cabins at the lake."

"A toast," Maggie said. Her cheeks were hot pink, her brown eyes slits.

"To?" Devin asked.

"To me," Maggie said. "To Effie. And to my new friend, Devin." She swallowed from her drink and hit me on the back. She whispered, "Now go dance. He's like one of those guys on MTV. Really."

"Maggie," I said, but Devin was just grinning and touching my hand and starting to stand. And, like every high school dance

215

I ever went to, the music turned slow, and my knees turned liquid. But this time I got the guy. This time it was Maggie sitting at the table, while I walked to the dance floor.

I had forgotten how to dance. Max and I never danced. In all the years we were together, we managed to never go to a single college function or other event that required this. Consequently, when Devin looked down at me and reached one arm around my back, I felt like laughing. I was thirteen again. But one of my hands found his hand, and the other found his shoulder and soon we were dancing. He was so tall, my face was even with his chest. I stared at the buttons on his shirt, noticed that one had chipped in half. And slowly, I gave in. I leaned in, and breathed him. Breathed the new smell of his detergent, felt the warmth of his skin through the flannel of his shirt. When the song ended, I didn't pull away, I only prayed for another slow song. But the music picked up and I would not attempt to do the two-step. I was accustomed to leaning, clinging, but dancing was something else all together.

At last call, Maggie was ready to go home. She had confetti in her hair courtesy of the bartender and a group of birthday greeters. She rested her head on Devin's shoulder.

"I think it's time for this one to get some sleep," he said.

"Me too," I said.

We managed to get Maggie from the bar to the truck; it took all of my strength to hoist her up onto the seat. The parking lot was almost empty. Devin got in the car, propped Maggie up, and turned the key. The engine trembled but didn't turn over. He tried three more times and then looked at me apologetically.

I looked out the window, wondering where Billy's brother might be hiding. Headlights illuminated the night and then turned toward the road. He turned the key again. Nothing. My heart started to pound so loudly I was certain he could hear it.

"Do you think we need a jump?" I asked.

"Probably. I'll run in and get Sue to help," he said. "You guys okay here?"

"Um-hum." I nodded. Maggie snored softly.

I watched him walk back to the bar. I was sweating even though I could almost see my breath. I was waiting for Ted to come out of a dark car. I was waiting for someone to get hurt. I nudged Maggie, but she wouldn't wake up. I felt like I was going to throw up.

But then Devin and Sue were pulling jumper cables out of her car, and creating a lifeline between one and the other. "Thanks a bunch," he said when the truck roared to life.

Ted was not here. He probably had forgotten about Devin completely by now. And I hated myself for always being frightened of what was already gone.

Devin helped me carry Maggie up the stairs to her bedroom. I kicked a pair of her panties under the bed. Alice was at her grandmother's, thank God. Maggie blew kisses as we left. I locked the door behind me, and checked two times to make sure it was locked.

"Are you tired?" he asked.

"Kind of."

"You wanna go home?"

"No," I said. "I mean, I'm not really tired."

"You want to come hang out at my house? I've got some chili."

"Chili?"

"And cornbread. Mama's recipe." I noticed then how kind his eyes are. Laugh lines like small rivers. Dimples like small canyons.

"Sounds good."

. . .

We sat on his porch eating chili until the sun started to turn the sky pink. The roof of my mouth was burned and there were cornbread crumbs in my hair. His right leg was touching my left leg. We sat like this, barely touching, chili turning cold in our bowls until the sky filled with light. We talked, but I was uncertain of the words. The only thing I was certain of was this shade of the sky and the way his arm fit across my shoulder. In the circle of his arm I was Alice. *Drink me.* And I didn't mind so much being small.

I could feel the air turning. Ever so slightly, there was a change in the scent of Gormlaith. It filled me with the strange familiar sadness of other summers' ends. But it was only August. This was only the prelude. There was, for now, nothing to fear.

Devin held the ladder as I climbed up to the tree house. My legs were shaky, uncertain now that we had torn so much away from the structure. I stepped into the musty room and waited for him.

"You sure we can fix this?" I asked.

"Promise," he said. His breath felt like heavy feathers on my shoulder.

All day we worked. Mostly I carried things, kept things steady. The plans were all inside his head. I didn't ask questions.

By the time the air began to chill and the sun fell behind Franklin, I was standing on the miracle porch staring out over Gormlaith. I couldn't tell how I was suspended. There was no evidence to suggest that we weren't standing on air.

"There," Devin said, brushing sawdust from his shirt. "Whatcha think?"

"It's great," I said. "Thank you."

"My pleasure," he said and sat down on the edge of the porch, his legs swinging below him. He looked like the giant at the top of Jack's beanstalk.

The sun melted into the water in dream colors and the porch swayed beneath us. I grabbed my sweatshirt from inside the dark tree house and pulled it around my shoulders. I sat down next to him and looked through the veil of leaves.

"It always ends too quick," he said.

"What's that?" I asked.

"Summer at Gormlaith." He smiled, helping me with a stubborn sleeve.

"I know." I nodded.

The darkness fell around his shoulders as the dream colors turned from orange-red-blue into indigo. When he closed his eyes, he disappeared. I reached for him to make sure he was still there.

Back at his house, he brought me hot cider in a glass beer mug.

"Sorry, all the dishes are dirty." He sighed and motioned toward his kitchen. "I wouldn't go in there if I were you. That kitchen's tempermental if you ask me. Temper tantrums. I swear to God. It damn near exploded today."

I took the mug and held it with two hands. The smell of cinnamon and cloves filled my head like a hushed secret. It brought back all sorts of longing. For summer to linger. For other autumns.

"It's a little early for cider," I said. "It's still summer."

"I couldn't resist," he said. "They had some at the Farmer's Market and I figured what the hell."

I sipped from the mug and let autumn fill me. *It might be easier this way*, I thought, *to welcome fall.*

"When do you go?" I asked. I couldn't look at him.

"Labor Day weekend," he said. "Classes start the day after Labor Day. Nothing like waiting until the last minute."

219

"Oh," I said.

"Good?" he asked then, pointing to my mug.

"Good." I smiled and finished the sweet warm cider.

I felt a yawn coming, my body giving in to the exhaustion brought on by a day spent working in the tree.

"Can we stay in the tree house one night?" he asked, reaching for my hand. "Before I leave?"

A thousand yeses. A thousand small aches. I nodded.

I woke up and didn't know where I was. The air smelled different. The quilts on my shoulders were unfamiliar, the fabric thick and soft but strange. I pulled myself from the confusion, sitting up to figure out where I was. The glass mug was still on the coffee table. Devin's flannel shirt was laid neatly across the back of an overstuffed armchair. The curtains were drawn and when I pulled them back to see what time it might be, I could see the light on in Devin's studio.

In Devin's tempermental kitchen, the clock said twelve-thirty. I was certain it was morning, that I had slept through an entire night. I felt rested and alive. I opened the back door and slipped a pair of Devin's boots on. I could barely walk, they were so big. I must have looked ridiculous standing in the open doorway of the studio when he turned away from his work and saw me standing there.

"Effie," he said, startled. He was kneeling on the floor over an enormous piece of paper.

"Hi." I smiled.

"Come in," he said, holding his hand out to me. I put my hand inside his and walked to where he was working. The room smelled of turpentine and tobacco.

"I'm sorry to bother you," I said, suddenly feeling like I should have stayed on his couch or silently slipped into the night.

"Don't be," he said, pulling me gently down to the floor. "Look."

I looked down at the paper carpeting the small room. It took several moments before I realized what the sketches were. Because they were so large. Because the hair on this woman was like a small river. Because her breasts and hands and eyes were bigger than mine. *But mine.*

Devin reached his hand out and put it in the open palm of the charcoal woman. With his other hand, he pulled me in close to him. Then he took my hand and pressed it into hers. As his fingers spread over mine, we almost fit. I was that large. And when he turned the silver key on the oil lamp, lowering the wick, and extinguishing the light, I couldn't tell which was his hand or *mine* or *hers*.

In the cold dawn inside the studio, Devin's breath felt like summer captured in my hair. There was a note on the worktable: *Gone to town, I'll give you a call this afternoon.* I pulled the blanket over my shoulders like a giant cape and went outside into the cool morning air. I gathered my shoes and my sweatshirt and left the blanket folded on his couch. I walked down the road toward the camp, smiling, as if sleepwalking. I could see Magoo, the steam from his coffee, the steam of his breath, and the smoke of his pipe.

Perhaps I knew that there would be a gift waiting. Perhaps I felt it in his fingers when he made me sleep. I was not surprised when I walked to the steps of the unused door and saw the box sitting there. I was not startled when I picked it up and saw that he had, again, taken great care to make a small world for me.

I unhooked the silver clasp and lifted the lid.

Inside was Gormlaith at night. Water, the same color as it had been last night when I had found him in his studio, lost in the giant drawing of my hair and hands. But it wasn't really water, it couldn't be. Paper? Glass? The sky of this world was the exact indigo of dreams. Stars like fireflies, electric and bright. And above this miniature dream-lake was a silver moon, not suspended but ascending over the water. My barrette, waxing in this night sky.

I must have left the barrette at his house. I must have forgotten it on his steps when he heated the rain to wash my hair. My heart began to beat like a bird caught in the glass cage of my chest as I looked at the barrette suspended inside the box. How else could I explain this moon? I couldn't bring myself to walk upstairs to see if the barrette was there. Instead I drove into town, fighting the recollection of setting the barrette on the bureau the day before. Fighting the recollection of clipping the other silver moon into Keisha's hair.

Maggie was waiting for me at the diner. She was sitting at a table near the window, sipping a big glass of Coke with a lemon perched delicately on the edge. Her car was broken. *Beyond hope*, she had said, shaking her head. And so I had been taking her to and from work. I helped her get Alice wherever she needed to go.

"Hey, Effie," she said. "You hungry?"

"No," I said.

"I just ordered. Will you sit with me?"

"I need to know something," I said, reaching across the table and grabbing her hands.

"Are you okay?"

"No," I said, my heart thudding in my chest.

One of the second-shift waitresses brought Maggie a plate with a thick gray piece of meatloaf and a small white mound of mashed potatoes, colorless corn.

"What's going on?" she asked.

"What do you know about Devin?"

"You aren't having man problems already, Effie? They are definitely in your head. I can guarantee it. I see the way he looks at you."

"It's not that, Maggie," I said. "I need to know what people have said about him. About why he's here."

"I don't know," Maggie said. "Morris in the kitchen said he thinks he's related to that girl who drowned or something. I told him that just because they were the only two black people in Gormlaith doesn't make them *related*."

"He said they were related?" I asked, tears hot in my eyes.

"Yeh. Her brother, or cousin or something. I suppose it makes sense, if you think about it. I can't figure out why he'd come here otherwise. That and the way people are so nice to him. Even Ted Moffett. I've never seen him walk away from a fight. That's not exactly *typical* behavior around here. It would make sense though if his sister drowned. Quimby's got a sense of guilt if nothing else."

My ears were hot and stars were swimming in front of my eyes. *Andromeda. Cassiopeia. Orion.* Her hand swam out to me through the starry sky. *Cassiopeia. Keisha. Keisha.*

"It can't be true," I said, fighting tears.

"You're probably right," she said. "Morris doesn't know his head from his ass."

She ate all of the meatloaf and left the watery corn on her plate. I stared at my hands to keep the stars from descending again. My ears buzzed.

After I dropped Maggie off at home, I ran upstairs to the loft. I searched the cluttered dresser top for the barrette. *Silver moon barrette in a child's hair. A circle of white faces over her dark body on the moon-drenched grass that night.*

Underneath a dog-eared paperback I saw a sliver of silver. Gently, I moved the book away and picked up the barrette. I squeezed it in the palm of my hand, until the sharp tips of the crescent poked into my skin, bringing tears to my eyes.

I stumbled back down the stairs. In the kitchen I found the box as I had left it, hinged door open to the miniature night, and stared inside at the other barrette. At the other moon I had given her that summer three years ago.

Outside, a small wind skipped across the lake, lifted my hair from my shoulders as I walked across the road. Sleepwalking, I carried the box to the edge of the lake. Sleep-touching, I let the other barrette pierce my skin. Sleep-howling, I sat down on the rock and began to moan, stuttering white silent breath into the air. I sat at the edge of the water, trying to breathe, but I could only shiver, *her brother, her brother, her brother.*

August 24, 1991

∾ ∾ ∾ A recollection of hands. The way her hand looked like a small piece of chocolate in my own as we walked away from the swing. Hands reaching up to touch the bristles of hair at my neck when Max spoke. My hand reaching for the doorknob. He must have known by the end of the day that I had been rehearsing. He must have known that each movement was a small step closer to leaving.

Outside it is twilight. Orange melting into blue. Remarkably warm. Max is in the kitchen after dinner, still sitting at the kitchen table. I move away from him onto the porch, lie down on the daybed, hold a book to my chest like a shield. But the edges of the cover are too sharp to comfort me, the paper too likely to cut. I close my eyes and listen to the sounds of the summer people.

In the other room, he drinks his mother's face. Too much mascara and too little patience. *When she cried,* he said, *she looked just like you. Pathetic.* And through the ice cube panes, her face becomes mine. She makes him drunk. I make him drunk. She and I identical now. Sisters in this effort to drive him insane.

I recollect my hands tracing the edges of the embroidered sheets, thinking of Gussy pulling flowers from a simple white cloth while Grampa read in the other room. I long for this peace, for something I can't understand anymore amid this noise. The sun melts orange in the blue water, disrupts the blue with strange fire.

In the other room, he knows that I am ready. I can hear him fighting, staring me down in the rum rust of his drink. Willing me to stay. To wait with him a little while longer. Orange becomes blue. Waking becomes sleep. Day turns into night. In the other room he turns into the tiger behind the door I am trying to close. Hours of silence. Only the clanking of ice against glass.

I recollect my hands working across the bones of my body, identifying, classifying, making sure that all of me was there. Collar, clavicle, rib, pelvis, shin. I must make sure that I still have my bones to carry me.

It is midnight and I am some strange Cinderella, the glass slipper shattering into a thousand gestures. I use each gesture as a reminder that it is time to leave. Open palm across my face, nails dug into my shoulders, fingers laced like a noose around my neck. Fists meeting bone, bone, bone.

The bones of my legs carry me slowly from the porch across the living room floor to the kitchen. I can see the back of his head, bobbing, fighting me still in the melted ice. I pray for the silence of these old floors. *Do not moan tonight, be quiet. Let me go.*

But as I walk into the kitchen, he stands up and goes to the refrigerator.

"Have we got any more club soda?" he asks.

"No," I say, my heart pounding dully in my chest.

"Ginger ale?"

"No."

"Shit."

"Why don't you go to Hudson's?" I ask.

He looks at me, hatred and shame, and I know it will not be this easy. He won't just leave me alone here.

"Why don't I just drink something *else?*" he says and slams the thick-bottomed bottle on the kitchen table.

"Why don't you just fuck yourself?" I whisper when he leans into the refrigerator.

Pick a door. Pick a door. I am looking for the tiger. I am tempting him with a bloody piece of meat. I am ready for his attack.

"Excuse me?" he says and sways drunkenly away from the refrigerator.

"I *said,* 'Why-don't-you-just-fuck-yourself?' " My heart is steady, beating against the walls of my chest.

He slams the refrigerator door and stares at me in disbelief. Threatening me with his silence. His hands are curled into fists at his sides.

"Do it," I say.

He doesn't move.

"You goddamned coward." I stare at him, at his face, and it makes me laugh. "You're pathetic."

And then he gives me what I have asked for. Hands curled into fists, striking at my face. The sudden swell of my lip, the metallic taste of blood in my mouth. I feel my heart beating in the place where his knuckles have met my bone. And then I recollect my hand on the latch to the door, the simplicity of the silver hook, the ease. It has always been there, this door. What have your hands been doing?

226

I can hardly believe that I am moving, that the road is beneath me and that I can go faster now than he could run. I recollect my hands, skin stretched tightly over knuckles, holding the steering wheel tightly. I can see the lake in my rearview mirror. I can see everything reflected in reverse, and it isn't familiar anymore.

When I park the car in Gussy and Grampa's driveway in Quimby, I remember Keisha.

She will be expecting me soon. I promised I would meet her there, that I would be there after everyone was asleep.

This is more important, I think. *I am here.* There is no turning away from this.

I open the car door and run to the edge of Gussy's garden to vomit. I shiver and vomit, my body heaving and trembling with the poison filling me. The grass is cold and wet under me. My fingers dig into the cold ground as I become empty. I imagine that they would not see me if I went to the door. That there is nothing left at all except bones and that they too will turn completely to dust.

The house is quiet. Gussy's calico, Franny, is watching me through the window. I imagine Grampa has fallen asleep with a book on his chest. That Gussy is softly snoring next to him on the bed. I imagine the green glow of a digital clock, the smell of tuna casserole or honey-glazed ham and sweet potatoes still in the air. Dishes drying in the wooden rack next to the sink.

I think of his face, his hands, pleading. I see him standing at the edge of the road, watching his mother disappear. The smell of gasoline, and the way her hair flew out the driver's side window. I wonder if he stood outside as I drove away. If he cried into his hands. If he is only waiting for me to turn around and come back.

I watch my feet moving away from the house. I watch myself reflected in reverse, going nowhere, going *back.* The pull of the

227

bottom of the lake, the irresistible need to breathe. And I am somewhere in between. *This is drowning.*

In the car, I can't feel my hands on the wheel anymore. I am only an apparition. I am already gone. I drive slowly away from my grandparents' house, through town where everyone is sleeping, and turn onto the dirt road that will take me back to Gormlaith.

When the trees clear, I see a new red and blue. Not sun, not sky, but lights spinning across the water, dipping into the water like transparent hands. I stop the car when I see the summer people standing like ghosts at the edge of the water, white faces illuminated by the moon.

I leave the car in the road and run to edge of the water. Blue night. Blue lights making patterns on the water, on my hands. It is cold and I am shivering in my summer dress. I am shivering and tearing at my cuticles when they pull her body out of the water and lay her on the moon-drenched indigo grass.

Max pulls the boat out of the water and I hear the scream of the wooden bottom scraping against the rocks. He looks at me as he tethers the boat to the tree stump. He looks at me, and his flat drunken eyes say, *Because of you. This is all because of you.*

As he walks away, explaining to the officer how he came to find a dead girl in the middle of the lake in the middle of the night, I kneel next to her on the ground. My fingers pull the satin edge of the blanket over her hair, beaded with glistening drops of water. And I envy the way she seems to sleep, warm and quiet beneath a blanket of light. I envy her, because I am colder than water, colder than air. I am colder than this girl who gave me someplace safe.

PART

THREE

၈ ၈ ၈ *Silence falls in the empty spaces between before and now. There is no hush, no prelude; there is only the abrupt end to the words. But in this space is memory, and in this memory is unbearable pain.*

If I do not speak, if I slip into this white space like a sheer cotton summer dress, I may be safe. Because where there are no words, there is no danger. In this summer dress, there is nothing but the empty where before resides as memory and after is not yet born.

It is quiet here, without words. I could almost sleep. I could almost lie down in this white forest, lay my head across a bed of white needles, and rest. But I know that in these trees are ghosts, clinging to the branches, stirring in the transparent leaves. And if you listen closely, the ghosts' voices are louder than horns, louder and more seductive than Sirens, beckoning sailors to shipwreck.

And so I look for a way out of these white trees, out of this terrible playground. I stumble across the white ground, tripping on invisible rocks and scraping my legs on invisible branches. I know from these ghosts that silence is deceptive. That it isn't safe at all.

But what you are forgetting when you ask for words is that breaking silence is like breaking glass. The consequences are sharp, draw blood, leave slivers of pain in your fingers. The words may not be what you wanted at all. They may lodge themselves like broken glass under the tender skin of bare feet on pavement. They may crack open old wounds, make an old bruise blue again.

Do not ask me for haunted, because the slivers of haunted are sharper and more exacting than swords.

August 1994

∾ ∾ ∾ I tried to make it not true. Inside the patchwork cave I made, I dreamed his words explaining everything undone. As the late summer sun descended outside my window, I dreamed his hand pressing mine, his voice saying, *No, no. I knew of her, of course, but no, no.*

When night fell, I willed it untrue with remembered childhood prayers and wishing games. In the soft cavern of quilts, I pleaded like a child for it to go away. I considered every explanation, every possible coincidence, every discrepancy. I imagined them together and then separately, as I knew them, until I couldn't tell the difference between them anymore.

But at the library I had pulled out the yellowed newspapers from that summer, bound in a large leather book. I had found the article about her, tucked into the center of the newspaper where people might be less apt to find her. *Fresh Air Fund Child Drowns in Lake Gormlaith.* And as I stared at the words, smudged and precarious on the page, I realized that I hadn't known her at all. *Keisha Jackson.* Hadn't even known her last name.

When Devin called later that day I told him that I had errands to run, groceries to get, that I would be busy all day. I told him the weather would be blue again tomorrow, that the lake was warm, so I would not have to tell him the other things.

I drove back toward town, blinded by sun. I drove blindly around the lake reciting the shopping list like a mantra: *bread, milk, eggs, rice.* But when I got to Hudson's, I didn't go inside. Instead, I walked past the trucks and station wagons. Past three children with runny noses and dirty feet playing soldiers while their parents shopped inside. Then I walked through the tall grass into the woods where I first loved Billy Moffett.

The rusty trash was still there, in piles of knobs and doors and glass windows. I stepped carefully across the metallic hills, through the rivers of broken glass. The sun reflected in an oven door, and I felt my blood hot and liquid inside. I yanked a metal pipe out from under the debris and started to swing. I smashed the cold metal against anything that was not already broken.

The sound of metal on metal made me grind my teeth together. It felt like chewing on tinfoil, the metallic pain of tin on silver fillings. But still I pounded the pipe into everything that was still whole. I hit until nothing was intact anymore.

And then I sat down in the grass and looked at my destruction. Sweat ran down my arms in small rivers. I wiped the back of my hand across my forehead, felt the cool sweat under my hair. I sat there until my heart had stopped pounding so hard, until my breaths were regular and steady again.

My hands were sore, my palms already beginning to blister.

Instead of returning to the camp, I drove all the way into Quimby. I drove across the covered bridge and up the winding hill to Quimby High. School was in session again already. I imagined all of the restless kids inside, peering out the windows at the sunshine. The smell of chalkboards and new pink erasers.

I parked near the cafeteria and walked to the cemetery fence. I opened the gate and wandered slowly, winding my way through the stones, to my grandfather. The dominoes had moved. The white dots dizzying in this intricate game of aligning and matching. Gussy had also been there recently. There were fresh flowers in the jelly jars; the water clear. His pipe still lay on the cool granite, the grassy tobacco loose inside the hollow wooden bowl. I ran my finger along its gentle spine.

No one else was in the cemetery. There wasn't even the familiar hum of the groundskeeper's lawn mower. I laid down on the ground on my back, and stared at the sky. Clouds moved like white phantoms across the expanse of blue. Beyond this there were no birds, nothing but brightness. When I closed my eyes, I could still see the sun, like a black glowing ember behind my eyelids.

Behind my eyes, I saw Max waiting for me at the kitchen table. Perhaps drifting off to sleep and then waking, realizing that I was still gone. I watched him slam his empty glass on the table and look over his shoulder as if I might suddenly appear. I saw him stand up, one of his legs asleep, perhaps, numb and needles. I watched him walk through the dark living room turning on light after light, lighting every corner where I might be hiding. I saw him walk up the winding stairs, his pace quickening as he found each corner empty of me. I watched him panic then, his expression becoming uncertain. Scared, even, I watched him rub his hand across the top of his head, pressing down his hair, ruffled from sleep.

Outside he may have looked to the woods. He may have looked for the moon on my pale skin through the trees. He may have muttered my name, called me back home. He may have figured I'd only gone for a drive. That I would be back soon. That I only needed to ride with the windows rolled down, that I only needed a little night wind on my face.

Because then, on the back of my eyes, he walked calmly to the water and untied the boat from the tree stump. Breathing steadily, he crawled into the boat and pushed himself away from the shore. He dipped the oars into the water and slowly headed for the center of the lake.

He must have drifted off out there, because when he woke up he was disoriented, couldn't tell where he was in all that water. Remembering my absence, he must have shuddered a little and picked up the oars again to go back home.

There were no lights. No lights at all near the Foresters' camp. But if he could find the outline of the shore then he could find his way home. So he rowed toward the red dock, bobbing, making sounds like hands clapping. And when he was close enough to see the shadowy outline of the Foresters' camp and the edge of the water, he must have sighed a little, leaned back a little on the seat.

When he hit the piece of wood in the water, he worried first about scraping the bottom of the boat. He pushed hard against the wood to move away from it. But instead of resisting, the wood yielded and then disappeared. Dizzy and drunk still, he realized that it wasn't what he had thought. When she floated to the surface and he saw her skin, the same color as the dark water, he must have believed that this was a dream. That soon he would wake up, wrapped around me again, safe.

She was heavy, I imagined. Heavier than an eleven year old should be. The weight of her sleep, the weight of water. He touched her for the first time, and she felt cold. He thought that her dark skin would collect warmth like a dark shirt collects sunlight. Like pavement or charcoal. But she was cold, and heavy. It must have seemed that she had appeared in the lake like an apparition, a ghost child who had lost her way.

The story was easier than the truth. *He found her, found her, found her.* Floating like a piece of driftwood in the night water. He and she were alike then. Both lost in the lake, both drunk and dizzy, both already dead.

I opened my eyes and stared at the sun. I stared until my eyes fought and blinked. I rolled over and stared at the stone. *True,* etched in granite above my grandfather's name.

I pressed my ear to the ground. Listened for something, any-thing. The low aching wail of bagpipes. The sound of drums. The signal, the cue.

It began with blue. Blue sky, blue lake, and white paper sail-boats. I whispered into the ground, whispered into waiting ears. I uttered the first blue. Of the small flowers Max picked for me and taped all around my dorm room door so that when I came out, I was surrounded by forget-me-nots. Of the ink he used to write my name, so he could conjure me when I was not with him. Of the walls in the small bathroom of our first apartment. He tried to paint me the sky, but it came out the color of turquoise stones. *It's okay. I love it. It reminds me of my mother's Navajo ring.* Of the bowl he filled with sliced peaches and sugar when I was sick and sad one summer afternoon. Of the broken cobalt glass in the sink. His hands working quickly to stop mine from bleeding.

I whispered the secrets of how this began. Against drums. I whispered until my words became their own rhythm, their own melody, until they became music instead of pain. Until each rec-ollection became a small note, strung together on threads of blue.

Later, I returned to my cave. I returned to the bed where I hoped sleep would erase this. And that night, while Devin tapped at the door and later threw pebbles at my window, I dreamed them apart. I separated her face from his in my memory, tore the thread that bound them with trembling fingers. I dreamed him with pale eyes first, eyes that looked nothing like hers. And then I slowly dreamed the rest of his color away to make all of this impossible. In my mind he became transparent, water beneath the memory of my fingers.

But it *was* true. True. Because inside the box was Gormlaith at night, and above it, her moon.

• • •

"You told me that you were from D.C., that your family lived in D.C.," I said as I stared at his dark shape behind the screen door. "You said that your father worked at the Smithsonian."

"I am," he said. "He did. But my family moved to New York about ten years ago. My father works at the Guggenheim. Are you okay?"

"No," I said, my eyes hot and wet. "You should have told me. Why didn't you tell me?"

I pushed the screen door open and he stood there, his hands in his pockets, his eyebrows raised and waiting for an explanation. When he didn't speak, I felt a pounding in my throat and chest. When he closed his eyes, he disappeared into the backdrop of night. And I lunged into the space that was him, pounded my fists into his chest to bring him back. Like a child, I cried and pounded my fists.

When the strength in my arms was gone and I couldn't hit anymore, he carefully, tentatively, put his arms around me and pulled me into him. My eyes made his shirt wet, and I listened closely to the damp sounds of his fear.

We stood like this in the darkness for a long time. Finally, I looked up into his face, reached with my hands for his face and pleaded with my fingers for him to make this not true.

But his color, her color, were the same. It could not have been a coincidence here in this colorless place. I hated myself for trying to pretend that his color and hers had nothing to do with each other. That he was in any less danger just because he was larger, stronger. They were the same. My fingers pleaded but only found the same cavernous dimples, same insistent chin, same gently bowed lips.

Inside the box was Gormlaith that night. The night I broke my promise. A broken promise made of paper or glass. The night I went back when I promised myself I would never return, only to find that Max could do more damage when I was gone than when I was there. That night was captured in Devin's box. And above the water was her futile moon.

"You knew her," he said. I felt the words with my fingers. "My sister."

And I realized then that I loved him in the beginning and now because they *were* the same. I loved her first when I found her swimming at night, disappearing into the night. And then I loved him, for his darkness, for his resemblance to her, to night. I loved him *because* all of this was true.

We moved into the house like ghosts. He may have been carrying me. I could not feel the floor. Pressed into him, I couldn't feel anything except his heart beating like drums against my chest. There were no lights, nothing to guide our bodies through the rooms. The small fire I had built to keep the camp warm was just a pile of glowing embers in the fireplace.

He led me through the darkness to the porch. Moonlight shone blue through the glass. I did not feel my feet leave the floor, did not feel anything but the rhythm of the drums in his chest. The tentative rhythm of his fingers, of his hands, on my skin. In the cave he made over me with his body, I felt nothing but the beating of our blood in veins, taut and trembling. The gentle beating of blood like birds' wings. Like loons lifting out of Gormlaith and rising up into the night.

In this foreign country, this place of drums, I listened for the signal, the cue to begin. I waited for the rhythm to change, for the melody of the blue black of his skin, of her skin, to change. But the drums were insistent. I did not speak, did not sing, did not break.

The darkness enclosed us like hands. His body enclosed mine like night. His skin, her skin, covered me. I was invisible now. I had finally disappeared. I was only water in his hands.

Then, the silence of breathing. The silence of blood beating. The silence of this moon in the window, and that moon in her hair.

"I'm sorry," he whispered. "I should have told you."

I pressed my fingers to his lips to keep his words inside. I wanted nothing anymore except for the rhythm of his breath on my neck, like bird's wings or a child's flickering eyelashes.

We fell asleep this way, the harmony of our breaths new and strange. I awakened only when I heard the sound outside the kitchen door. The small motion of my waking woke Devin, and he sat up startled by me and this unfamiliar place.

"What is it?" he asked.

"I don't know," I said. I pulled on my dress, which lay empty on the floor, and slipped my shoes on my bare feet.

Outside the sound was louder. It sounded like a cat crying, like one of Mrs. Olsen's cats screaming. My heart quickened as I walked around the side of the camp. It sounded horrible, wrong.

When I got to the front yard I saw Alice sitting, rocking on the front step. The hem of her nightgown and her feet were covered with mud. Her eyes were wide and startled, her hair tangled.

"Daddy," the voice said.

My shoulders ached.

"Daddy's killing Mommy."

And then I was carrying Alice, her small body curled against mine, pressed against mine. Devin came running outside after me.

"What's happening?"

"We need to go to Maggie," I cried.

Alice lay curled in the backseat of the car as Devin and I went into Maggie's house. Inside, it was quiet and still. Nothing looked any different than it had earlier today. Nothing was out of place. There was a half-full glass of lemonade on her kitchen table, a pizza box on the counter. In the living room, the TV was on with the sound turned down. Blue light fluttered on the walls like moths.

In the bathroom, Maggie was lying on the floor, her arms draped across the rim of the toilet. Blood was pouring from cuts above her eyes and her mouth. Vomit stained her blouse. Devin picked her up and cradled her in his arms like a child.

"Alice?" she asked, her voice gurgling with too much liquid inside.

"She's with us. He didn't get her," I whispered into the red tangles of her hair.

This is not happening not happening not happening, I thought as we walked through her still house and out onto the porch into this still night. *This is not happening again,* I thought.

And later in the bright artificial light of the emergency room, with Alice's head on my lap and Devin's arm across my shoulders I wanted to scream. I wanted to make the sounds that Alice made that woke me from my dream. I wanted to shatter air with my voice. I wanted to pierce the strange stillness and white of this night. I wanted to find Bugs and kill him with my bare hands, break his eardrums with a song I have never dared to sing.

Maggie's bones were broken. The bones that held her face together (her smile suspended, her eyes wide) were fractured into slivers. Her wrists. The bones of her fingers. He broke her and then walked away into the night.

"Welcome to hell," she said when I came into the room hiding behind flowers.

"Maggie," I said, and set the flowers in the blue plastic pitcher of water on the nightstand. I sat down in the chair next to the bed and reached for her. But everything was blue or broken.

"How's Alice?" she asked, pulling the thin white sheet up to her chin.

"She's okay," I said. "She's at your mom's. Devin and I brought her some Cherry Garcia."

"Is she talking?" Beyond the blue of her bruises, I could almost see her. I could almost see hope. But the purple and blue were so distracting I couldn't look long enough to find it.

"Not yet." I smiled.

Maggie turned her head and looked out the window. Her profile looked strange and swollen. Her head was an odd mix of color. The fire of her hair and the blue, blue water of that new face. But for all that blue, the trembling of her shoulders was the only evidence of tears.

The girl at the bank was the same one who let me into the safe deposit box before. I watched the back of her heels as we walked down into the basement. Two small runs like scars traveled up the back of her small calves. Her perfume smelled like the perfume counter at the J. C. Penney, or like the scent of a fashion magazine. Indecisive and thick.

"Just buzz when you're ready," she said. She stopped at the foot of the stairs and turned to look at me. "You mind if I ask what you got in there? I mean, we're not supposed to ask, but sometimes I would just love to know what some people keep locked up. Sounds stupid, huh?" Then she shook her hand dismissively, "Forget it. I'm sorry."

"Home," I said.

"Excuse me?" she asked.

"Gold," I said.

"Wow," she said, her eyes widening. "Like bars of gold?"

"Um-hum." I nodded.

I took the coins and savings bonds and put them in my pocket. I unrolled the blue prints and wound my fingers along the spiral staircase banister.

I took the stairs two at a time upstairs to the bank lobby. My blood was running quickly, my heart thudding, reminding me of the walls of my chest. The girl who helped me smiled from behind the marble and glass wall.

"I'd like to make a withdrawal," I said.

Gussy brought the last of Grampa's fish that night. "Well, this is it," she said. "That darned fish is finally gone."

"Have you heard from those people at all? The Kings?" I asked, opening the oven door and peering in at the fish sizzling under the broiler.

"Not yet," she said. "Soon, I'd think, if they're interested."

"I don't like them."

"I know you don't honey, but it's not likely we're going to be able to find somebody that you do like."

"What does that mean?" I asked.

"I mean, you love this old place. There isn't gonna be a single person you'd want living here." Gussy poured two glasses of milk and set them on the table.

"That's not true," I said.

"It is true. And it's okay. But it's time for me to sell this place. It belonged to your Grampa, and now he's gone. I can't hold on to it, Effie. I have to let it go."

I stood up then and went to the porch. I opened Grampa's desk and pulled out the cigar box. I carried it to the kitchen and set it next to Gussy's plate.

"What is this?" she asked, raising her eyebrow. "It's not my birthday for another month."

"Open it," I said. My palms were damp. I put them in my lap and touched the dampness to my shorts.

She opened the lid slowly, and looked at me.

"I want to buy the camp. There's a lot of money in there. Enough to make a down payment, the bank says."

Gussy's hand flew up to her chest.

"If you would rather rent to me," I said, "I can pay rent and for all the utilities and for the property taxes."

Gussy sat quietly staring at the cracked cover of the cigar box.

"I know that Mom and Dad were hoping I'd spend Grampa's money on school. But I don't think I'm going to go back to school anytime soon."

Gussy looked up from the box and into my eyes. "You are absolutely sure that you want to be here?"

"It's home," I said to Gussy, my throat thick with relief.

We ate dinner quietly. The phone ringing startled me.

"Effie?" My mother's voice was high-pitched and excited on the other end.

"Um-hum," I said, holding on to the last bit of lemony fish before I swallowed it.

"I've got some good news!" she said. "Colette just called. She and Yari are getting married!"

"Did you tell her?" my father asked excitedly in the background.

"Yes, yes. What do you think?" she said.

"That's great," I said to her. "Colette's engaged," I said to Gussy.

"That's wonderful," she said, standing up from the table, wiping her hands on a napkin.

"Is Gussy there with you?" my mother asked.

"Uh-huh, hold on," I said and handed Gussy the phone.

Gussy smiled as my mother told her all of the details of Yari's proposal. Something to do with hiding the ring in her toe shoe.

"We have to have a party," Gussy said then, reaching for the calendar hanging on the wall. "For the engagement. Let's have it here over Labor Day weekend. Talk to Colette and call me at home tomorrow," Gussy said. "Tell her I love her."

After Gussy left, I ran the dirty plates under hot water. Labor Day would be Devin's last day at Gormlaith. After Labor Day he would return to New York, and I would be alone. I filled the sink with water so hot I could barely touch it and let the steam and heat bring tears. When the water had cooled and all of the dishes were clean, I picked the bones out of the sink and laid them inside the small nest next to the robin's egg.

Devin's house smelled of tomatoes and carrots, zucchini and beets. We spent all weekend harvesting the overgrown garden, picking the ripe vegetables, salvaging the ones that had already started to turn back into earth. We worked so we didn't have to speak. There were no words for what happened between us. For what happened to Maggie. We brought the truck into town and bought glass jars, large pots, and the other things the library book said we needed to preserve the generosity of his garden.

His kitchen was thick with steam, the pressure canner rocking on the small stove, the glass jars tinkling inside. In the living room we spread newspaper across the coffee table, and Devin set the basket of beans in front of me. I began by carefully cutting the sharp tips from each bean and then finally gave up on tidiness and started to snap the ends off in efficient crisp rhythms.

"Okay, give me what you've got," he said, emerging from the steamy kitchen, his sleeves rolled up to his elbows.

"Here you go," I said, passing him the basket of ready beans.

"I have no idea what I'm doing," he said.

"How do they look?"

"Like vegetables in jars. Hot vegetables in jars."

"Sounds like you're doing it right," I said and started snapping the next pile of beans.

"What time do you want to get to Maggie?" he asked.

"Three or so," I said. "I'm going to get Alice at Maggie's mom's first."

"Maggie like beets?"

"Maybe." I laughed.

Maggie was going to leave the hospital today. We offered to give her a ride home. Her car still wasn't fixed, and she couldn't have driven anyway because of her wrists. Devin and I were going to stay with her that night. She said she wasn't scared, that he wouldn't be back, but she didn't argue when we insisted. Alice hadn't seen her yet, but now that the bruises were fading, we suggested that Alice come home now too.

After I finished the last of the beans, I went to the kitchen and watched Devin fill the jars with the colors of his garden, watched him carefully seal the lids with the pink rubber seals, and lower the glasses into the water. His concentration was perfect, his hands sure and steady. The counter was covered with the finished jars. All of the colors of the spectrum. Tomatoes, carrots, wax beans, zucchini, beets, like a harvested rainbow. It smelled like the garden in here. Like the earth.

"It smells good," I said. "Like summertime."

"You sure you don't mind keeping these for me?" he asked, securing the lid of the metal contraption on the stove.

"Not at all," I said.

"You made the right decision," he said. "About the camp."

"I know." I smiled.

Maggie's mother lives out by the fish hatchery at the farm where Maggie grew up. Her father was born on this farm, back

246

when farmers could actually make a profit here. Now they barely sustain themselves on this shrinking piece of land. The winter before they had sold fifty acres to a couple from Connecticut. Skiers who wanted to build a summer home near the mountain.

Alice was sitting on top of a tractor in the driveway eating a popsicle. Her lips were stained purple, and her little white T-shirt was dotted with popsicle drippings. Maggie's mom was sitting on the porch, trying to comb a burr out of her German shepherd's fur. Jezebel had just had puppies. Her teats were pink and hanging from her body like eager fingers.

"Hi, Effie," Maggie's mom said loudly, waving the bright pink comb at me.

"Hi, Rose," I said.

Alice jumped down off the tractor and came running to the porch. She hugged my legs and the last bit of her Popsicle fell into the dirt.

"Hi, pumkin," I said, bending down to Alice. "You are a *mess*."

"She's had a very busy day," Rose said, freeing the burr from Jezebel's tresses. "We canned some tomatoes, watched *Sesame Street* and *Days of Our Lives*, helped Jezebel with her new puppies."

"You suppose your mom's gonna let you have a puppy?" I asked Alice. She beamed at me and then shrugged.

"We're working on her." Rose winked. "I'm gonna work on you too. Come with me."

Alice took me by the hand and led me to a closet inside the house. There were blankets on the floor and five wriggling pups. They squeaked like toys when we came close and then Jezebel was pushing between my legs to get to them. She turned around several times and then heaved her weight down onto the floor, somehow avoiding them. And then they were all fighting for milk, all scrambling and burying their faces in her belly.

"You almost got me," I said. I thought for a fleeting moment, then, of having a dog. Of waking up each morning and reaching for the leash hanging on the back of the closet door. Of taking her to the water and letting her swim. "Almost."

Alice crawled into the passenger's side of the Bug and fastened her seat belt.

"Any luck finding Bugs?" I asked Rose.

"Course not. He's probably back in Florida by now. We've got a restraining order. Like that'll make a difference."

"We're going to stay with her tonight. She'll be fine," I said softly.

"I know she will, honey. It's Alice I'm worried about."

I got in the car next to Alice. "See you later," I said, waving to Rose. She stood on her porch and kept waving until we couldn't see her anymore.

"We'll go get your mom in just a little bit," I said.

Alice nodded. She reached onto the dashboard and picked up a wilted flower I had forgotten there. Something I picked from the side of the road in town.

"Are you hungry?" I asked.

She shook her head and twirled the brown stem around her fingers.

"Thirsty?"

She smiled.

"You want a shake?" I asked.

She nodded and smiled. She still had all of her baby teeth. They were small and white, separated by huge spaces.

There is greasy spoon drive-in on the way from Rose's house to the lake. Sometimes I took Alice to get vanilla shakes. I knew she liked them, and Maggie didn't mind, but mostly it was for me. I loved the way they served the trays right to your car, attaching the metal handles of the tray to your window. I loved pouring the thick sweet shakes from the big silver canisters into paper cups. Usually I got one and split it with Alice. And we didn't drive away until it was all gone. Today, I let the cold shake numb my hands and tongue. Let everything freeze, until I couldn't feel anything anymore.

We brought Maggie three jars of tomatoes. Alice motioned for us to stop at the grocery store and ran directly to the chip aisle where she reached for a giant bag of salt and vinegar chips, Maggie's favorite. In the hospital parking lot, Devin stayed in the car with Alice, who was dressed up in her favorite blue dress and her cowboy boots. She had six different plastic bunny barrettes in her hair.

Maggie was packing her things when I got to her room. She took the cards down from the corkboard and laid them across her nightgowns and slippers. "My grandmother sent a sympathy card," she said, waving a pastel greeting card. "Her eyesight either sucks or she thinks I'm dead."

"I'm glad you're coming home," I said.

"Me too. If I had to watch another episode of Little House on the Prairie, I would have wanted to be dead," she said, motioning to her roommate, an elderly woman who stared intently at the TV suspended from the ceiling across the room.

As we walked down the cool hallway to the elevators, I could hear her wince a bit with each step.

"I'm buying the camp from Gussy," I said as the doors opened. "I'm staying at Gormlaith."

She smiled and we stepped into the elevator. When the doors closed and we were alone, she reached out for my hand. The plaster cast was rough and thick around her fingers. "Effie?"

"Yeh?"

"I thought he killed me this time. I thought I was dead."

• • •

Alice wouldn't let go of Maggie's legs. Not when she crawled out of the backseat of the Bug and ran to us in the parking lot, and not later when we got to Maggie's house and started making dinner for them. She held on and Maggie let her. It must have hurt terribly, the way she clung to her. But Maggie walked slowly to accommodate the child attached to her. And finally, we made them both sit down and we brought the TV trays into the living room so that Maggie wouldn't have to get up again.

Alice fell asleep as soon as the sun went down. Devin carried her up to her room like a little bag of laundry.

"Will you stay with her awhile to make sure she stays asleep?" Maggie asked.

"No problem," Devin said and winked at her. His footsteps were heavy on the stairs.

"Can we go outside for a bit? I've been cooped up for over a week now," Maggie asked.

"Sure. Do you need some help?"

"Nah, I'm fine. Just grab that pillow for my butt," she said.

I helped her ease her body into the rocking chair, careful to arrange the pillow so that her body was protected from the sharp wicker.

We sat for a long time watching the water. It was a quiet night, a lot of the summer people had started to return to their suburbs and cities.

"What did she say?" Maggie asked, her voice small and scared.

"Alice?" I asked.

She nodded.

"She said he was killing you," I said, staring at her hands.

"He was so gentle," she said, closing her eyes. "With me. After that night when I burned him. He promised he would never hurt me again, that he would never do anything to hurt us. He stopped going out so much. He would do these things for me, things he never used to do. Like doing the dishes, like making my coffee in the morning. Like putting the toilet seat back down."

A bird flew across the water, dipping in, looking for food.

"It took me completely by surprise," she said. "It was like he snapped. He wasn't even drunk. I was hanging clothes on the line and somebody called. Some guy from work or something. He was inside watching a basketball game and the phone rang. He must've missed something, a big shot or something. Because the next thing I know he's standing in the doorway holding the phone, screaming at me. All I could think was I hope no one's on the other end. I hope nobody is listening to this. I had clothes-pins in my mouth, wet sheets in my hands, and he's standing there screaming at me about the phone call. So the first thing I think to do is to get it all inside, you know what I mean? I put down the laundry and walked toward him, trying to get him to go back inside. Alice was in the backyard, playing in the sandbox. She didn't need to listen to this crap. She was singing, I remem-ber. That bus song, you know the one . . ." Maggie opened her eyes and hummed a little. "The wheels on the bus go round and round . . . something she learned at day care. One of those an-noying kid's songs."

I tried to imagine Alice singing, sifting sand and singing about the wheels of a bus.

"And it worked. We got inside and he calmed down. By the time I got whoever it was off the phone, he was watching the game again, like nothing ever happened. I even forgot about it. Funny how I used to be able to do that." Maggie laughed. "But he went out drinking that night. I told him to go have fun. I wanted some time alone. That was back when Alice would still take a bath. I gave her a bath, and the water looked so nice, I decided to take one myself. I ran the nicest bath, water so hot it turned my legs red. I used some of her Mr. Bubble even. I felt like I was in one of those Calgon commercials. You know, peace-ful. Happy.

"He got home just after I got in the tub. I heard the door open and close downstairs and I remember feeling relieved. He couldn't be that drunk. He'd come home early. I even felt a little excited when I heard him coming up the stairs. Like I did when we first lived together. Like when we first got married and used to walk around naked just because we could.

"But as soon as he opened the door, I knew he wasn't right. He was mumbling about my 'boyfriend' at work, if he'd come to see me, if that's why I was taking a bath. And before I even had a chance to think of something to say to calm him down, he was pushing me under the water. He didn't even roll up his sleeves. He just shoved me under and held me there until I could feel the water filling up my lungs. I kept kicking at the edge of the tub, but he was too strong.

"And then he let go. I sort of floated up and thought that maybe I was dead, but there was soap in my eyes and water in my ears and nose. And Alice was standing there watching us. She was rubbing her eyes the way that kids do, the way that just about breaks your heart. And she was watching her daddy kill me. And when she opened her mouth up to scream, there was nothing there. Not a single sound came out. And that scared me more than anything that Bugs could ever do to me."

"He took her voice," I said. "He took it."

"I wish he were dead, Effie. This won't stop until he's dead."

On the back of my eyelids, Max sat crouched in the corner of his apartment, urine-yellow surgical tubing wrapped around his arm. I imagined the way his body must have rushed with the familiar feeling of artificial bliss. Of the way he might not have known that anything was going wrong. The nausea a small price to pay for this joy. Love, love, love relaxing his body until it made his heart explode. Did his chest fill with the fleshy shards of his heart? Did his lungs expand until they burst like a child's balloon? Or did everything just stop?

Moonlight struggled through the leaves above us, making a

small cathedral of trees. I felt my heart quickening.

"Maggie?"

"Yeh?"

"His sister *is* the one who drowned, you know," I whispered.

"Shit," she said.

I closed my eyes for a moment, concentrated on the way the cool air felt on my skin.

The sound of drums filled my ears like water. "I was there that night."

"At the lake?" she asked.

"I made him mad. I made him mad enough to hit me. I *wanted* him to hit me. I thought that if he hit me hard enough it would be real. Then I could leave." I pulled my knees to my chest and rocked gently. "When I drove to Gussy's I kept running my tongue across the cut in my lip. It was like evidence, you know? Like the only way I could justify leaving. I kept opening up the cut."

Maggie looked straight ahead at the lake.

"I shouldn't have left," I said.

"No," she said shaking her head.

I nodded. "Max was the one who found her. He was out there too." The drums pounded in my ears, the low moan of bagpipes, of a woman's cry. "After I left, he went out in the boat."

Maggie shivered.

"She went swimming every night. I was the only one who knew that. Sometimes we'd swim for hours out there. Just her and me. We didn't even talk, we just floated. It was quiet. Sometimes I'd think about swimming with her all day. I couldn't wait sometimes for him to fall asleep so I could be with her out there on the water. I was supposed to be there that night. I promised her I would be there."

I could feel tears running into the corners of my mouth.

"He must have thought her body was a rock. He was drunk.

Confused in the dark, probably." I touched Maggie's hand to feel her bones. To feel the hard frame of her beneath her skin. "It was my fault."

"Effie," she said, her voice low and stern.

I stared at my hands.

"Look at me, Effie," she said.

I lifted my head. Tears were running, searing my skin in hot rivers.

"I let Bugs come back too. That time I told you about. I let him come back into my house." She stopped rocking and leaned forward. "I used to blame myself for what he did to Alice. But it was *his* fault. He's the one."

It was so quiet, I could almost hear my own heart beating.

"Devin doesn't know," I said.

"He can't hurt you anymore, Effie. He can't hurt anybody else either. And it won't do anybody any good to bring him back from the dead now." Maggie leaned forward, touching my face with her broken fingers. "It's all over. I would give the world for that."

September 1994

◈ ◈ ◈ Devin pulled into the driveway before I had time to put the coffee on. The back of his truck was filled with the things I would keep for him: jars and jars of vegetables, the boxes he couldn't take back with him, his summer clothes.

"Morning," he said, jumping down from the truck.

"Hi," I said. "Let me get this coffee going and then I'll help you unload."

"No hurry," he said and came into the kitchen.

254

I got the coffee beans from the freezer and plugged in the grinder. Soon the room smelled of fresh coffee, the water gurgling and hissing with promises of wakefulness.

"Oh shit," Devin said. "I forgot. I brought breakfast."

He disappeared outside and returned again with a grocery bag.

He set the bag on the table and started to pull things out. A carton of my favorite kind of orange juice, four raspberry muffins, white Styrofoam containers from the diner with steaming yellow eggs and bacon and biscuits inside.

"You didn't forget," I said. "Why did you do all this?"

"Why not?" he shrugged.

I nodded and poured coffee into two matching mugs.

When he went back out to the truck for a forgotten newspaper I sat down at the table and let myself imagine, for a minute, next summer. I imagined other mornings here. His dark hair over the top of a newspaper, his hand reaching across this Formica for mine. As I spooned the eggs and bacon onto Gussy's plates, I let myself fall into a place I never imagined would belong to me.

After the food was gone, I showed Devin the work I had done in the shed. I had completely emptied it out first, struggled against cobwebs and dead insects and unidentifiable rusted junk. When it was empty, the driveway looked like a yard sale. Then I had set about making a place for the jars. I knew that when winter came I would need to move them inside, but for now this would have to do. We carried the jars carefully to the shed and soon the old bookcases and wooden crates were filled with Devin's glass garden.

Inside, I had done some similar work in the closet. I emptied drawers in the upstairs dresser for his summer clothes. I cleared off shelves to make room for his magic boxes. It didn't take long before the truck was empty and Devin's things were like strange stowaways in the camp.

"I have some work to do today," Devin said, slumping down in the couch. His legs stretched out nearly to the middle of the room. "But I'd like to see you tonight."

"Whatcha want to do?" I asked.

"I don't care," he said and motioned for me to sit beside him.

I curled up into the crook his body made. I could have stayed like that forever. There I could almost forget that he would be gone in less than a week.

Magoo was better now. He didn't need me to go into town for him anymore, but I kept bringing him books anyway. He spent much of his day outside in an Adirondack chair by the woodpile, reading and puffing on his pipe. Today he was out early, Police-man curled up at his feet.

"Good morning, Mr. Tucker," I said after Devin drove away.

"Mornin', Effie."

"I'm staying," I said. "You'll have a neighbor all year 'round now."

"Gussy told me." He smiled and filled his pipe. "You gonna brave the winter here too, huh?"

"Yep," I said and reached down to pet Police's head.

"You'll be needing some wood."

"I know. Where do you get yours?"

"Guy named Peterson. Real reasonable. They'll split it for you too."

"I'll get his number from you," I said.

"You know your Grampa always wanted to stay here through the winter. Course Gussy would never have stood for it. Too isolated for a butterfly like her. But I think he would have been happy here. Every chance he got he'd sneak up here, you know."

"Really?" I asked.

"Gussy would go to church or to one of her meetings and

he'd have the chains on his truck faster than you could say 'Gormlaith.' She knew what he was doin'. She's smart as a whip. Sometimes he'd just come up here to walk out on the ice. Swore he could measure how thick it was just by the way it felt under his feet." Magoo set the book he had been reading down on a stump next to him that served as an outdoor end table. "Winter up here will clear your head. Sure as sugar."

There was a chill in the air that day, despite the blue sky and sun. It looked like summer still, but it smelled of early autumn. There was an edge to the air, a crispness that signaled fall.

I held on to the minutes. I held on to them as if I could keep them from passing, like a mother holding on to a child that insists on growing up. And each moment became somehow precious. I missed him already, and he wasn't even gone.

That night he took me on a walk. That's all. He wanted to walk all the way around the lake. He'd never done it before.

The wind off the water made the air cold. As we walked along the dirt road, I wished that I had worn mittens. Now that the summer people were all gone, most of the camps were dark, sealed shut tightly until next summer. Magoo's camp was the only one nearby with the warm orange glow of someone living inside. We hadn't talked about Keisha since the night that Bugs came back. But she was between us, a ghost. It was like those nights when we swam silently next to each other, not speaking, only floating. And each recollection felt like a blow. Like Max wasn't gone at all. Like he was still here too.

"I love it here," Devin said. "When everyone's gone."

I nodded in the darkness. Our feet shuffled across the cold dirt road.

"My great-grandfather picked this place because it was so quiet," I said. "Back then, it was always like this. There were only three or four camps on the entire lake. He probably thought it would stay like that forever. My grampa always said that if he were rich he'd buy up all the land and tear the houses down so that it could be like it used to be."

"He would have hated New York." He laughed. "You cold?"

"A little," I said. He reached for my hand and suddenly it was enveloped in the warmth of him.

The Foresters' camp was dark. The untended dock was dipping into the water. The yard grew wild, grass tickling the edges of the windows. As we walked around the lake, we could have been the only people on earth.

We walked to Devin's empty house. My fingers were numb, my toes cold inside my boots. I shivered when we entered the kitchen and turned on the lights.

"Do you want to build a fire?" I asked. "It's cold enough tonight."

"I'll go get some wood," Devin said.

As Devin disappeared into the shed to search for some kindling and logs, I started to ache. At first I thought it might be the cold in my bones, the shivering of marrow. But the longer he was gone, the deeper it went, and I realized that it was only sadness. Only missing.

Later, I fell asleep in front of the fire. Flames leaped across the back of my eyelids. His fingers wound their way through my hair, made circles on my scalp, until the aching stopped and I felt warm again. I woke up once in the middle of the night and thought that I was in Seattle. In the darkness, I could have sworn that rain was beating against the windows. But it was only the sound of flames touching the metal door of the woodstove, the sound of his breaths. When I fell asleep again, I dreamed rain. Dark and warm. I dreamed his coffee hands on my face, raining on my eyelids. I dreamed her hand like chocolate in mine. I dreamed the words that might explain to him how she died.

• • •

Tess arrived for Colette and Yari's party before anyone else.

I was taking sheets down from the clothesline. I had Maggie's laundry too. I told her I would take care of the things that she was still too weak to do. I used lavender soap and collected the end of summer in the crisp cotton. I couldn't wait until she buried her face in the clean sheets and smelled this rare scent of sunshine.

"Effie Greer, my dear," Tess said, skipping to me across the front lawn. I smiled at her knobby knees and cutoff shorts. I smiled at her braids. "Wanna catch some crawdads for supper?"

"Tess," I said.

"I'm serious." She smiled. "I've got a trunk full of hot dogs."

She hugged me, and I could smell the Teaberry gum that only Tess chewed.

"So Colette's getting married. She pregnant?"

"Doubt it," I said. "Too hard to get en pointe with a big belly."

"What's he like?" she asked, helping me fold the sheets.

"Yari?"

"Yeh," she said.

"He's nice," I said. "He lets Colette boss him around."

"A match made in heaven." She smirked. "Let's go swimming," she said.

"Okay, let me get finished here," I said and made a tidy pile of sheets in the wicker basket at my feet.

Fall had come early. Usually, leaves stayed green until late September. But as we walked through the woods to the pool, the green of summer foliage was interrupted every so often by the sudden explosion of orange or red. Sunlight streaming through the empty spaces made the color even more brilliant. Like small fires amid all that green.

When we got to the water, Tess untied her shoes, peeled off her socks, and laid them across a smooth gray stone. She unbuttoned her shirt and unzipped her shorts. And then she was inside the water, her beautiful head floating across the top of the water.

I put my clothes next to hers on the rock. Our empty clothes like ghosts. I looked at Tess floating in the water, her body easy and careless. Naked, I climbed up onto a large rock that hung over the pool, a small cliff. Trees shaded this place from the incessant sunshine. I curled my knees to my chest.

Through an opening in the leaves September sun burned on my shoulders as I whispered to the beat of the new drums. The steady cry of the bagpipes, strange melody of blues. Of each bruise. Of each bruise.

Below me, Tess floated in the water, a pale votive. Eyes closed. And while she swam, perhaps mistaking my song at first for the sound of water or wind, I told the story of the first time. Of the first time he bruised my shoulders, in the spring when lilacs bloomed and cherry blossoms exploded in white bursts all over campus. Of the next morning when the floor of my dorm room was covered with the snow of cherry blossoms, sweet and white. Max had left no note, no pleas, just this. How all day his apologies filled my head with the smell of spring. And how when I turned on the hot water and sank into the shallow bathtub, there was no evidence of the night before on my skin. There were no bruises. I told her I thought I only dreamed his fingers. That I only dreamed the violet stains of fingertips. That I only dreamed this color because of the way the lilacs looked that spring against all of that white, white snow.

Tess spread a towel across the flat rock. She motioned for me to join her, and I crawled down from my strange perch and laid next to her under the strange mix of green and red and orange leaves. The sun was warm, but her hand was cold when it found mine.

I closed my eyes and listened to the creek running gently into this warm, still pool. I listened until I heard the low moan of the bagpipes, the low moan of a woman's voice looking for love, and I recalled all of that blue. Of each bruise after that day, of each bruise. I imagined each bruise from the needle, and wondered if he was only trying to become me with each prick. If maybe, after I was gone, he finally felt sorry for everything he had done.

That afternoon, Colette and Yari arrived. In their wake was my parents' station wagon and Gussy. While Tess and I stretched the badminton net between two trees in the front yard, I watched the strange ritual of my family. My mother scurrying about with bags and Tupperware. My father muttering behind her. Gussy's slow, steady movements, singular and strong. The odd exchanges between Yari and my father, handshakes and awkward hugs, pats on the back. My mother's arms like fleshy vises, insistent embraces. I watch the strange choreography, the familial dance, changed by the years and distance between us. And I felt as though I were waiting in the wings. That I was waiting for some cue to make my own entrance into this peculiar performance.

It came in the form of my mother's waving arm, noticing me finally, sitting with my back against the trunk of the tree.

"Effie," she hollered. "Come help me with the cake."

My knees were the knees of a child, rising at the sound of my mother's voice, carrying me to her, my feet dragging behind.

"You bought a cake," I said in disbelief as I stared at the enormous pink box in the back of the station wagon.

"It's a carrot cake. Cream cheese frosting. Colette's favorite."

"What does Yari like?" I asked.

"Well, I don't know," she said, putting her hands on her hips. "I didn't think to ask him."

Of course not, I thought. "Ready?" I asked, lifting one side of the box.

She nodded and lifted the other end.

The temptation was strong, but I did not let the box fall, not even when my mother stumbled a bit over the threshold. The kitchen counters were covered with grocery bags. My father had already put all of the Styrofoam packages of meat in the fridge and had escaped to the backyard where he was lifting the dome lid of the barbecue, peering at the gray charcoal that had been there since the Fourth of July.

I escaped through the crowd in the kitchen to find him in the backyard.

"Hi, Dad," I said.

"Hi, honey."

"You need some help?" I asked, sitting down at the picnic table.

"That's okay." He smiled. He pulled the dirty grill out of the barbecue and set it on the grass. "Your mother is in her element." He laughed.

"This will be nice." I smiled. "For Colette."

"He's a nice guy," he said. "Lets Colette boss him around."

I grinned.

"You'll find someone someday too, I imagine. Then we'll have to do this all over again."

As my father busied himself with the barbecue, I watched how careful he was. How meticulous he was with this ritual. Precise. Certain. I found here something I had seen in Colette, the perfection of even simple movements. Grace.

"Dad, when did you know that you loved Mom?" I asked.

"When?" he said, reaching for the wire brush. "When she first brought me here, I suppose. I had just finished my last final, medieval history, and she pulled me out of the classroom. She was standing outside the classroom door waiting for me to put my pen down. She dragged me out of there so fast I didn't know what hit me." He started to scrub the blackened grate.

"She didn't tell me where we were going, and I trusted her in that stupid way you trust people you are just starting to love, and she brought me here. She got two lawn chairs out of the shed and set them facing the lake. We sat there all afternoon. She told me exactly who she planned to be and that person fit exactly with who I planned to be. And she had this way of making everything feel okay. Even though I knew I had failed that exam and I would have to go to summer school to graduate, she pretended that it didn't matter. It's hard not to love somebody who can do that."

He turned on the hose and started to spray the grate. The water made a small river at my feet.

"She doesn't want to hear things sometimes," I said.

"What do you mean?"

"I mean, maybe she needs to stop pretending everything's okay sometimes and listen. She doesn't know about Max and me. About how bad he was."

I waited for his surprise. I had been practicing this moment, rehearsing this part of the dance, again and again.

"Yes she does, Effie," he said, turning off the hose and laying it gently on the grass. "She was listening, you just weren't telling her anything. She was only waiting for you. We were both just waiting for you."

The rust-gold-orange-purple of the woods behind him blurred through the spray of the hose, the water in my eyes, the thickness in my throat.

"It's done now," I said. "You can tell her that, if you want."

"Good." He smiled.

I nodded and stood up from the picnic table. I started to walk toward Tess in the front yard. She was trying to get the birdie out of the tree with her racquet.

"Effie?" he said.

I turned around. "Yeh?"

"I'm glad you're staying."

"Me too." I smiled.

Maggie brought Alice with her. Alice and Tess played bad-minton until both of them had grass-stained knees. Maggie and I sat at the picnic table, while Colette and Yari took a walk and everyone else cooked. Through the window, I could hear the sound of Gussy and my mother as they prepared the salads. The air smelled wonderful, the scent of stolen summer.

Maggie and I had brought a bottle of cold pink wine from my mother's reserves and were drinking it out of plastic cups. My tongue was dry, my head pleasantly fuzzy.

"When does Devin go back to New York?" Maggie asked.

"Monday morning," I said.

"Is he coming tonight?"

"Later," I said. "He's still packing."

"You'll miss him," Maggie said, picking at a piece of red paint peeling away from the wooden tabletop. "But, I'll be around. Me and Alice. To keep you company, you know."

"I know," I said. I reached across the table for her hand. Most of her bruises were gone now. Faded away like so many summer afternoons.

Colette and Yari came back soaking wet and giggling. I found them clean towels in the closet and helped Colette dry her hair. Yari changed into some dry clothes and we started carrying every-thing outside.

My mother had strung Chinese lanterns all over the backyard. She turned them on as the sun began to fall. Magoo waddled over just as we were all sitting down to eat.

"I was wondering when you'd get here." Gussy reprimanded me.

"Just finishing up a book." He smiled at me.

"They're *history* books," Gussy said. "You already know what's going to happen." At the picnic table, we were illuminated by the lanterns' strange yellow glow. Gussy moved with absolute grace, passing the colorful dishes until everyone's plates were full. Laughter rose from the table in small crescendos from the steady chatter and the sound of forks and glasses clanking.

The faces of my family, animated by conversation, by lanterns, and by moon suddenly made me feel strangely content. The smell of Gussy's lavender soap. Maggie's fire-hair. My father raising his plastic champagne glass to meet the rest of ours as my mother cut into the sweet white frosting on the cake. The smell of Magoo's pipe after the dishes were all gone. *This is home,* I thought. *Right here.*

Devin rode his bicycle up as I was wiping off the vinyl tablecloth, and Tess was trying to roast a marshmallow on the barbecue.

"Hi." he said.

"Hi." Tess smiled, dropping the gooey marshmallow into the fire. "Oops."

"This is Devin, Tess," I said.

"Pleased to meetcha," she said and shook his hand.

I had planned to keep him a secret, not to subject him to my whole family. But something about the way he shook Tess's hand and smiled triggered something in me.

"You want to meet the other Greers?" I asked.

"Sure." He smiled.

I took his hand and led him inside, into the bright kitchen where the after-dinner dance had already commenced. Gussy washing, Colette drying. My father trying to make the reception on the radio clearer by moving the antenna back and forth, up

265

and down. Yari sitting in the kitchen nook, Magoo asleep on the couch.

"Everybody?" I said. "This is my friend, Devin. He's been living over at that house with the swing this summer."

Heads turning. Synchronicity of surprise.

"Hi," he said. He looked so big next to everyone, except for my mother, who was coming down the stairs with a blanket for Magoo.

"Hi," Colette said, wiping off a soapy hand and reaching for his.

"Effie's told me a lot about you," Gussy said, smiling, nodding.

My mother stared at his large hands, fumbling for a place to go. "Did Effie get you anything to eat?" she asked.

"I had a late lunch." He smiled. "I don't need anything."

"Of course you do," she said. "You like carrot cake?"

"We're going out in the boat," I said.

"Oh."

"Bring a sweater," my father said. "It's cold out on the water."

"It was nice to meet you." My mother smiled.

"You too," Devin said. "All of you."

We untied the boat from the tree stump and I got in first. Devin stepped in after me, the boat dipping first to the left and then to the right with his weight. When he took the oars and spread his arms out to row, he was as wide as the boat.

"It was nice to meet them," he said.

"Sorry if it was overwhelming," I said.

"I'm not easily overwhelmed." He smiled. "I grew up in a house with seven kids. You can only imagine what dinner at our house was like."

I looked up at the starless sky. The water was calm beneath us. I thought of his family around a table. Children's elbows and knees bumping, his mother trying to get some control over all that noise. I imagined him, the second oldest, trying to help her. How he might have shushed his brother and then tickled Keisha under the table to make her giggle.

"Why did you come here," I asked. "The first time?"

He pushed the oars forward and they rose out of the water like birds.

"I came to see this lake," he said. "I guess I imagined it was like a giant black hole. Sinister or something. I knew that if I could see the lake that pulled her under, then I might be able to fight it somehow. Beat it, you know?"

I nodded and pulled Gussy's sweater around my shoulders. My heart was beating steadily, hard and insistent.

"But when I got here, it wasn't like I'd imagined at all. It was beautiful. The first day I got here I spent hours just looking into the water. For some sort of monster to show his face. But the water was perfectly blue. There was nothing hiding in there."

He stopped rowing and the boat remained still in the water.

"After a while, I guess I realized that there wasn't any battle to be fought. Nothing was going to bring her back anyway. You can't punch water, you know? It doesn't offer any resistance. It's weak."

He started rowing again, slowly. "And so I stopped fighting. It wasn't easy, of course. I've had my share of temper tantrums. Finally, I realized that it had taken my sister, but it was giving me something in return. It's the way the world works, I think. You look for something you've lost, and you wind up finding something else. That sound stupid?"

"No," I whispered.

"And then, it gave me you. The first time I saw you, I knew you were a gift."

My heart, my head pounded with the sounds of the drums.

"Why didn't you tell me she was your sister?" I asked, the

267

moaning of bagpipes, the moaning of something lost. Or stolen.

"I don't know. I guess I didn't know how. I made my peace with Gormlaith a long time ago. I didn't want you feeling sorry for me, I guess. People around here feel bad about it. I know that's the only reason why they welcomed me here the first time. I didn't want that from you."

"I loved her," I said, covering his large knuckles with my hands. "She was my friend."

"I know," he smiled.

I ran my fingers across the peaks and valleys of his knuckles. He moved ever so slightly, dipping the oars in and out of the water. I moved from the seat then and stretched out on the bottom of the boat. I fit neatly under the seats, my legs between his on the bottom of the boat.

"When I was little," I said, "my Grampa and I would come out here sometimes and I would fall asleep on the bottom of the boat. He would paddle me around for hours like that."

I laid on my back and turned my head to the side. I pressed my ear to the wooden bottom and waited for the drums. I listened for the signal to begin my story, the cue to tell him, to let go of Max's secret.

But the music was gone. There was only the sound of water beneath me. Only the gentle rocking of the boat. Only the sound of Gormlaith at night. And, quite suddenly, Max was gone too. That night dissolved into the sound of the oars dipping into the water. The sound of Devin's low hum. *It wasn't my fault.* I couldn't protect her, save her. But the lake was giving me another chance. The secret didn't matter, because it didn't belong to me. And the bruises Max had left on Devin's life had already begun to fade. Blue turning slowly from indigo to black.

EPILOGUE

෧ ෧ ෧ *Time does not heal wounds. It's a body's ritual that does. The instinctual cleansing with rain or other waters, the application of salves. Despite the sting. Even neglected, the body begins to take care. To repair itself. Blood clots, tissues regenerate, flesh scars. Soon, the thin white line is the only evidence of the pain. It is the body, not time. Time does nothing except create distance between the body and that which caused it harm.*

Recollection of fear can be stronger than the original fear itself. Similarly, bliss is sometimes more vivid when recollected. How else do you explain longing? Longing for what has already passed. That's the real pain.

But you insisted, you pried with your fingers to see. You returned to me after I turned away. You made me recollect for you, collect again and again for you, interrupting the healing with your curiosity.

Now that I have given you the words, you may long for them. You may miss me. You may try to find the notes to the song again and again and won't be able to find them. Perhaps, the wounds I made will already have begun to scar. Maybe the body will have begun its ritual of forgetting.

I told you not to ask for haunted, not to ask me to recollect. Because recollection is like tearing at closed wounds. Like peeling back the careful tissue put there by the body to make it safe. And because remembered pain is always worse than the original pain, because this time it is expected. This time you already know how much it will hurt.

January 1995

ᔆ ᔆ ᔆ It is winter here.

I found a dusty Crock-Pot in one of Gussy's cupboards, and I am making stew from frozen stew meat and the memory of other winters in Gussy's kitchen.

This morning I awoke to six inches of new snow, splinters of glass still swirling furiously outside my window. Before I attempted to fight through the blizzard to put chains on the van, I listened to the radio for the listing of schools that would be closed due to the storm. I felt like I was seven years old again, praying for a snow day. Answered prayers, every school that I visit with the mobile library would be closed. I shivered with cold and excitement and went to the shed in my bathrobe for more wood for the fire.

Inside I built a fire that roared and crackled, and then set about finding the necessary ingredients. Stew meat, garlic, thyme. I went to the closet, rearranged to accommodate Devin's garden, and grabbed two jars of red tomatoes.

Now, I peel fresh carrots and potatoes, leaving their skins in brown and orange heaps in the sink. I crush the pungent garlic with a fork and find thyme hiding behind salt and baking powder in the cupboard. I put everything in the Crock-Pot and then open the seal on the tomatoes. The sweet smell of summer makes me dizzy. Recollections of the giant's garden captured in a glass jar. *I might survive winter this way,* I think.

When the crock is full, I turn the dial, putting my hands on the sides to make sure that it still works. It heats up as quickly as the woodstove in the other room.

Rump is whining at the door to be let out. I am reluctant to open the door again; heat escapes so quickly. But she insists, and I relent. She is still a puppy really, and I should be proud of her. Alice and Maggie's pick of the litter, Rapunzel, is not nearly as obedient and considerate. Alice named them both, Rumpelstiltsken and Rapunzel. She whispered their names to me before I had even decided to take her home. But now, in winter when Maggie's visits are necessarily made less frequent by the weather and when Magoo hibernates for days on end, I am grateful for her company. Sometimes when I am sleeping, she finds me buried under the covers and curls her warm body against mine, making me feel not quite so alone.

"Come on Rump," I say, standing in the doorway, shivering in my robe.

She begs me to be patient with her wet brown eyes. She is particular about where she pees. She is usually fond of the side of the shed, but today the snow is obstructing her path. I watch her swim through the fresh snow looking for a more accessible spot to relieve herself. Finally, she finds a place and then finds her way back to me through the white ocean and shakes the white crystals off all over my bare legs.

"Get in," I say.

Inside she goes straight to the flannel dog bed my mother bought her for Christmas that I have put close to the woodstove. I follow her and try to warm my hands near the fire.

"Should we shovel the driveway today?" I ask her, but she is already dreaming. She chases dream rabbits, dream squirrels in dream summertime.

Outside it continues to snow, but inside everywhere I look there are pieces of summer. Oblivious to the storm outside, Lenny and George paddle through the summer water, lie prone under the warmth of artificial sun. In the closet, on shelves I made from boards and bricks, the colors of Devin's garden are captured in clear glass jars. In the living room, among Grampa's books, Devin's boxes hold suns that do not set, butterflies in eternal flight, and flowers that never wilt. It is easy here to believe in spring.

I pull on my new Sorrels, their felt linings thick and warm around my wool clad feet. As I begin the daunting task of uncovering the van, I think, *Winter will not last forever. Spring is inevitable.* But for each path I clear, each straining muscle in my back, there is more snow falling from the sky to replace it. Like Sisyphus in this ridiculous task. I am able, after an hour, to make a pathway from the door to the road. On either side are cold, white walls.

But rather than returning to the warmth of the house, and the warmth of Rump's body against mine, I decide to walk. The wind blows snow into my eyes like small pieces of glass. Winter is so much more beautiful under the moon or the sun. But today, the whole world is white, and I can't feel my toes.

In winter, you can't tell where the lake begins or ends. And after snow, it is almost impossible to differentiate earth from water. I trudge through the snow toward the lake, my only reference point the trees, tired and heavy in their white dresses.

I am alone here. Only a few people are stupid enough to brave this, to spend three, sometimes four months in this white dimensionless world. I could scream or sing at the top of my lungs and the snow would swallow my sound. My words would only freeze in the air, splinter and fall to the ground in shattered pieces.

I think of my mother coming here to escape from us. While Colette and I fought and sulked and played the TV too loud, when we grew bored with each other, with winter, our mother would come to this place. Grampa, too, loved winter here. Like my mother, he must have come here to be alone. To disappear into this white. I imagine him walking across the frozen water, judging the thickness by the sounds of his footsteps.

I walk to where the old stump sticks its wrinkled head up from a mountain of snow and look out toward the island. Wind tears through the trees, lifting the cloaks from their shoulders, leaving their branches bare and exposed.

I step onto the ice, tentative and scared. But after a few steps, I see that the ice is thick, my footsteps light. They make dull soft thuds as I move farther away from land. In this tentative way, I walk until I can't see the camp anymore. I walk until I am completely enclosed by white snow, white air, white sky.

Devin was wrong about the lake. It can resist a fist; it is not weak at all. Its strength is in its resistance, not in its pull. And now, it holds me up. *It holds me up.*

But you must be careful. You must not tread too heavily, must not threaten it with the temper or carelessness of stomping feet. You must treat it with tenderness, forgiveness. You must trust its hands. Then it will take care of you. Then it will keep you safe.